Samlor stepped forward and swung at the demon . . .

He chopped for a wrist. Instead of slipping through like light in mist, the caravan master's steel clanged as numbingly as if he had slashed an anvil. The demon seized the blade and began to chitter in high-pitched laughter.

All of the demon but its right leg had pulled free of the wall. That leg was still smokily insubstantial, but the claws of the left foot cut triple furrows in the concrete as they strained to drag the creature wholly out of the stone. The left hand—forepaw—was reaching for Samlor's face while the right gripped his knife . . .

Don't miss these other exciting tales of Sanctuary ™: the meanest, seediest, most dangerous town in all the worlds of fantasy. . . .

THIEVES' WORLD
(Stories by Asprin, Abbey, Anderson, Bradley, Brunner, DeWees, Haldeman, and Offutt)

TALES FROM THE VULGAR UNICORN
(Stories by Asprin, Abbey, Drake, Farmer, Morris, Offutt, and van Vogt)

SHADOWS OF SANCTUARY
(Stories by Asprin, Abbey, Cherryh, McIntyre, Morris, Offutt, and Paxson)

STORM SEASON
(Stories by Asprin, Abbey, Cherryh, Morris, Offutt, and Paxson)

THE FACE OF CHAOS
(Stories by Asprin, Abbey, Cherryh, Drake, Morris, and Paxson)

WINGS OF OMEN
(Stories by Asprin, Abbey, Bailey, Cherryh, Duane, Chris and Janet Morris, Offutt, and Paxson)

THE DEAD OF WINTER
(Stories by Asprin, Abbey, Bailey, Cherryh, Duane, Morris, Offutt, and Paxson)

SOUL OF THE CITY
(Stories by Abbey, Cherryh, and Morris)

BLOOD TIES
(Stories by Asprin, Abbey, Bailey, Cherryh, Duane, Chris and Janet Morris, Andrew and Jodie Offutt, and Paxson)

AFTERMATH
(Stories by Asprin, Abbey, Brunner, Drake, Morris, Offutt, and Perry)

DAGGER
DAVID DRAKE

ACE BOOKS, NEW YORK

This book is an Ace
original edition, and has
never been previously
published.

DAGGER

An Ace Book/published by arrangement with
the author

PRINTING HISTORY
Ace edition/April 1988

ISBN: 0-441-80609-0

To
Bob Asprin,
who in October 1979 asked,
"Have you read Thieves' World yet?"

CHAPTER 1

"YOU NEED A dagger, caravan master," said the stranger to Samlor hil Samt as he began to bring a weapon slowly out from under his cloak.

The man hadn't spoken loudly, but there were key words which rang in the air of the Vulgar Unicorn. Weapon words were almost as sure a way to get attention in this bar as the mention of money. Conversation stopped or dropped into a lower key; eyes shifted over beer mugs and dice cups.

Samlor was already in the state of tension which gripped any sane man when he walked into this bar in the heart of Sanctuary's Maze district. More than the word "dagger" shocked him now, so that his right hand slipped to the brass pommel and hilt—of nondescript hardwood, plain and serviceable like the man who carried it—of the long fighting knife in his belt sheath.

At the same time, Samlor's left arm swept behind him to locate and hold his seven-year-old niece Star. She was with him in this place because there was no place safer for her than beside her mother's brother . . . which was almost another way of saying that there is no safety at all in this life.

Almost: because for forty-three years, Samlor hil Samt had managed to do what he thought he had to do, be damned to the price he paid or the cost to whatever stood between him and duty.

The stranger shouldn't have called him "caravan master." That's what he was, what he had been ever since he had determined to lift his family from poverty, despite the scorn all his kin heaped on him for dishonoring Cirdonian nobility by going into trade. But no one in Sanctuary should have recognized Samlor; and if they did, he and Star were in trouble much deeper than the general miasma of danger permeating this place.

There were people in Sanctuary who actively wished Samlor dead. That was unusual; not because he'd lived a life free from deadly enemies, but because fate or the Cirdonian caravan master himself had carried off most of those direct threats already.

When he bedded his camels at night on the trail, Samlor walked the circuit of the laager prodding crevices and holes with a cornel-wood staff flexible enough to reach an arm's length down a circuitous burrow.

If there were a hiss or an angry jarring of fangs on the staff, he either blocked the hole or, as the mood struck him, teased the snake into the open to be finished with a whip-swift flick of the staff. That was the only way to prevent beasts and men from being bitten when they rolled in their sleep onto vipers sheltering against mammalian warmth.

The caravan routes were a hard school, but applying the lessons he learned to human enemies had kept Samlor alive longer than would otherwise have been the case.

Sanctuary, though, was a problem better avoided than solved—and insoluble besides. Samlor had no intention of seeing and *smelling* the foulness of this place ever again, until the messenger arrived with the letter from Samlane.

It could have been a forgery, though the Cirdonian script on the strip of bark-pulp paper was illegible until it had been wound onto a message staff of the precise length and diameter of the ones Samlor's family had adopted when they were ennobled seventeen generations before. But the hand was right; the message had the right aura of terse presumption that Samlor would do his sister's will in this matter—

And the paper was browned enough with age, despite having been locked in a banker's strong room. The document might well have been written before Samlane died with her brother's knife through her belly and through the thing she carried in her womb.

Samlor couldn't imagine what inheritance could be worth the risk of bringing Star back to Sanctuary, but his sister had been foolishly destructive only of herself. If the legacy which would come to Star at age seven were that important, then it was Samlor's duty as the child's uncle to see that she received it.

It was his duty as the father as well, but that was something he thought about only when he awakened in the bleak darkness.

So he was in Sanctuary again, where no one was safe; and a man he didn't know had just identified him.

Star put a hand on her uncle's elbow, to reassure Samlor of her presence and the fact that she understood the tension.

The trio of punks by the door glanced sidelong with greasy eyes. They were street toughs, too young to have an identity beyond the gang membership they proclaimed with matching yellow bandanas and high boots that made sense only for horsemen. They were dangerous. Like baboons, they stank, yammered, and let vicious hostility toward outsiders serve in situations where humans would have found intelligence to be useful.

Four soldiers, out of uniform but obvious from the way their hair was cut short to fit beneath helmets, sat at a table near the bar with a pimp and a woman. The pimp gave Samlor and the situation an appraising look. The woman eyed the caravan master blearily, because he happened to be standing where her eyes were more or less focused.

And the soldiers, after momentary alertness at the possibility of a brawl, resumed their negotiations regarding a price for the woman to go down on all four of them in the alley outside.

There were a dozen other people in the tavern, besides the slope-shouldered tapster and the bar maid—the only other woman present—who slid between tables, too tired to slap at the hands that groped her and too jaded to care. The drinkers, solitary or in pairs, were nondescript though clothed within a fair range of wealth and national origin.

They could be identified as criminals only because they chose to gather here.

"I don't need a dagger," said Samlor, releasing Star to free his left hand as his right lifted the wedge of his own belt knife a few inches up in its sheath. "I have my own."

There was nothing fancy about Samlor's weapon. The blade was a foot long with two straight edges. The metal had no ornamentation beyond the unsharpened relief cuts which would permit the user to short-grip the weapon with an index finger over the crosshilt. It was forged of a good grade of steel—though again, nothing exceptional.

Recently, a few blades of Enlibar steel had appeared. These were worked from iron alloyed with a blue-green ore of copper which had been cursed by earth spirits, kobolds. The ore could be smelted only with magical means, and it was said to give an exceptional toughness to sword blades.

Samlor had been interested in the reports, but he'd survived as long as he had by sticking to what he was sure would work. He left the experiments with kobold steel to others.

"You'll want this anyway," said the stranger, lifting his dagger by its crosshilt so that the pommel was toward Samlor.

Not a threat, only a man with something to sell, thought the Cirdonian as he sidled away from the stranger to get to the bar. Harmless, almost certainly—but Samlor moved to his left, guiding Star ahead of him so that his body was between her and the weapon that the other man insisted on displaying. The fellow had sized up Samlor as he entered the Vulgar Unicorn, guessing his occupation from his appearance. A con man's trick, perhaps; but not an assassin's.

There was no reason to take chances.

"When are we going to sleep, Uncle?" asked Star with a thin whine on the last syllables which meant she was really getting tired. That was understandable, but it meant she was likely to balk when she needed to obey. She might even call him "Uncle Samlor" despite being warned that Samlor's real name would make both of them targets.

Star was an unusual child, but she was a child nonetheless.

"Two mugs of blue john," said the Cirdonian, loudly enough for the tapster halfway down the bar to hear him. They already had the attention of the fellow, an athlete gone to fat but still powerful. He was balding, and his scars showed that he had been doing this work or work equally rough for many years.

If something had cost him his left thumb during that time—he was still the one walking around to tell the tale, wasn't he?

"*I* want—" Star piped up.

"And two beers to wash it down," Samlor said loudly, cutting her off. As his left hand reached down for his belt purse, he let it linger for a moment where Star's hood covered the whorl of white hair that was the source of her name. She quieted for the moment, though the touch was gentle.

Star's mother had immersed herself in arts that had ultimately killed her—or had led her to need to die. Her child had terrifying powers when necessity and circumstances combined to bring them out.

But Samlor hil Samt had no need of magic to frighten anyone who knew him as well as the child did. He would not cuff her across the room; not here, not ever. His rage was as real as the rock glowing white in the bowels of a volcano. The Cirdonian's anger bubbled beneath a crust of control which split only when he chose that it should, and he would never release its destruction on his kin, blood of his blood . . . his seed.

Star was old enough to recognize the fury, and wise enough to avoid it even when she was fatigued. She patted her protector's hip.

The coin Samlor held between the middle and index finger of his left hand was physically small but minted from gold. It was an indication to the sharp-eyed tapster that his customer wanted more than drink, and a promise that he would pay well for the additional service. The man behind the bar nodded as he scooped clabbered milk from a stoneware jug under the bar.

There was no drink more refreshing than blue john to a dusty traveller, tired and hungry but too dry to bolt solid food. It was a caravaner's drink—and Samlor was a caravaner, obvious to anyone, even before he ordered. He shouldn't have been surprised at the way a stranger had addressed him.

Samlor's cloak was pinned up now to half-length as he would wear it for riding. When he slept or stood in a chill breeze, it could cover him head to toe. The fleece from which it was tightly woven had a natural blue-black color, but it had never been washed or dyed. Lanolin remaining in the wool made the garment almost waterproof.

The tunic he wore beneath the cloak was wool also but died a neutral russet color. Starting out before dawn on the caravan road, Samlor would wear as many as three similar tunics over this one, stripping them off and binding them to his saddle as the sun brightened dazzlingly on the high passes.

The bottom layer against his skin of silk, the only luxury Samlor allowed himself or even desired while he was on the road.

He was a broad-shouldered, deep-chested man even without the added bulk of his cloak, but his wrists would have been thick on a man of half again his size. The skin of his hands and face was roughened by a thousand storms whipping sand or ice crystals across the plains, and it was darkened to an angry red that mimicked the tan his Cirdonian genes did not have the pigment to support.

When Samlor smiled, as he did occasionally, the expression flitted across his face with the diffidence of a visitor sure he's knocking at the wrong address. When he barked orders, whether to men or beasts, his features stayed neutral and nothing but assurance rang in his chill, crisp tones.

When Samlor hil Samt was angry enough to kill, he spoke in soft, bantering tones. The muscles stretched across his cheekbones and pulled themselves into a visage very different from the way he normally looked; a visage not altogether human.

He rarely became that angry; and he was not angry now,

only cautious and in need of information before he could lead Star and her legacy out of this *damnable* city.

The clabbered milk was served in masars, wooden cups darkened by the sweating palms of hundreds of previous users. As the tapster paused, midway between reaching for the coin now or drawing the beer first, Samlor said, "I'm trying to find a man in this town, and I'm hoping that you might be able to help me. Business, but not—serious business."

That was true, though neither the tapster nor any other man in this dive was likely to believe it.

Not that they'd care, either, so long as they'd been paid in honest coin.

"A regular?" asked the balding man softly as his hand did, after all, cover the gold which Samlor was not yet willing to release.

"I doubt it," said the Cirdonian with a false, fleeting smile. "His name's Setios. A businessman, perhaps, a banker, as like as not. Or just possibly, he might be, you know . . . someone who deals with magic. I was told he keeps a demon imprisoned in a crystal bottle."

You could never tell how mention of sorcery or a wizard was going to strike people. Some very tough men would blanch and draw away—or try to slit your throat so that they wouldn't have to listen to more.

The tapster only smiled and said, "Somebody may know him. I'll ask around." He turned. The coin disappeared into a pocket of his apron.

"Uncle, I don't *like*—"

"And the beers, friend," Samlor called in a slightly louder voice.

There was little for a child to drink in a place like this. Star didn't have decades of caravan life behind her, the days when anything wet was better than the smile of a goddess. The beer was a better bet than whatever passed for wine, and either would be safer than the water.

"This is a very special knife," said a voice at Samlor's shoulder.

The Cirdonian turned, face flat. He was almost willing to disbelieve the senses that told him that the stranger was pursuing his attempt to sell a dagger. In *this* place, a tavern where unwanted persistence generally led to somebody being killed.

"Get away from me," Samlor said in a clear, clipped voice, "or I'll put you through a window."

He nodded toward the wall facing the street, where wicker lattices screened the large openings to either side of the door. The sides of the room were ventilated by high, horizontal slits that opened onto alleys even more fetid than the interior of the tavern.

Samlor meant exactly what he said, though it would cause trouble that he'd really rather avoid.

Star wasn't the only one whom fatigue had left with a hair trigger.

The man wasn't a threatening figure, only an irritating one. He was shorter than Samlor by an inch or two and fine-boned to an almost feminine degree. He wore a white linen kilt with a scarlet hem, cinched up on a slant by a belt of gorgeous gold brocade. His thigh-length cape was of a thick, soft, blue fabric, but his torso was bare beneath that garment. The skin was coppery brown, and his chest, though hairless, was flat-muscled and clearly male.

The stranger blinked above his smile and backed a half step. Samlor caught the beers that the tapster glided to him across the surface of the bar.

"Here, Star," said the Cirdonian, handing one of the containers down to his charge. "It's what there is, so don't complain. We'll do better another time, all right?"

The beer was in leathern jacks, and the tar used to seal the leather became a major component of the liquid's flavor. It was an acquired taste—and not one Samlor, much less his niece, had ever bothered to acquire. At that, the smoky flavor of the tar might be less unpleasant than the way the brew here would taste without it.

The tapster had crooked a finger toward a dun-colored man at a corner table. Samlor would not have noticed the summons had he not been sure it was coming, but the two men began to talk in low voices at the far end of the bar.

The tavern was lighted by a lantern behind the bar and a trio of lamps hanging from a hoop in the center of the room.

The terra-cotta lamps had been molded for good luck into the shape of penises.

There was no sign that the clientele of this place was particularly fortunate, and the *gods* knew they were not well lighted. The cheap lamp oil gave off as much smoke as flame, so that the tavern drifted in a haze as bitter as the faces of its denizens.

"Really, Master Samlor," said the stranger, "you *must* look at this dagger."

The Cirdonian's name made time freeze for him, though no one else in the Vulgar Unicorn appeared to take undue notice. The flat of the weapon was toward Samlor. The slim man held the hilt between thumb and forefinger and balanced the lower edge of the blade near the tip on his other forefinger—not even a razor will cut with no more force than gravity driving it.

Samlor's own belt knife was clear of its sheath, drawn by reflex without need for his conscious mind to react to the danger. But the stranger was smiling and immobile, and the dagger he held—

The dagger was very interesting at that.

Its pommel was faceted with the ruddy luster of copper. The butt itself was flat and narrow, angling wider for a finger's breadth toward the hilt and narrowing again in a smooth concave arc. The effect was that of a coffin, narrow for the corpse's head and wider for his shoulders until it tapered toward his feet again.

The hilt was unusual and perhaps not unattractive, but the true wonder of the weapon was its blade.

Steel becomes more brittle as it becomes harder. The greatest mystery of the swordsmith's art is the tempering that permits blades to strike without shattering while remaining hard enough to cleave armor or an opponent's weapon.

A way around the problem is to weld a billet of soft iron to a billet of steel hardened with the highest possible carbon content. The fused bar can then be hammered flat and folded back on itself, the process repeating until iron and steel are intermingled in thousands of layers thinner than the edge of a razor.

Done correctly, the result is a blade whose hardness is sandwiched within malleable layers that absorb shock and give the whole resilience; but the operation requires the flats to be cleaned before each refolding, lest oxide scale weaken the core and cause it to split on impact like a wand of whalebone. Few smiths had the skill and patience to forge such blades; few purchasers had the wealth to pay for so much expert labor.

But this stranger seemed to think Samlor fell into the latter category—as the caravan master indeed did, if he wanted a thing badly enough.

The blade was beautiful. It was double-edged and a foot long, with the sharpened surfaces describing flat curves instead of being straight tapers like those of the knife in Samlor's hand. The blade sloped toward either edge from the deep keel in the center which gave it stiffness—and all along the flat, the surface danced and shimmered with the polished, acid-etched whorls of the dissimilar metals which comprised it.

Because of their multiple hammered refoldings, the join lines between layers of iron and steel were as complex as the sutures of a human skull. After the bar had been forged and ground into a blade, the smith polished it and dipped it into strong acid which he quickly flushed away.

The steel resisted the biting fluid, but some of the softer iron was eaten by even the brief touch. The iron became a shadow of incredible delicacy against which the ripples of bright steel stood out like sunlight on mountain rapids. Even without its functional purpose, the watermarked blade would have commanded a high price for its appearance.

Samlor's eyes stung. He blinked, because in the wavering lamplight the spidery lines of iron against steel looked like writing.

The stranger smiled more broadly.

"Unc—" began Star with a tug on the caravan master's left sleeve.

The iron shadows in the heart of the blade read, "He will attack" in Cirdonian script. A moment before, they had been only swirls of metal.

The stranger's hand slid fully onto the hilt he had been

pinching to display. He twisted it in a slashing stroke toward Samlor's eyes.

Samlor didn't believe the words written on steel. He didn't even believe he had seen them. But part of his nervous system—"mind" would be too formal a term for reflex at so primitive a level—reacted to the strangeness with explosive activity.

The Cirdonian's left hand shot out and crushed the stranger's fingers against the grip of his weapon, easily turning the stroke into a harmless upward sweep. The metal that Samlor touched—the copper buttcap and the tang to which scales of dark wood were pinned to complete the hilt—were cooler than air temperature despite having been carried beneath the stranger's cape.

Samlor's right hand slammed his own dagger up and through the stranger's ribcage till the crosshilt stopped at the breastbone. The caravan master could have disarmed his opponent without putting a foot of steel through his chest, but reflex didn't know and instinct didn't care.

The stranger—the dead man, now, with steel from his diaphragm to the back of his throat—lifted at the short, powerful blow. His head snapped back—his mouth was still smiling—and hammered the hoop which suspended the lamps. They sloshed and went out as the heavy oil doused their wicks.

"Star, keep behind—" Samlor ordered as the light dimmed and his right hand jerked down to clear his weapon from the torso in which he had just imbedded it. The stranger flopped forward loosely, but the blade remained stuck.

Somebody's hurled beer mug smashed the lantern behind the bar. The Vulgar Unicorn was as dark as the bowels of Hell.

Samlor ducked and hunched back against the bar while he tugged at his knife hilt with enough strength to have forced a camel to its knees.

There was a grunt and an oak-topped table crashed over. Somebody screamed as if he were being opened from groin to gullet—as may have been the case. Darkness in a place

like this was both an opportunity and a source of panic.
Either could lead to slaughter.

Samlor's dagger wouldn't come free. He hadn't felt it
grate bone as it went in, and it didn't feel now as if the tip
were caught on ribs or the stranger's vertebrae. The blade
didn't flex at all, the way it should have done if it were held
at one point. It was more as if Samlor had thrust the steel
into fresh concrete and came back a day later in a vain
attempt to withdraw it.

One advantage to winning a knife fight is that you have
the choice of your opponent's weapon if something's
happened to yours. The Cirdonian's left hand snatched the
hilt from the unresisting fingers of the man he had just
killed, while his right arm swept behind him to gather up his
niece.

A thrown weapon plucked his sleeve much the way the
child had done a moment before. The point was too blunt to
stick in the bar panel against which it crashed like a
crossbow bolt.

Star wasn't there. She wasn't anywhere within the sweep
of Samlor's arm, and there was no response when he
desperately called the child's name.

Steel hit steel across the room with a clang and a shower
of orange sparks. Someone outside the tavern called a
warning, but there was already a murderous scuffle blocking
the only door to the street.

That left the door to the alley on the opposite side of the
tavern; stairs to the upper floor—which Samlor couldn't
locate in the dark and which were probably worth his life to
attempt anyway; and a third option which was faster and
safer than the other two, though it was neither fast nor safe
on any sane scale.

Samlor gripped the body of his victim beneath both
armpits and rushed forward, using the corpse as a shield and
a battering ram.

His niece might still be inside the Vulgar Unicorn, but he
couldn't find her in the darkness if she didn't—or couldn't—
answer his call. Star was a level-headed girl who might
have screamed but wouldn't have panicked to silence when
Samlor shouted for her.

He was much more concerned that she had bolted for the door the instant the lights went out, and that she was now in the arms of someone with a good idea of the price a virgin of her age would fetch in this hellhole.

Somebody brushed Samlor from the side—backed into him—and caromed off wailing in terror. Samlor did not cut with his new dagger at the contact because Star could still be within reach of his blade. . . .

He was willing to be stabbed himself to avoid making that sort of mistake.

Samlor stumbled on an outstretched limb which gave but did not twitch beneath his boot. Then the corpse hit the screen to the right of the door and the Cirdonian used all the strength of his back and shoulders to smash the wickerwork out into the street.

The screen was dry with age, and many of the individual withies were already splitting away from the tiny trenails that pinned them to the frame. The wicker still retained a springy strength greater than that of thin board shutters, and Samlor felt a hint of infuriating backthrust against his push.

The frame snapped away from the sash, letting the corpse carry the collapsing wickerwork ahead of it into the street.

There was enough haze to hide the stars and sliver moon, but the sky glow was enough ʾɔ fill the window sash after the lattice had been torn away. Samlor dived over the sill, keeping his body as low as possible. He could have boosted himself with his empty right hand so that he landed feet first instead of slamming the street with his shoulder—

But if he had done that, the knife that flicked through the air above his rolling body would instead have punched between his shoulder blades. Some brawlers, like sharks in a feeding frenzy, don't need a reason to kill: only a target.

"*Star!*" the caravan master bellowed as he hit, the shock of impact turning the word into more of a gasp than he had expected. His cloak and shoulder muscles had to break the fall, because his left hand, the downside hand, held the long knife that could be the margin of survival in the next instants.

The door of the tavern beside Samlor was blocked by two men, the larger holding the smaller and stabbing with mindless repetition. The only sound the victim made now was the squelch of his flesh parting before the steel.

A watchman had stepped from a door down the street. The lantern he raised did not illuminate figures, but its light wavered from metal in the hands of half a dozen men scurrying toward the altercation.

Samlor had heard that there were local militias raised from every few blocks of the Old City. They differed from street gangs in their expressed determination to keep order and protect their enclaves—but that didn't mean it would be healthy for an outsider to fall into their hands after starting a brawl on their turf. Militiamen rarely saw the need for a trial when there was already a rope or a sword handy.

The squad marching toward the noise from the other direction *was* paid to enforce the law, but the priorities of the men comprising the unit tended to be more personal. They were regular army, and the quicker they silenced the trouble, the quicker they could get the fuck back to the patrol station where they didn't have to worry about showers of bricks and roofing tiles.

One of the soldiers carried a lantern on a pole. The glazing was protected by wire mesh, and similar metal curtains depended stiffly from the brims of the squad's dented helmets. They carried pole arms, halbreds and short pikes, and they shuffled forward with such noisy delibera- tion that it was obvious they hoped the problem would go away without any need for them to deal with it.

Samlor was willing enough to do that. The problem was how.

Star wasn't in the street and wasn't answering him. He'd find her if he had to wash Sanctuary away in the blood of its denizens, but first he had to get clear of this mess into which Fate seemed to have dropped him through no fault of his own.

Why had that clumsy, suicidal stranger attacked him? Why had the fellow even accosted him?

But first, survival.

Samlor switched the dagger to his right hand, master hand, and dodged into the alley nearest him.

The passageway was scarcely the width of his shoulders,

but a door—strapped and studded with metal—gave onto it from the building on the other side. The Cirdonian slapped the panel as he dodged past it. Had it opened, he would have dived in and dealt with those inside in whatever fashion seemed advisable.

But he didn't expect that; and as he expected, the door was as solid as the stone to either side of it.

The alley jogged, though Samlor didn't recall an angle from inside the Vulgar Unicorn's taproom. He slid past the facet of masonry, into an instant of pitch darkness before someone within the tavern reignited a lamp.

There were two slit windows serving this side of the taproom. The grating still covered one, but the light silhouetted the crisp rectangle of the other from which the wickerwork had been torn since the caravan master last saw it inside.

Even so, the opening was too narrow to pass an adult.

Samlor's mouth opened to call, but the child in the midst of four men was already screaming, "*Uncle Samlor.*"

CHAPTER 2

THERE WERE THREE of them between him and Star, packed into the passageway so that the child's dust-whitened garments were only a shimmer past their legs. They were the punks from the table by the door. Beyond them was a fourth man, tall and hooded, closing Star's escape route.

Light in the passageway was only the ghost filtering through the tavern windows and reflected from the filth-blackened wall opposite, but it was enough for Samlor's business. He drew the push dagger from its sheath under the back of his collar and held it so that its narrow point jutted out between the fourth and index fingers of his left hand.

Before the caravan master could lunge into action, the hooded man stepped past the cringing Star and held his staff vertically to confront the trio of toughs. Either the hood was flapping loose or something tiny capered on the fellow's shoulder.

"What are you doing with this child?" he demanded in a clear voice. "Begone!"

"Hey," said the nearest thug, doubtful enough to step back and jostle a companion.

The staff glowed pale blue, a hazy color which seemed to hang in the air as the object trembled. The face beneath the hood was set with determination which controlled but did not eliminate the underlying fear. The staff shook because the man holding it was terrified.

Reasonably enough.

Samlor paused. If the toughs *did* turn away in fear of what confronted them, he didn't want to be launched into an attack intended for their backs.

He didn't know what was going on. Sometimes you had to act anyway—but just now, Star was out of immediate danger, so there was no point in going off half-cocked.

Something—a *man*, there was no damned doubt about it, but he was only a handspan tall—stood on the right shoulder of the man with the glowing staff. The little fellow hopped up and down, then piped, "Do not be afraid to do that in which you are right!"

A thug swore and swung his weapon at the staff.

Instead of blades or ordinary clubs, this trio of street toughs carried weighted chains which Samlor had mistaken in the tavern for items of armor or adornment when they were coiled through an epaulette loop on each youth's shoulder. Each chain was about a yard long, made up of fine links which slipped over one another like drops of water. They were polished glass-smooth and then plated for looks—silver for two of the thugs, gold for the third who now swung his weapon in a glittering arc.

Both ends of the chain were weighted by lead knobs the size of large walnuts, armed with steel spikes. The knobs were heavy enough to stun or kill but still so light that they could be directed handily and with blinding speed. A skilled man in the right situation could pulp an opposing knife artist, and he could do so with the sort of flashy display which on the street counted for more than success.

It was the wrong weapon for an alleyway which even at his widest point was straiter than the span of the chain fully extended, but the hooded man seemed to have no idea of how to defend himself. The weighted end of the chain wrapped itself tight against the staff—it clacked like wood, despite the glow which suggested it was of some eerie material—and the tough jerked it toward him.

The hopping manikin disappeared with a high-pitched shriek of terror. The hooded man staggered forward, managing to keep a hold on his staff only by lurching toward the punk whose weapon had snatched it. The blue glow was snuffed out as if the gold-plated chain had strangled the life from the wood.

The hooded man was a magician, *had* to be with his staff and capering manikin. Samlor—and probably the street toughs as well, though psychotic pride ruled the actions of their leader—expected magical retribution for the attack. A thunderbolt might shatter them, or icy needles from nowhere might lace their bodies into bloody sieves.

Nothing happened except that the leading thug gripped his opponent by the throat and shouted, "*Finish* 'im, dungbrains!" to his fellows as the victim struggled to free his chain-wrapped staff.

The caravan master waded in to do the job that magic wouldn't take care of after all.

One of the three youths hung a half step behind his fellows. Samlor punched the base of his skull left-handed. The steel cap concealed beneath the bright bandana rapped the knuckle of the Cirdonian's index finger, but the bodkin point of Samlor's push dagger plunged in to its full length.

The youth turned and cried out, pulling clear of the two-inch blade that left a trickle of gore crawling toward the collar of his studded vest. He'd been spinning his chain between the thumb and index finger of his right hand, waiting for an opening to slap the weight into the hooded man. One of the balls gouged Samlor's thigh, but that was accident rather than deliberate counterattack.

The youth dropped his weapon and stumbled off down the alleyway, kicked in passing by the man still struggling for his staff. Star flattened herself against the wall to let him go. Her eyes and the white swirl in her hair were pools of reflected light as she stared at her uncle.

Samlor cut at the neck of the next thug with the watermarked dagger while drops of blood still winked in the air as they flew from the neck of his first target. The hilt of the unfamiliar weapon was slimmer in his hand than the knife he'd left in the corpse, but the blade's relative point-heaviness gave heft to the slashing blow. The youth got his left arm up in time to block the edge with his forearm while his leader sprayed curses and tried to clear his chain from the staff which now held *it* rather than the reverse.

There wasn't enough hilt for Samlor's hands. The shock threatened to jar the knife away from him as the blade sank deep in the leading armbone and cracked it through when the Cirdonian twisted. The youth squealed in hopeless panic, but luck or practice spun one end of his weighted chain in a loop around the weapon that had crippled him.

Samlor punched the tough in the chest left-handed, then jerked down on the butt of his coffin-hilted dagger. The youth's leather vest was sewn with flat metal washers: the narrow point in Samlor's left hand scratched across the face of one before it sank deep enough into unprotected flesh to prick a lung.

Whether or not the metal in the daggerblade had spelled Samlor a warning, it served well enough for a fighting knife. At the Cirdonian's swift tug, the edges sawed through the silvered chain and freed themselves. The severed knob spun to the muck on the alley's cobblestones with its bit of attached chain twitching like a lizard's tail.

The thug lost his footing and fell backwards. He should have tangled himself with his leader, but the youth with the gilded chain danced clear. On his toes, buttocks flattening against the tavern wall as his fellow sprawled beneath him, he whirled a spiked knob at Samlor in a downward arc that split the difference between vertical and horizontal.

The stranger's hood had flopped back and his cape was twisted so that its broach closure was at his left shoulder instead of his throat. When the street tough dropped him to deal with Samlor, the man raised a hand and began to stutter words in a language the caravan master did not know. As the spiked chain spun at Samlor's skull in a curve as dangerous as a sword stroke, the stranger stopped talking and prodded the youth between the shoulders with his staff.

Samlor dodged back to avoid the spikes, forgetting the bulge in the wall behind that rocked him to a halt. The knob sparked across the stone and tore the Cirdonian's left ear as the youth tried to recover from the push that sent him off-balance.

He didn't get the chance.

The youth wore a necklace strung with the protective charms of at least a dozen faiths, and the front of his vest

was strengthened with gilt and silvered studs. None of that
helped him when Samlor stabbed upward from groin level.
While the punk thrashed like a gigged frog on the twelve-
inch blade, the caravan master punched him repeatedly with
the push dagger, aiming at the base of the jaw just below the
bandana and the steel cap it covered.

The youth collapsed. His eyes were open and his lungs
were still working well enough to form bubbles in the blood
that drooled from the corner of his mouth. A mixture of
body fluids and digestive products followed the blade of the
long knife as Samlor withdrew it. Their foetor was briefly
noticeable even in this alley.

He was probably fourteen years old or so. He looked
younger, but bad diet pinched and stunted the faces of those
born here into permanent childhood.

"Now the others," chirped a little voice. "Do not kill a
snake and leave its tail!"

The caravan master was on his knees. He did not recall
closing his eyes, but he opened them now. The man with the
staff was on his feet again and straightening his disordered
cape. The manikin was back on his shoulder, strutting
proudly with hands on hips.

"You," said Samlor very distinctly. "Shit it in or you'll
join 'em."

The little figure yelped and disappeared again.

Samlor, Star, and the stranger were alone with the dying
youth. The other two toughs had disappeared down the
alley, and no one else seemed to have entered the passage
behind the caravan master. There were voices from within
the taproom, deep and hectoring, but Samlor didn't care
enough to try to understand the words.

His niece, shivering also, minced over to him without
looking down and put her arms around Samlor's shoulder.
"I'm sorry you hurt your ear, Uncle," she said in a voice
that trembled with the child's attempts to control it. "I
shouldn't have—"

She hugged him harder. "But I thought I could climb up
from the bench when it was dark and I *didn't* know where
you were—" Her words tumbled out like flotsam in the
current of the sobs wracking her little body.

"—and the, those *men* came and I couldn't *do* anything!"

"You did fine, darling," the Cirdonian muttered. He encircled the child with his left arm, careful that the point of his push dagger was turned outward. He couldn't put it away until he cleaned it—as his right hand was cleaning the watered steel of the longer knife on the pantaloons of the boy whose breathing had ceased in a pair of great shudders. "But you've gotta listen to me, or really bad things could happen."

The blade of the long dagger showed a nick midway up on edge, but it had come through the struggle at least as well as any other knife was likely to have done. Samlor tried to sheathe it and found the new blade was a trifle too broad near the tip to fit in the scabbard meant for the knife it replaced.

He slid it beneath his belt instead; wiped the push dagger; and rose with that miniature weapon in his right hand while his left arm guided Star behind him again.

He thought he recognized the man who was fingering his staff now that his cape was rearranged.

"Who would you be, my friend?" Samlor asked without hostility or any other motion.

"My name is Khamwas," the fellow said in a cultured voice that tried to be calm. The peak of his hood must have added several inches to his height, because he was clearly shorter than the caravan master as well as being much more slightly built. "I'm a stranger here in your city."

The manikin silently reappeared on Khamwas' shoulder. The tiny features were unreadable in the dim light, but the figure's pose was apprehensive.

"Did you have a friend in that tavern?" asked the caravan master softly. When his right thumb turned to indicate the wall of the Vulgar Unicorn, the point of the push dagger winked knowingly toward Khamwas' eyes. "A brother, maybe?"

Reaching out on a sudden whim, Samlor jerked open the other man's cape. He *knew* the body he'd thrown ahead of him through the tavern window was dead, but the faces were so much alike. . . .

There were no bloodstains on this man's clothes and the

garments themselves were different—though of a not dissimilar fashion. A linen tunic bared Khamwas' right shoulder but covered most of his chest, and the belt that cinched it at the waist was of dark brocade, red or blue—certainly not gold.

"I beg your pardon," Khamwas said, touching his cape closed again with cautious dignity. "I have no brothers, and I don't *know* anyone in this city. I'm a scholar from a far country, and I've come to ask a favor here from a man named Setios."

"Uncle, that—" blurted Star, catching herself before Samlor's free hand could waggle a warning.

"A bird who flies to the nest of another," chirped the manikin sententiously, "will lose a feather."

"What in *hell* is that?" asked the caravan master deliberately, pointing at the manikin with his right index finger. The bodkin-bladed push dagger parallelled the gesturing finger as if by chance.

The manikin eeped and cowered. Khamwas reached across to his right shoulder with his cupped hand, as if to shield and stroke the little creature simultaneously.

"He does no harm, sir," the self-styled scholar replied calmly. "I—when I was younger, you understand—prayed to certain powers for wisdom. They sent me this little fellow instead. His name is Tjainufi."

The manikin stared balefully at Khamwas, but his tiny arm reached out to pat the hand protecting him. "A fool who wants to go with a wise man," he said, "is a goose who wants to go with the slaughter knife."

Samlor blinked. He was confused, but that probably didn't matter, not compared to a dozen other things. "You know my name, then?" he said, harshly again, sure that Khamwas had to have some connection with the stranger in the tavern. A sorcerer who knew your name had the first knot in a rope of power to bind you. . . .

"Sir, I know *no* one in your city," Khamwas repeated, drawing himself up and planting the staff firmly before him with his hands linked on it. "I have a daughter the age of your niece, so I—tried, I should say, to intervene when she seemed to be in difficulties."

He paused. For an instant his staff glowed again. The grain of the wood made ripples in the phosphorescence, and a haze of light wrapped Khamwas' hands like a real fog.

Star reached past her uncle and touched the staff.

The glow flickered out as Khamwas started, but a tinge of blue clung to the child's fingers as she withdrew them. Samlor did not swear, because words had power—especially at times like these. His left hand caressed his niece's hair, offering human contact when he could not be sure what help, if any, the child required.

If Khamwas' toying had done any harm, he would be fed his liver on the point of a knife.

Star giggled while both men watched her with fear born of uncertainty. She opened her fingers slowly and the glow between their tips grew and paled like the sheen of an expanding soap bubble. Then it popped as if it had never been.

Khamwas let out his breath abruptly. "Sir," he said to the caravan master, "I didn't realize. Forgive me for intruding in your affairs."

Tjainufi, who had disappeared when Star lifted light from the staff, now waggled an arm at Khamwas and said, "Do not say, 'I am learned.' Set yourself to become wise."

Khamwas would have stepped by and continued up the alley, but Samlor restrained him with a gesture that would have become contact if the scholar had not halted. "You saved Star from a bad time before I got here," he said. "And likely you saved me, besides distracting the little bastards. My name's Samlor hil Samt." He sheathed the little dagger behind his collar. "You and I need to talk."

"All right, Master Samlor," agreed the other man, though the way his lips pursed showed that the suggestion was not one he would have made himself. He gestured up the passageway, the direction from which the Cirdonian had come, and added, "There are more suitable places to discuss matters than here, I'm certain."

"No," said Samlor flatly, "there's not."

It wasn't worth his time to explain that the direction in which Khamwas was headed would be a no-go area for at least the next hour. The passageway was narrow enough to be defended by one man, and both flanks were protected by masonry that would require siege equipment to breach. If their luck were really out, they could be attacked from both directions simultaneously, but that risk was better than being trapped in a cul-de-sac with no bolthole.

Given the nature of Sanctuary, this was probably the safest place within a league in any direction.

"What do you know about Setios?" the caravan master demanded, no more threatening than was implicit in the fact that he had already demonstrated his willingness and ability to kill.

Star was squatting, her skirts lifted and wrapped around her thighs to keep the hem from lying in the muck. A tiny glow spun within the globe of her hands as she cooed. Its color was more nearly yellow than the blue which had washed Khamwas' staff.

The glow was reflected faintly by the eyes of the dead youth.

Khamwas' face worked in something between a grimace and a moue of embarrassment as he watched the child. "Ah," he said to Samlor. "That is, ah—are you . . . ?"

The caravan master shook his head, glad to find that the question amused him rather than arousing any of the other possible emotions. "On a good day," he said, "I might be able to recite a spell without stumbling over the syllables— if somebody wrote 'em out for me really careful." That was an exaggeration, though not a great one.

"My sister, though," he added, embarrassed himself for reasons the other man should not be able to fathom, "that was more her line."

To the extent that anything besides sex was Samlane's line.

"I see," said Khamwas, and he continued to glance down at the child even as he returned to the earlier question. "I don't know Setios at all," he explained, "but I know— I've been told by, well—"

He shrugged. Samlor nodded grimly; but if this fellow called himself scholar rather than wizard, he at least recognized that the latter was a term of reproach to decent men.

"Serve your god, that he may guard you," said Tjainufi, stroking his master's—could Khamwas be called that?—right ear.

"He has," Khamwas went on after the awkward pause, "a stele from my own land, from Napata—"

"Of course," Samlor interrupted, placing the stranger at least. "The Land of the River."

"The river," Khamwas agreed with a nod of approval, "and of the desert. And in the desert, many monuments of former times—" he paused again, gave a gentle smile "—greater times for my people, some would say, though I myself am content."

"You want to—retrieve," said Samlor, avoiding the question of means, "a monument that this Setios has. Is he a magician?"

"I don't know," said Khamwas with another shrug. "And I don't need the stele, only a chance to look at it. And, ah, Samlor—?"

The caravan master nodded curtly to indicate that he would not take offense at what he assumed would be a tense question.

"I will pay him well for the look," the Napatan said. "It's of no value to him—not for the purpose I intend it—without other information. It will give me the location of a particular tomb, which is significant to me for other reasons."

The light in Star's hands was growing brighter, throwing the men's shadows onto the wall of the alley. Khamwas' face looked demonically inhuman because it was being illuminated from below.

Samlor touched his niece's head. "Not so much, dearest," he murmured. "We don't want anybody noticing us here if we can help it."

"But—" Star began shrilly. She looked up and met her uncle's eyes. The light shrank to the size of a large pearl, too dim to show anything but itself.

"She didn't know how to do that before," said Samlor, as much an explanation to himself as one directed toward the other man. "She picks things up."

"I see," said Khamwas, and maybe he did. "Well."

He shook himself, to settle his cape and to settle himself in his resolve. "Well, Master Samlor," the Napatan continued, "I must be on." He nodded past Samlor toward the head of the alley.

"Not that way," said the caravan master wryly, though he did not move again to block the other man.

"Yes, it is," Khamwas replied with a touch of astringence. He stiffened to his full height. The manikin on his shoulder mimicked the posture, perhaps in irony. "The direction of Setios' house is precisely—" he extended his arm at an angle toward Samlor; hesitated with his eyes turned inward; and corrected the line a little further to the right "—this way. And this passage is the nearest route to the way I need to follow."

"Do not do a thing you have not first considered carefully," Tjainufi suddenly warned.

The caravan master began to chuckle. He clapped a hand in a friendly fashion on Khamwas' left shoulder. "Nearest route to having your head stuck on a pole, I'd judge," he said. The Napatan felt as fine-boned as he looked, but there was a decent layer of muscle between the skeleton and the soft fabric of his cape.

"Look," Samlor continued, "d'ye mean to tell me you don't know where in the city Setios lives, you're just walking through the place in the straightest line your— friends, I suppose—tell you is the way to Setios? Are these the same friends who gave you wisdom?"

The caravan master nodded toward Tjainufi.

"I think that's my affair, Master Samlor," said Khamwas. He strode forward, gripping his staff vertically before him. His knuckles were white.

The manikin said, " 'What he does insults me,' says the fool when a wise man instructs him."

Khamwas halted. Samlor looked at the little figure with a frown of new surmise. There was no bad advice—only advice that was wrong for a given set of circumstances. And, just possibly, Tjainufi's advice was more appropriate than the Cirdonian had guessed.

"All I meant, friend," Samlor said, touching and then removing his hand from the other man's shoulder, "was that maybe there aren't any good districts in Sanctuary—but your straight line's sure as death taking you through the middle of the worst of what there is."

Star had stood up when Khamwas started to walk away. The light which now clung to her left palm had put out tendrils and was fluctuating through a series of pastels paler than the colors of a noontime rainbow. Impulsively, she hugged the Napatan's leg and said, "Isn't it *pretty?* Oh, thank you!"

"It's only a—little thing," Khamwas explained apologetically to the child's uncle. "It—I don't know how she learned it from seeing what I did."

Samlor noticed that the staff glowed only when Khamwas could concentrate on it, but that the phosphorescence in Star's hand continued its complex evolutions of shape and color even while his niece was hugging and smiling brightly at the other man.

The light glinted on the bare blade of Samlor's new dagger, harder in reflection than the source hanging in the air seemed.

The caravan master blinked, touched his tunic over the silver medallion of the goddess Heqt on his breast, and only then slid the weapon back from its temporary resting place beneath his belt. The twisting phosphorescence gave the markings a false hint of motion; but they were only swirls of metal, not the script he thought he had again seen.

Khamwas watched with controlled apprehension. Deciding that it was better to go on with his proposal than to wonder why Samlor was staring at the knife whose guard still bore dark stains, the Napatan said, "Master Samlor, you understand this city as I do not. And you're clearly able to deal with, ah, with violence, should any be offered. Could I prevail on you to accompany me to the house of Setios? I'll pay you well."

"Do not walk the road without a stick in your hand," Tjainufi said approvingly.

"*We* need to find Setios, Uncle Samlor," said the child in a voice rising toward shrill. She released Khamwas and instead tugged insistently on the elbow of her uncle's right sleeve. "*Please* can we? He's nice."

Cold steel cannot flow, twist, parse out words, thought the caravan master. The nick in the edge was bright and real: this was no thing of enchantment, only a dagger with an awkward hilt and a very good blade.

Star pulled at Samlor's arm with most of her weight. He did not look down at her, nor did his hand drop. That arm had dragged a donkey back up to the trail from which it had stumbled into a gulley a hundred feet deep.

"*Please*," said the child.

"Friend Samlor?" said the Napatan doubtfully. The knife was only that, a knife, so far as he could see.

Go with him, spelled the rippling steel at which Samlor stared.

The words faded as the glow in Star's hand shrank to a point and disappeared.

"I was ready," said the caravan master slowly, "to find a guide in there."

He did not gesture toward the tavern. He was speaking to himself, not to the pair of living humans with him in the alleyway. They stared at Samlor, his niece and the stranger, as they would have stared at a pet lion who suddenly began to act oddly.

"So I guess," Samlor continued, "we'll find Setios together. After all—" he tapped the blade of the coffin-hilted dagger with a fingernail; the metal gave a musical ping.

"—we're all four agreed, aren't we?"

Star leaned toward her uncle and hugged his powerful thigh, but she would not meet his eyes again or look at the knife in his hand. Khamwas nodded cautiously.

"We'll circle out of the Maze, then," said Samlor matter-of-factly. "Come on."

The way down the alley meant stepping over the body of the youth he had just killed.

This was Sanctuary. It wouldn't be the last corpse they saw.

CHAPTER 3

THE BODY SPRAWLED just inside the alley would have passed for a corpse if you didn't listen carefully—or didn't recognize the ragged susurrus of a man breathing while his face lay against slimy cobblestones.

"Mind this," said Samlor, touching first Star, then Khamwas so that they would notice his gesture toward the obstacle. Human eyes could adapt to scant illumination, but at this end of the alley the dying man's breath was all that made it possible to locate him.

The manikin on Khamwas' shoulder must have been able to sense the situation, because he said, "There is no one who does not die." His voice was as high as a bird's; but, also like a bird's, it had considerable volume behind it.

The Napatan "scholar" reached toward his shoulder with his free hand, a gesture mingled of affection and warning. "Tjainufi," he muttered, "Not now. . . ."

Samlor doubted that Khamwas had any more control over the manikin than a camel driver did over a pet mouse which lived in a fold of his cloak. Or, for that matter, than Samlor himself had over his niece, who was bright enough to understand any instructions he gave her—but whose response was as likely to be willful as that of any other seven-year-old.

Now, for instance, a ball of phosphorescence bloomed in the cup of the child's hand, lighting her way past the dying

29

man despite the caravan master's warning that illumination—magical or otherwise—would be more risk to them than benefit, at least until they got out of the Maze.

Star put a foot down daintily, just short of the victim's outflung arm, then skipped by in a motion that by its incongruity made the scene all the more horrible. The ball of light she had formed drifted behind her for a moment. Its core shrank and brightened—from will o' the wisp to firefly intensity—while the whirling periphery formed tendrils like the whorl of silver-white hair on Star's head.

The child turned back, saw the set expression on Samlor's face, and jerked away as if he had slapped her physically. The spin of light blanked as if it had never been.

"Is he . . . ?" asked Khamwas as he stepped over his mind's image of where the body lay. "One of those we—met a moment ago?"

"The gang who came after us with chains, sure," said the caravan master as he followed with a long stride. The passageway was wide enough for him to spread his arms without quite touching the walls to either side; in the Maze, that made it a street. It held only the normal sounds of feral animals going about their business and, from behind shutters, bestial humans. "They're all dead, the two who ran off as sure as the one who didn't. Turn left here."

"The House of Setios is more to the—"

"Turn fucking *left*," Samlor whispered in a voice like stones rubbing.

"Do not be a hindrance, lest you be cursed," said Tjainufi on the Napatan's shoulder. The manikin bowed toward Samlor, but the caravan master was too angry to approve of anything.

Mostly he was angry at himself, because he'd killed often enough during his life to know that he really didn't like killing. Especially not kids, even punk kids who'd have dished his skull in with weighted chains and raped Star until they sold her to a brothel for the price of a skin of wine. . . .

Sanctuary might be incrementally better off without that particular trio, but Samlor hil Samt wasn't Justice, wasn't responsible to his god for the cleansing of this hellhole.

If he really wanted to avoid killing strangers, he should have kept out of Sanctuary, and he *surely* should have avoided the Vulgar Unicorn, even though it had looked like the best place to learn what he needed to know. There were many cities where merchant guild offices would supply information to a stranger. In a few there were even licensed municipal guides. But this place. . . .

"All I wanted was a guide to the house of Setios," the caravan master said.

"Khamwas will take us there, Uncle," said Star. Her voice was falsely bright to suggest that she didn't remember having disobeyed Samlor a moment before. She tucked her hand into that of the Napatan scholar.

The exchange frightened Samlor, because he *hadn't* meant to speak aloud.

"First," the caravan master said to his companions now that they could walk abreast, "we're going to get out of the Maze. *Then* we'll worry about a safe route to where we want to be."

Khamwas murmured assent. Star, glad to be included, patted her uncle's arm.

Samlor should have explained sooner instead of snarling orders and expecting to be obeyed because—because, in unvarnished truth, he was a dangerous man in a foul mood, and the long knife in his hand had killed at least once this evening. Maybe he *did* belong in Sanctuary.

Or dead.

"What would you do without me, hey, kid?" the caravan master said cheerfully to his niece. His left hand tousled her hair beneath the hood. "Hope the legacy Setios's keeping for you's worth the effort."

Hell, Samlor didn't want to die. And the rest, well—he'd worry about innocent bystanders, but he wouldn't lose sleep over punks who'd known the rules of the game they lost.

"Ah, legacy?" asked Khamwas, caught between an unwillingness to intrude and a near necessity of knowing what was going on.

"My mommie left me something," said Star, falling into the sing-song by which children remember information whose import is still beyond their grasp. Samlor let her

prattle on. Light through warped shutters up the street had
blanked and brightened as it would if someone moved in
front of it.

"She's dead, my mommie," the child continued, "but
she gave somebody a message to give to Uncle Samlor
when I'm seven which I am, so now we have to find Setios
who has my mommie's present."

Samlor stepped in front of his companions and stopped,
crying to the darkness, "*Try* it, fucker, and see what it buys
you!"

He didn't know how many there were or whether there
might be somebody behind him. He'd back away if he had
to—and had the chance—praying that Khamwas would be
alert enough to warn of trouble in that direction.

The Napatan whispered something. An ill-timed question, Samlor thought, but the words weren't meant for him
or for anyone human. Khamwas' staff glowed as it had
when the caravan master first saw the man; then the glow
detached itself from the wood and began to grow into a
manlike figure that staggered down the street in front of
them.

The figure didn't really walk, didn't move at all in the
normal sense. At the intervals of a heartbeat, the shape
displaced forward, limbs at changed angles as if it had
stepped from one point to another, though it had not visibly
crossed the intervening space. Beyond the figure hung its
afterimages, fading slowly from the transparent orange of
the original through stages of a violet that was itself almost
an absence of light.

As it advanced, the figure made an angry hissing like that
of a firebrand flung into a puddle.

Two men crouched in a doorway three yards away. One of
them wore a cavalryman's back-and-breast armor; both had
helmets of military weight and pattern. Between that
protection and the swords ready in their hands, Samlor
would have been a dead man had he tried to stop their
rush—and he couldn't flee without abandoning Star.

The muggers' eyes burned like those of beasts trapped by
the light of a hunter's lantern.

The shape's arm reached—*was*—toward them. One man

screamed and both bolted down the street in a clash of
falling equipment. The glowing figure stopped and disappeared as slowly as a lampwick cooling to blackness.

"Heqt be praised," muttered Samlor hil Samt. His left
hand had fumbled for the silver medallion hanging from his
neck. He could not feel the embossed features of the toad-
faced goddess beneath the fabric of his tunics, but the
unintended homage had been answered by a feeling of cool
stability.

Stability was worth a lot just now to Samlor.

Star was chattering to Khamwas, her words those of a
young child but her intent clearly that of an artist who wants
to learn a new technique. It was pitch dark in the street
when the last of the lurching figures disappeared.

A thing like a minnow of lambent red fluttered from
Star's hand.

"Not *now*," the caravan master snarled, terrified by the
implications of what Star had done.

The tiny fish gave a half turn in the air and collapsed
inward to a point of light and nothingness. Star looked
cautiously toward her uncle.

"Let's get on," said Samlor quietly, gesturing up the
darkened street.

"The strength of an army is its leader," squeaked
Tjainufi from Khamwas' shoulder.

Seeing the heavily-armed men flee in panic explained—
or might explain—how the Napatan had strolled into the
heart of the Maze alive. It still seemed incredible that
anyone would be naive enough to leave the caravan
encampment and walk in the straightest possible line toward
the house he wanted to visit. Khamwas' god—or a
demon—might point him unerringly toward Setios' house,
but the knowledge would do him little good if he were dead
and stripped in a gutter.

Still, Khamwas might have done just that. He was . . .
if not incredible, then a very strange man.

And the Napatan scholar was not nearly as strange as
Samlor's niece.

The Maze had administrative boundaries which were of
no more real significance than property lines on a swamp.

Samlor did not relax until he heard cracked voices up the street ahead of them. Two scavengers were pushing a handcart over the cobbles, pausing occasionally to scrabble for booty in the muck. They were singing, each of them a separate song, and from their voices the caravan master presumed they were either senile or very drunk.

But they were alive. If nobody had slit their throats for pleasure or the groat's worth of garbage they had scavenged, then Samlor had led his party out of the zone of most immediate danger.

Not that the caravan master was about to put away the long dagger he carried free in his right hand.

At the corner of a three-story building, locked and shuttered like a banker's strongbox, Samlor paused and said, "All right, Khamwas. *Now* you can point us toward Setios' house."

"Uncle, I want something to drink," said Star. "I didn't *like* the milk in that place."

"To the right, I think," said Khamwas, gesturing with his staff. The manikin had seated itself crosslegged on the Napatan's shoulder. The little figure was lounging with a hand leaned against Khamwas' neck as if it were the bole of a huge tree.

More than the level of risk had changed when Samlor's party got free of the Maze. The pavements were wider and somewhat more straight, and a number of door alcoves were illuminated by lamps in niches—closed against pilfering by screens of iron or pierced stone. The lights were intended to drive undesirables away from the building fronts, but they speeded travel without need for the drifting foxfire which Samlor's companions could provide.

"Why didn't you want me to light our way before, Master Samlor?" the Napatan asked.

Samlor stumbled, sure his mind had been read. Before he got out the threat that leaped to his tongue in response— "If you *ever* do that again—" reason reasserted itself.

Lamps on the buildings had made *him* think about the difficulty of staggering through the Maze in darkness. Therefore Khamwas might have thought the same thing, and spoken.

It didn't prove that the Napatan didn't read minds, but at least it permitted Samlor to continue believing that his thoughts were his own. He preferred a world in which that was true, and he didn't intend to go searching for proof that it wasn't.

"I suppose because it's, ah, a trick and not true light," Khamwas continued uncertainly. The other man's silence made the Napatan think that he'd said something wrong, and he was trying to smooth over the rift by closing the conversation that Samlor seemed unwilling to join. "It would have called attention to us."

A decent fellow, that one, thought the caravan master, for all his magical "scholarship" . . . and the fact that his face looked eerily similiar to that of the stranger whose dagger Samlor carried.

Since he'd been unable to free his own fighting knife after ramming it through the stranger's chest.

"No, not that," the caravan master replied. He chuckled. "I might've told you that, though. Truth is, I'm just scared of it. I figured things back there were tense enough without me scared and mad as blazes at you because of it."

"It's *simple*, Uncle," said Star, raising her hand with the palm cupped toward Samlor. "You just—"

"Not now, child," Samlor said, tensing again. *Not ever*, his mind added.

A party of six—or perhaps two parties of three, gravitating toward one another in a subconscious calculus of safety—were approaching them from the opposite direction.

"Star, in the middle," the Cirdonian caravaner muttered as he brushed the wall with his right shoulder. "And both of you behind me. *Watch* it." He heard Khamwas whispering to his staff or to the powers the scholar could key through it, but no apparition or—other sending—capered before them.

There was no need for that, nor for the water-marked steel of Samlor's dagger. The others edged by against the other side of the street. Samlor felt suicidally outnumbered, but he looked to those who saw him in shadow-streaked lamplight like certain death if anybody started something. Which was no more than the truth, not that he'd be alive

at the end himself. Not that he'd care about *that* either, so
long as he died with his teeth in a throat.

"A man's character is on his face," said Tjainufi, but
Samlor was motioning his companions ahead of him, poised
and wholly concentrated on the men disappearing down the
street behind them.

They probably weren't dangerous, just people with
somewhere of their own to go.

Sure. Probably headed for the meeting of a charitable
order, where they'd divide all their possessions among the
poor. *Nobody* in Sanctuary was too busy to prey upon the
helpless.

"When are we going to be there?" Star whined. Her
voice rose to a clear note that sounded like a shout in the
general stillness. "I'm *tired*." Nothing physical the child
could do would force her uncle to her will—but by speaking
loudly, she could call attention to their presence and
threaten all their lives.

A sure way to get attention, and a normal human
technique, sometimes modified for greater subtlety by
adults.

Samlor scooped his niece up with his left hand, resting
one of her hips against the jut of his pelvis. It was a gentle
movement and answered her complaint of being tired—she
could rest her head on his shoulder as they strode along, if
she cared to.

But it also reminded her of just how strong her uncle was,
and of how quickly he could move if he chose to.

"We'll get there, Star," Samlor said. "Don't fuss."

"Serve your father and mother," peeped Tjainufi, "that
you may go and prosper."

"Your friend," the caravan master remarked to Khamwas, "could get on a fellow's nerves."

The manikin, at eye level between the two adults,
suddenly disappeared. Khamwas smiled sadly and replied,
"Yes, but he was a useful warning to me. I asked the gods
for wisdom and—got him. I was young, and I was so sure I
could force my will on the gods. . . . What if I had asked
for something more dangerous than wisdom?"

"Luck turns away destruction by the great gods," called Tjainufi from the opposite shoulder, out of Samlor's sight.

"Besides," added Khamwas, cupping his hand on his empty shoulder. The manikin popped back there again, though with a nervous glance over the protective fingers toward the Cirdonian. "I'd miss him by now."

He smiled. Samlor smiled back in understanding, past the fluffy hair of his niece.

CHAPTER 4

Kнамwas directed them up one arm of a five-way intersection, past a patrol station. The gate to the internal courtyard was lighted by flaring sconces, and there was a squad on guard outside. An officer took a step into the street as if to halt the trio, but he changed his mind after a pause.

They were in the neighborhood of the palace now, a better section of the city. The residents here stole large sums with parchment and whispered words instead of cutting wayfarers' throats for a few coins.

And the residents expected protection from their lesser brethren in crime. The troops here would check a pair of men, detain them if they had no satisfactory account of their business; kill them if any resistance were offered.

But two men carrying a young child were unlikely burglars. Most probably they were part of the service industry catering to Sanctuary's wealthy and power-ful . . . and the rich did not care to have their nighttime sports delayed by uniformed officiousness. Samlor had no need for the bribe—or the knife—he had ready.

"We're getting close, I think," Khamwas remarked. He lifted his head as if to sniff the air which even here would have been improved by a cloudburst to ram the effluvium from the street down into the harbor.

Samlor grimaced and looked around him. He wanted to know how Khamwas found his directions . . . but he didn't want to ask; and anyway, he wouldn't understand if they scholar/magician took the time to explain.

Worse, Star likely *would* understand.

"I wonder what Setios is keeping for her," the caravan master whispered, so softly that the child could not hear even though Samlor's lips brushed her fine hair as he spoke.

They paused at a place where the pavement was almost wide enough to be called a square. A median strip, raised to knee height behind a stone curb, was planted with bushes and a tree which spread impressively even though its limbs had been lopped into sprays of young shoots by repeated prunings for firewood. A carriage could pass to either side of the median without threatening to scrape its gilding on the building fronts, though its postillion might have to duck to save his plumed shako from the jutting upper stores.

"Is it going to rain?" Star asked sleepily from the cradle of Samlor's arm.

The caravan master glanced at the sky. There were stars, but a scud of high clouds blocked and cleared streaks across them at rapid intervals. The edge in the air might well be harbinger of a storm poised to sweep from the hills to the west of town and wash the air at least briefly clean.

"Perhaps, dearest," the Cirdonian said. "But we'll be all right."

They'd be under cover, he hoped; or, better yet, back in a bolted chamber of the caravansary on the White Foal River before the storm broke.

Khamwas began to mutter something with his fingers interlaced on the top of his staff. Star shook herself into supple alertness and hopped off her uncle's supporting arm. She did not touch the Napatan, but she watched his face closely as he mouthed words in a language the caravan master did not recognize.

Left to his own devices—unwilling to consider what his niece was teaching herself now, and *barely* unwilling to order her to turn away—Samlor surveyed the houses in their immediate neighborhood.

It was an old section of the city, but wealthy and fashionable enough that there had been considerable rebuilding to modify the original Ilsigi character. Directly across from Samlor's vantage place, the front of the house had been demolished and was being replaced by a two-story portico with columns of colored marble. The spiked grating which enclosed the lot in lieu of a wall was temporary but looked sturdy enough to protect the gate of a fortress.

Beyond the grating, tools and building materials lay jumbled, awaiting the return of workmen at daylight. There was no sign that the house proper was occupied; it was hard to imagine that anyone who was rich enough to carry out the renovation would also be willing to live through the disruption it entailed. A lamp burned brightly on a shack within the enclosure, and a watchman's eyes peered toward the trio from the shack's unglazed window.

The other houses were quiet, though all, save the one against which Salmor's party sheltered, guarded their facades with lamplight. At this hour, business was most likely to be carried on through back entrances or trap doors to tunnels that were older than the Ilsigs . . . and possibly older than humanity.

It might be a bad time to meet Setios; but again, it might not. He'd been an associate of Star's mother, which meant at the least that he was used to strange hours and unusual demands.

He'd see them in now, provide the child with her legacy—if it were here. If it were portable. If Setios were willing to meet the terms of an agreement made with a woman now long dead.

Samlor swore, damning his sister Samlane to a Hell beneath all Hells; and knowing as he recited the words under his breath that any afterlife in which Samlane found herself was certain to be worse than her brother could imagine.

"*This* is the house," said Khamwas with a note of wonder in his voice. He and the child turned to look at the facade of the building against which the caravan master leaned while he surveyed the rest of the neighborhood.

"Looks pretty quiet," said Samlor. The words were less an understatement than a conversational placeholder while the Cirdonian considered what might be a real problem.

The building didn't look quiet. It looked abandoned.

It was a blank-faced structure. Its second floor was corbelled out a foot or so but there was no real front overhang to match those of the houses to either side. The stone ashlars had been worn smooth by decades of sidewalk traffic brushing against them; the mortar binding them could have used tuck pointing, but that was more a matter of aesthetics than structural necessity.

The only ground-floor window facing the street was a narrow slit beside the iron-bound door. There was a grate-protected niche for a lantern on the other side of the door alcove. The stones were blackened by carbon from the flame, but the lamp within was cold and dark. It had not been lighted this night and perhaps not for weeks past.

There was no sign of life through the slit intended to give a guard inside a look at whoever was calling.

"Perhaps I'm wrong," said Khamwas uncertainly. "This *should* be the house of Setios, but I—I can't be sure I'm right."

He made as if to bend over his staff again, then straightened and said decisively, "No, I'm sure it must be the house—but perhaps he doesn't live here anymore." The Napatan stepped to the street-level door and raised his staff to rap on the panel.

"Ah—" said Samlor.

The caravan master held the long dagger he had taken from the man he had killed in the Vulgar Unicorn. The weapon belonged in his hand when they prowled through the Maze, but it wasn't normal practice to knock on a stranger's door with steel bare in your fist.

On the other hand, this was Sanctuary; and anyway, the new knife didn't fit the sheath of the one Samlor had left in the corpse.

"Go ahead," he said to Khamwas. The Napatan was poised, watching the caravan master and waiting for a suggestion to replace his own intent.

Khamwas nodded, Star mirroring his motion as if hypnotized by tiredness. He rapped twice on the door panel. The sound of wood on wood was sharp and soulless.

"Won't be anybody there," said Samlor. His own eyes were drawn to the watermarked blade of the knife. *His* knife, now; the owner wasn't going to claim it with a foot of steel through his chest. The whorls of blended metals, iron black against polished steel, were only memories in the distant lamplight. There was no way Samlor could see them now, even if they began to spell words as he had watched them do—in defiance of reason—twice before.

The caravan master shook himself out of the clouded reverie into which fatigue was easing him. He needed rest as badly as his niece did, and it looked as though there was no way he was going to clear up his business tonight anyway.

"Look," he said, irritated because Khamwas still faced the door as if there were a chance it would open. "There's nobody here, and—"

Metal clanked as the bar closing the door from inside was withdrawn from its staples. The door leaf opened inward, squealing on bronze pivots set into the lintel and transom instead of hanging from strap hinges.

"No one will see you," said the voice of the figure standing in the doorway. Whatever else the doorkeeper might be, it was not human.

The creature was far shorter than Star. Fur clothed its body and long tail in ashen luster, but the frame beneath was skeletally thin. Its features had the pointed sharpness of a fox's muzzle, and there was no intelligence whatever in its beady eyes.

"Wait," said Samlor hil Samt as the doorkeeper began to close the portal again. He set his boot against the iron-strapped lower edge of the door. "Your master holds a trust f-for my niece Star."

"No one will see you," the creature repeated. Behind it was another set of door leaves, reinforced like the first. They combined to form a closet-sized anteroom which could probably be flooded with anything from boiling water to molten lead.

If there were anyone alive in the house to do so. The doorkeeper spoke in a thin, breathy voice, but its chest did not rise and fall.

"It isn't real," Khamwas said, speaking in some different universe in which Samlor was not focused in terrified determination on the unhuman—unalive—doorkeeper of this house. "It's a simulacrum like the—"

"No one will see you," the doorkeeper repeated without emphasis. It swung the panel shut, thrusting Samlor violently backward even though he tried to brace himself by stiffening his supporting leg behind him.

"I *have* Star's legacy!" the caravan master shouted as he hurled himself against the door, slamming into it with the meat of his left shoulder.

The panel thumped but did not rebound. The bar crashed into place.

"I *will*!" Samlor cried again. "Depend on it!"

His voice echoed, but there was no sound at all from within the house.

"It wasn't really present," said Khamwas, touching the other man's shoulder to calm him.

"It's there enough for me," said Samlor grimly, massaging his bruised shoulder with the faceted knife-hilt. "Might've tried t' stop a landslide for all I could do to keep it from slamming the door."

At a venture, he poked his daggerblade through the slit beside the door, in and out quickly like a snake licking the air. Nothing touched the metal, nor was there any other response.

"He who shakes the stone," said—warned?—Tjainufi, "will have it fall on his foot."

"I mean," said Khamwas hastily to deflect possible wrath from his manikin, "that it's no more than a part of the door. A trick only, without volition or consciousness. It's carrying out the last order it was given, the way a bolt lies in its groove when the master releases it. No one may be present."

"If we go in *there*," said Star distinctly, pointing at the door, "we'll be—*krrk*!"

The child cocked her head up as if her neck had been wrung. "Like chickens," she added as she relaxed, grinning.

Samlor's breath wheezed out. He had thought—

"Well, Star," said the Napatan scholar, "I might be able to keep the wraith from moving for a time, long enough for

us to get past the . . . zone of which it's a part. I *might*.
But I think we'd best not go in by this door until Setios
permits us to pass."

The two of them smiled knowingly at one another.

Samlor restrained his impulse to do something pointlessly
violent. He looked at the blade of his knife instead of
glaring at his companions and began in a very reasonable
tone, "In that case, we'd best get some sleep and—"

"Actually," said Khamwas, not so much interrupting as
speaking without being aware that Samlor was in the middle
of a statement, "neither of us have business with Setios
himself, only with items in his possession. I wonder. . . ."

"*I* want my gift *now*," said Star, her face set in the
slanting lines of temper. Either she tossed her head slightly,
or the whorl of white strands in her curly black hair moved
on its own.

Go in now read the iron letters on the blade at which
Samlor stared in anger. There was too little light for the
markings to be visible, but he saw them nonetheless.

"Heqt take you all to the waters beneath the earth!"
shouted the Cirdonian in fury. He slashed the air with his
dagger as if to wipe away the message crawling there in the
metal. "I'm not a burglar, and coming to this *damned* city
doesn't make me one."

"When you are hungry, eat what you despise," said the
manikin on Khamwas' shoulder. "When you are full,
despise it."

"Anyway," said Star, "it's going to rain, Uncle Samlor."
She looked smug at the unanswerable truth of her latest
argument.

The caravan master began to laugh.

Khamwas blinked, as frightened by the apparent humor
as he had been by the anger that preceded it. Emotional
outbursts by a man as dangerous as the caravan master were
like creakings from the dike holding back flood waters.

"Well," the Napatan said cautiously. "I suppose the
situation may change for the better by daylight. Though of
course neither of us were considering theft. I want to look at
a slab of engraved stone, and you simply wish to retrieve

your niece's legacy from its caretaker—who seems to be absent."

"We don't know what it *is*," said Star. "My gift."

"Ah," said Khamwas, speaking to the girl but with an eye cocked toward her uncle. "That shouldn't be an insurmountable problem. If we're inside—" he nodded toward the door "—and the object is there also, I should be able to locate it for you."

"Will you show *me* how?" Star begged, clasping her hands together in a mixture of pleading and premature delight.

"Ah. . . ," repeated the Napatan scholar. "I think that depends on what your uncle says, my dear."

"Her uncle says that we're not inside yet," Samlor stated without particular emphasis. "And he'll see about getting there."

Without speaking further to his companions, the Cirdonian walked to the corner of the building.

The sidewall of Setios' house was not common to the building beside it. Each was a self-standing structure set back a foot from the property line between them. That air space provided insulation in event of a fire and prevented the occupants of one house from invading their neighbors after tunneling at leisure through a common wall.

In Sanctuary, the second was apt to be a greater threat than the first.

There were no ground-floor windows in the sidewall, but the second story was ventilated by barred openings. Samlor stepped through the gap, too narrow to be called an alley anywhere but in the Maze. He ignored his companions, though they followed him gingerly in lieu of any other directions.

The vertical bars of the window above him were thumb-thick and set with scarcely more room between them. Star might have been able to reach through one of the spaces, but the caravan master was quite certain that his own big hands would not fit.

"Are there going to be things like that door-monkey waiting by the windows?" Samlor asked the other man quietly. He nodded upward to indicate the opening he had studied.

Khamwas shrugged in darkness relieved only by the strip of clouded sky above them. "I would expect human servants if anything," he said. "They're—more trustworthy, in many ways. And from what I've gathered, Setios is a collector the way I'm a scholar. Neither of us, you understand, are magicians of real power."

He paused and tucked his lip under his front teeth in doubt, then added, "The way your niece here appears to be, Master Samlor."

"Yeah," said the caravan master without emotion. His left hand tousled Star's hair gently, but he did not look down at the child. "And he collected a demon in a bottle, among other things."

Samlor grimaced, then went on. "Let's get out t' the street again. You wait, and I'll go talk to the fellow across the way there."

CHAPTER 5

WITH HIS COMPANIONS shuffling ahead because the passageway was too strait to let him by, Samlor returned to the front of the house. The two adjacent buildings, Setios' and the one beside it, were of similar construction, but they *felt* radically different to the Cirdonian as he stood between them. Neither showed signs of life or activity at the moment, but a hand on the other building's stonework transmitted hints of movement. *Something* was alive there.

But not in Setios' house.

"If he thinks," said the caravan master in a conversational tone, "that he can skip to avoid paying over Star's legacy, then that's something we'll discuss when I find the gentleman.

"Which I will."

Samlor shrugged, settling his cloak and disengaging his mind from a doubtful future. There was the present to deal with, and that was quite enough.

"Ah, Samlor . . . ?" Khamwas said.

"Just wait here," the Cirdonian repeated. "I'm going across the street to talk with the watchman there." He nodded toward the guard shack on the construction site opposite.

"Yes, of course," Khamwas said with enough disinterest to hint at irritation. "But what I wanted to say was—Setios, you see, may not be avoiding you. There's been a recent upheaval in the structure of, you see—magic. He may have been frightened and fled from that.''

The Napatan grinned. ''He'll have left behind the stele I want to read, surely. Probably his whole collection, if *that* fear is why he left. And, as for this child's legacy—'' he touched Star's cheek affectionately ''—if we don't find it here, I'll help you locate it. Because you've helped me. And because I am honored to help someone as talented as your niece.''

''The plans of god are one thing,'' said the manikin on his shoulder. ''The thoughts of men are another.''

''Yeah, well,'' said the caravan master as he slipped the dagger back under his belt. It was the least obtrusive way to carry the weapon until he got a proper sheath. ''Best get on with it unless we want t' grow roots down into the pavement.''

He strode across the street with a swaggering assurance which immediately set him apart in a city where lone men habitually slunk. The watchman edged back from his window so that his eyes no longer reflected light.

''Ho, friend,'' Samlor called a half step back from the high iron fence. He spoke loudly enough for the watchman to hear him without difficulty; but he didn't want to arouse the entire street. There was a lot he had yet to do around here, and the last thing he needed was for somebody to start hammering on an alarm gong.

''Git yer butt away er I'll stitch ye right through the middle wi' me crossbow!'' crackled a terrified voice from within the guard shack.

The air was dead still now, under heavy clouds, and noticeably warmer than it had been during the early evening. Samlor shivered, though the concern did not show on his face.

It wasn't likely the watchman had a crossbow; that was an expensive piece of equipment and not at all suited to the job for which he had been hired.

Besides, if the nervous bastard *had* a missile weapon chances were he'd've cut loose at the caravan master as he crossed the street. There were a lot of people who hadn't any business being armed. Through some sort of cosmic

balancing of accounts, they tended to be the folks who most
wanted enough hardware to equip an assault company.

"All I want to do is buy a little information, friend," said
Samlor, reaching deliberately into the purse which balanced
the long knife on the other side of his belt. He hoped the
lantern on the guard shack illuminated his movement
clearly. The sky'd gotten dark as a yard up a pig's ass, and
he *really* didn't want this jumpy fathead to think that the
threat level was going up.

Samlor carried five pieces of Rankan gold wrapped in
chamois to keep the mint marks sharp and the metal bright.
They were useful in just this sort of situation, where you
had to convince somebody unmistakably that his best
interests were your interests.

Now Samlor spilled the coins from his right hand to his
left, letting them fall far enough through the air to wake
shivers of light. Not even brass could mimic that color or
the particular music of gold ringing on gold.

"Buy it at a pretty good rate, too," the caravan master
added, relieved beyond measure to hear a sigh of wonder
from the guard shack. There were enough people who
wanted Samlor hil Samt dead that being killed by accident
would be ridiculous.

"Here," he added. "Catch."

The Cirdonian spun one of the gold coins off the thumb of
his left hand, aiming it between the bars of the fence and
into the dark rectangle of the shack's window ten feet
beyond.

There was a crash of objects within, a thump, and then
the barely distinct pinging of the coin bouncing onto the
floor despite the watchman's desperate attempts to catch it
in the air.

Samlor waited, his face neutral, while the hidden
watchman shuffled on his hands and knees and bumped the
walls of his shack repeatedly. There was no light inside
beyond what slipped between the boards, and the coin—the
price of an excellent donkey or a horse that might or might
not carry an adult twenty miles—was not large physically.

The noises stopped. The watchman reappeared at the
window and stuck his arm out so that he could see the coin

in the light of the lantern on the shack's front. It winked, and Samlor winked cheerfully at the amazement of the man whom he saw for the first time.

Money was generally the best way to approach a stranger. "What d'ye wanna know?" said the watchman. His voice was no less suspicious than before, but now it was pitched an octave lower. The coin disappeared somewhere out of sight as soon as he realized that he was flashing it to the world.

"How long you been here?" Samlor asked. Then, realizing that he knew exactly what answer he would get—*Huh? Since sundown*—he added, "How many weeks, I mean?"

The watchman's hands reappeared in the light. He was counting on his fingers while his lips mouthed one, two, three—

He paused. "Pay me," he demanded.

"When I'm satisfied," the caravan master said, "you get all the rest of this. If I'm not satisfied, I'll take back the first, and I'll have your guts for garters."

Gold danced from one hand to the palm of the other in time with Samlor's broadening smile. The mixed message suddenly got home in the watchman's brain. He jumped back away from the window.

"No *problem*, friend," said Samlor. "I *want* to give you this money."

"Three weeks. An' a day," came the voice from the dark. "Look—"

"And have you seen any signs that anybody lives in the place opposite?" Samlor continued, trampling steadily over the notion that the watchman had something useful to say that wasn't an answer to a direct question. "People going in or out? Food deliveries? The lantern by the door lighted?"

"Gods and demons," the watchman mumbled, leaning forward again in his shack. "Well, I dunno, I—what was that last thing again?"

Like working with a camel, thought Samlor, except that a good camel was probably smarter. "The lantern by the doorway there," he repeated gently, pointing with the hand which held the money. "Has it ever been lighted while you're on duty here?"

"There's no lantern," said the watchman, stretching as far forward as he could from the window. He was a scrawny man, and the effect was rather that of a turtle trying to grasp a berry hanging well above it. "Say, but yer *right*, there *was* a light over there back. . . . Well, I dunno for sure, but there was a light."

That was going to have to do, the caravan master realized. There had been at least some evidence of occupancy at Setios' house three weeks ago, and now there wasn't. Samlor'd never been a big one on finesse if it looked like a quick and dirty way was going to accomplish the job.

"Fine," he said aloud to the watchman. "Now you bring me that screw jack over there—" he pointed "—and I give you this.

"Better yet—" he went on, because he saw the watchman's mouth drop open before the fellow skipped out of sight again in fear "—I'm going to drop the gold right here."

Samlor reached inside the grating and let the coins fall with a glittering song. "Now," he repeated. "All you have to do is bring me that jack. Then I'll go away, and you can scoop up the money safe as can be. Right? Look at it."

Despite himself, the watchman did peer out of his shack again. "But if they miss a tool. . . ," he said in a tone of desperate pleading.

"I'm paying you more than you'd make in a year doing this," said the caravan master reasonably. The coins shone on the ground as invitingly as the eyes of the most beautiful whore in the world. "For that matter, I'll bring the jack back if I've got a chance—but what d'*you* care?"

The watchman sidled out of his shack. As the caravan master had suspected, the fellow's weapon was not a crossbow but a pike which had been sawed off—or broken and smoothed—to a total length of about five feet, butt to point. It was useless except for prodding away a drunk who tried to climb into the site, but serious trouble was for soldiers summoned by the alarm gong—not for the cretin to deal with by himself.

"I dunno," the fellow muttered, but he picked up the

heavy jack with as much assurance as he managed with anything.

"The bar too," Samlor directed. "To turn it."

The watchman blinked, fumbled, and then laid down his pike to bring the iron rod which drove the mechanism.

The jack was a solid iron screw which the contractor's men were using to drive into place the quarter-ton blocks which had to interlock with the existing fabric of the structure being renovated. A frame clamped to the front of the building provided a base from which the jack could be screwed. Its steady thrust would move stones smoothly, instead of shattering them as would result from an attempt to hammer them into place.

The watchman had approached within six or seven feet of the fence. Then he lobbed the pieces of the jack underhand in the direction of Samlor and skipped back like a keeper who had just fed a restive lion. Iron bounced from the ground into iron with exactly the sort of clangor which Samlor had hoped to avoid.

"*Idiot!*" the caravan master snarled under his breath as he tried to damp the ringing bars by squeezing them in his hands. It didn't help a lot—the grating vibrated in a hundred separate harmonies—but it was a good release for the fury that wrapped Samlor for the moment. As well get mad at a dog for barking. . . .

He reached through the grate and lifted the screw jack. Maybe the watchman, holding his pike again in the terrified certainty that he would need it, wasn't as frail as he looked. The bar and screw weighed a good thirty pounds, and the handle was solid enough to be a crushingly effective weapon in a strong man's hands.

The noise hadn't aroused any obvious interest. It wasn't exactly that residents of this district minded their own business. Rather, they were wealthy enough that noise in the night implied criminality of too trivial a nature to be profitable to them.

"Spend it wisely, friend," said Samlor as he tucked the jack under his cloak. No point in giving a view of the proceedings to anyone who chanced to be peering through a window. He backed a few paces away from the fence and bowed sardonically to the watchman, who was hopping from one foot to the other as if executing a clumsy dance with his pike.

Samlor turned and strode back to his companions. Behind him, he heard the fellow diving for the gold which he could at last safely retrieve.

Well, the fool had already outlived the caravan master by a couple decades, so it wasn't absolutely certain that possession of that much money was the kiss of death. They'd made a bargain, and Samlor had kept his part of it. The results beyond that weren't a concern of his.

"If a fool follows his heart," said Tjainufi from the Napatan's shoulder, "he does wisely."

Samlor started, looking at the manikin with appraising eyes. "Do you think so?" he asked, then grimaced to find himself talking to the unnatural little—thing. "Khamwas," he said gruffly, "come help me with the window."

Star was curled in the corner of the door alcove, dozing with the Napatan's cape for a pillow. Khamwas stood in front of her, watching the street as well as the caravan master. He was very slim without the bulk of the outer garment, and his bare chest was no garb for this night.

"I, ah," he said, looking down at the child. "I thought it would be good if she got some rest, so. . . . She's very like my own daughter, you know."

"Wish I had more talent for what she needs," said the caravan master quietly, staring at the child also. "Wish I *knew* what she needs, what any kid needs. But you do what you can."

He grimaced again. "Bring 'er along, will you? I need you at the side to hand me this jack when I'm ready for it—" he fluffed his cloak open to display the tool "—and I don't want her in plain sight on the street, even though it means getting her up again."

The sky had closed in above the passage between the two buildings. It was as dark as a narrow cave, and for the time being the air was as motionless as that of a cavern miles below the ground. Samlor found his location by subconscious memory of the six cautious paces which had brought him beneath the window when he could see it.

He put down the jack and began the task of ascending the wall.

The houses were built close enough to one another that the caravan master could brace himself against opposite walls, first with his hands and then by wedging his hobnails into narrow cracks in the masonry. He mounted to the second floor window like a frog swimming, his legs lifting him each time his arms had locked on a fresh hold.

When Samlor's left palm touched the window ledge, he explored it by touch with all the care required of a possible trap with razor edges. Beneath him he heard his companions, Khamwas murmuring a response to Star's whine. He was glad he had the other man along on this business, not least because Khamwas *could* look after the child.

The bars were set solidly into stone lintels, and they were just as tight together as Samlor had thought. There were glazed windows within, swung back in sashes and apparently hooked to keep breezes from banging them to and fro.

There was no light in the room beyond, and utterly no sound.

Samlor set both his feet against the wall of Setios' house and braced his back on the adjacent building. If he'd thought things through, he might have redoubled his cloak before he set his shoulders on the rough stone, but he'd be all right for the brief while he expected to cling here. The important thing was that his hands were free.

"Khamwas," he called softly, "hand me up the jack. And *don't* let the handle fall out of it, right?"

"Just a mo—oh," said the Napatan. "There. . . ."

Samlor twisted his torso against the wall and reached down as far as he could with his left hand. He could not see Khamwas, but the scrunch of wood suggested that the Napatan had wedged his staff between the walls and was using the slant to raise himself, even though one of his hands was full of the heavy jack.

"Hold it," Samlor whispered. His fingers brushed one of the crossholes by which the jack was turned. By squeezing down a fraction further, the caravan master managed to hook the rod between his index and middle fingers, though the strain on them and the web of his hand was agonizing.

"*There*, you bitch!" he snarled at it as he lurched up against pain that he had to ignore for the instant before his right hand closed on the barrel of the jack and took the strain. Straightening up was difficult—at one angle, the chain closure of his cloak threatened to throttle him—but it felt so good not to have a tearing weight on his fingers that he could easily ignore lesser problems.

He set the jack sideways on the window ledge, angling it so that the screw top touched a bar while the base was firmly against the stone sash. The handle rotated the screw slightly before binding against the ledge. Samlor removed the handle, set the end into the other crosshole (offset ninety degrees from the first) and cranked the screw up another quarter turn. The base scrunched and the top gave an iron-to-iron squeak.

The caravan master grinned and began pumping the screw higher. The bars protecting the window were sturdy, but Samlor's powerful arm muscles were multiplied by the handle's leverage and the shallow-pitched threads of the housejack. The combination would have torn apart the stone sash if that were necessary.

It wasn't, but chips of cement spalled away before the bar set in it fractured. The jack slipped. Samlor swore and clamped it with the hand that had been resting on the barrel more for his support than its.

"Are you all right?" Khamwas whispered in concern.

"Yeah, it's all right," the caravan master replied. He didn't want to arouse people in the house behind him—by this time he was convinced that Setios had decamped with all his household in the past three weeks—but explaining the situation to his companion calmed both of them. "The bars're brittle, cast instead of worked. It surprised me when it broke, but it makes the job simpler.

"A single plowing does not produce the crop," said Tjainufi.

"Don't get your bowels in an uproar," the caravan master grunted back.

He began levering more furiously, each stroke requiring him to reset the jack handle. The crack of metal breaking had been unexpected; and right now, the things the caravan master *did* expect included some that were really unpleasant.

The bar had broken at its lower end, where it took the strain of the jack. The top, where the displacement was less acute, remained in its stone transom—but it was just a matter of time before that gave way as well.

Each thrust of the handle now was against increased resistance. Samlor's shoulders were more than equal to the job, but the palm of his right hand felt as if it might be starting to bruise under the strain. The calluses were no help in this.

The second bar, driven by the broken end of the first, bent ahead of the jack's thrust until it touched the third. Samlor continued to crank.

Cement pattered down from the transom in bits ranging as large as fingernails. The bars were crushing their setting under a sidethrust which they had not been designed to resist.

The bar which had broken initially pulled free. Only luck and Samlor's reflexive grab kept it from dropping to the ground with enough inertia to crush any skull it met in its path.

"Heqt," the Cirdonian muttered as he found himself with a firm grip on the length of iron. "Heqt be praised." Before he resumed work, he pulled the silver medallion and its thong outside his tunic, so that the embossed face of the toad goddess could watch his efforts.

After a moment's consideration, he slid the bar inside Setios' house instead of trying to pass it on to Khamwas. The clunk-*cling!* it made on the hard flooring within was less noticeable than the squeal inevitable as the screw jack forced its way onward.

The grill was beginning to collapse. The bars were set in a trough in the hard limestone of the sill and transom. Any attempt to hammer the iron inward would be resisted by three inches of rock. The daubs of cement which held the bars apart within the trough were not nearly as strong.

Only the integrity of the whole construct preserved its strength. That ended when the jack inexorably tore out the first bar.

For the next few minutes, Samlor's major problem was to avoid dropping a bar or, worse, the jack itself. When the fifth bar came out, he gripped the next with his left hand instead of advancing the screw again. The bar quivered, then tore loose to his mighty tug.

The caravan master's whole body was under strain from the position it had been holding. Some of his large muscles were beginning to tremble. He responded with a burst of nervous energy, dropping the jack within the house to get it out of the way while his hand ripped away the remaining bars on the right side of the window.

If one of them had remained firm, Samlor would have had to pause for an hour or more, shuddering on the ground while his muscles purged themselves of fatigue poisons. There was no need. The cement bonding had been cracked already by asymmetric compression. Bar after bar came away until there were no more in the right half of the window. Metal rang as the caravan master dropped them, but he could no longer hear any sound except the hammer of blood in his temples.

He couldn't stop now, and he certainly couldn't take the time to reconnoiter the room he had just opened. There wasn't a damned thing to see—the room was as dark as the sky above—and the caravan master knew he'd be really lucky if he still had the strength to throw himself directly into Setios' house.

"Heqt help and sustain me in this enterprise which I undertook for my daughter Star," Samlor prayed, though the only sound that came from his mouth was the wheeze of his breath. He gripped the sash with his left hand and a bar with his right, then drew himself into the opening with the clumsy certainty of a toad hopping.

The Cirdonian's hobnails slipped an instant after his shoulders curved away from the adjacent wall, but his torso was already half inside the building. He wriggled, trying to pull himself the rest of the way through the narrow opening. His boots clashed on the wall which had supported his shoulders—and pushed him inside with no trouble at all.

If he'd been thinking straighter, he'd've planned it that way.

A boobytrap—a spring-driven blade or a nest of spikes—
would have gone off during Samlor's previous activities, but
there was still the chance that someone—human or not—
waited in the darkness to spear the intruder as he sprawled
totally helpless. The Cirdonian was so played out by the
sudden release of strain that he couldn't have moved for the
next few seconds if he'd *known* he'd be slaughtered instead
of just fearing it.

"Praised be Heqt in whom the world lives," murmured
Samlor as his senses returned him to the world beyond his
own effort and necessities. The marble floor beneath him
was cold and slick with water. The glazed windows had not
been closed the last time it rained; and that, from idle
chatter overheard at the caravansary, had been more than a
week ago.

Khamwas called from the alley, his words blurred but the
worry in them clear.

Samlor rolled onto his right side. There was a sharp pain
in his left thigh where the unsheathed dagger had prodded
him during his contortions. He didn't think it had drawn
blood through the double tunics.

"It's all right," the caravan master said, then realized that
he wasn't sure he could understand the croaked words
himself. He gripped the window ledge, brushing the
scattered bars into muted chiming around his knees.

"It's all right," he repeated, leaning back through the
opening by which he had entered. "Just a minute and I'll
find—" his hand brushed fabric, curtains or tapestries,
beside the window "—yeah, just a second and I'll have
something for you t' climb by."

The Napatan might have been able to mount the way
Samlor had, but Star was too small to fill the gap as
comfortably as either of the adult males. It was risky to
bring her into a magician's house, but a worse risk to leave
her in a Sanctuary alley.

Life was, after all, a series of gambles which every
creature lost on the final throw.

A fastening gave way; cloth tumbled down beside the
Cirdonian. It was embroidered, partly with metallic threads
that made it stiff to the touch. Something about the feel of

the fabric suggested to Samlor that he didn't want to see the design.

He slipped an end of the tapestry out between the remaining bars instead of tossing it directly through the opening he had torn. He no longer felt lightheaded, but he didn't trust his muscles to anchor his companions against a straight pull.

"Come on up," the caravan master directed, speaking through the window. "Star first." The tapestry, belayed around the grill, wasn't going to pull out of his hands.

The window was scarcely visible as a rectangle, and the still air smelt of storm.

There was a discussion below. Star came up the tapestry, flailing her legs angrily behind her. There was a pout in her voice as she demanded, "What *is* this old place? I don't like it."

Maybe she felt something about the house—and maybe she was an overtired seven-year-old and therefore cranky.

There wasn't time to worry about it. The caravan master gripped the child beneath the shoulders with his left arm and lifted her into the room. Star yelped as her head brushed the transom, but she should've had sense enough to duck.

"My staff, Master Samlor," said Khamwas.

The Cirdonian leaned forward and caught the vague motion that proved to be the end of an ordinary wooden staff when his fingers enclosed it. Behind him, the room lighted vaguely with blue pastel.

Star shouldn't have done it without asking; but they needed light, and a child *wasn't* a responsible adult. Samlor slid the staff behind him with his left hand while supporting the tapestry with his right hand and using his full weight to pin the end to the floor.

The Napatan scholar mounted gracefully and used Samlor's arm like the bar of a trapeze to swing himself over the lintel. Only then did the caravan master turn to see where they were and what his niece was doing.

Star had set swimming through the air a trio of miniature octopuses made of light. A blue creature drifted beneath the ceiling frescoed with scenes of anthropomorphic deities, a yellow one prowled beneath the legs of a writing table sumptuous with mother-of-pearl inlays.

The third miniature octopus was of an indigo so pale that it barely showed up against the carven door against which it bobbed feebly.

"Where's—" Samlor said as he looked narrowly at Khamwas. "You know, your little friend?"

Tjainufi reappeared on the Napatan's right shoulder. The manikin moved with the silent suddenness of an image in an angled mirror, now here and now not as the tilt changes. "The warp does not stray far from the woof," he said in cheerful satisfaction.

"Khamwas," the Cirdonian added as he looked around them, "if you can locate what we're after, then get to it. I *really* don't want t' spend any longer here than I need to."

"Look, Uncle," Star squealed as she pranced over to the writing desk. "Mommie's *box*!"

Samlor's speed and reflexes were in proper form after his exertions, but his judgment was off. He attempted to spring for the desk before Star got there, and his boots skidded out from under him on the wet marble. Because he'd swept the long dagger from his belt as part of the same unthinking maneuver, he had only his left palm to break his fall. The shock made the back of his hand tingle and the palm burn.

Khamwas had retrieved his staff. He stopped muttering to it when the Cirdonian slapped the floor hard enough to make the loose bars roll and jingle among themselves. "Are you . . . ?" he began, offering a hand to the sprawling bigger man.

"See, Uncle Samlor?" said the child, returning to the caravan master with an ivory box in her hands. "It's got mommie's mark on it."

"No, go on with your business," said Samlor calmly to the Napatan. He felt the prickly warmth of embarrassment painting his skin, but he wouldn't have survived this long if he lashed out in anger every time he'd made a public fool of himself. "Find the stele you're after, and then we'll see what Star's got here."

He took the box from the child as quickly as he could

without letting it slip from his numbed fingers. Even if it were just what it seemed—a casket of Samlane's big enough to hold a pair of armlets—it could be extremely dangerous.

Much of what Samlor's sister had owned, and had known, fell into that category, one way or another.

Khamwas' face showed the concern which any sane man would feel under the circumstances, but he resumed his meditation on—or prayers to—his staff.

Star's palm-sized creatures of light continued their slow patrol of the room. The caravan master seemed to have broken into a large study. There was a couch to one side of the door and on the other the writing desk with matching chair. The chair lay on its back, as if its last occupant had jumped up hastily.

Most of the interior wall space was taken up by cedarwood cabinets for books and scrolls. Even the palely drifting smears of light showed that the works ranged widely in age and quality of binding, but the varied types were intermixed within individual cabinets. Samlor did not doubt that the library was arrayed in a rigid order; but he was willing to bet that he would not be able to discover that order if he spent a year among the shelves.

His instinct about the tapestry he had dropped through the bars had been correct. Its counterpart still hung on the wall. The design worked into it in gorgeous color was religious . . . depending on one's definition of the term. The border was formed of curlicues, interrupted at regular intervals by nodes.

The indigo octopus pulled itself along the border, illuminating the pattern beneath the groping tentacles. The embroidered nodes were humans contorted with pain. The curlicues were intestines, pulled an anatomically reasonable distance from gaping bellies.

Setios appeared to be exactly the sort of man that Samlane could be expected to meet.

"*Open* it, Uncle!" Star demanded.

Samlor still had the coffin-hilted dagger in his hand. His glance around the room had been a professional assessment of the situation, not daydreaming. The child had her own

agenda, though, and this casket was—might be—the thing
that had brought them to Sanctuary to begin with.

Khamwas still murmured over his staff. The caravan
master got up with caution born of experience and walked
over to the writing desk. A triple-wicked oil lamp hung
from a crane attached to the desktop. It promised real
illumination when Samlor lit it with the brass fire-piston in
his wallet.

"There's no oil, Uncle Samlor," said Star with the
satisfaction of a child who knows more than adult. She
cupped her hand again and turned it up with a saffron glow
in the palm. The creatures of light still drifting about the
room dimmed by comparison. "See?"

The bowl of the lamp was empty except for a sheen in its
center, oil beyond the touch of the wicks. Only one of the
three wicks had been lighted at the lamp's last use. When
the flame had consumed all the oil, it reduced the twist of
cotton to ash. The other wicks were sharply divided into
black and white, ready to function if the fuel supply were
renewed.

Setios had really left in a hurry.

"Fine, hold the light where it is, darling," Samlor said to
his niece as calmly as if he were asking her to pass the bread
at table. The casket wasn't anything which the Cirdonian
remembered from his youth, but the family crest—the
rampant wyvern of the House of Kodrix—was enameled on
the lid. Beneath it was carven in Cirdonian script the motto
An Eagle Does Not Snatch Flies.

Samlor's parents had never forgiven him for running high
risk, high profit caravans like a commoner instead of
vegetating in noble poverty. But they'd lived well—drunk
well, at least—on the flies he snatched for them, and the
money Samlor provided had bought his sister a marriage
with a Rankan noble.

Which couldn't save Samlane from herself, but was the
best effort possible for a brother who didn't claim to be a
god.

The light hanging beneath Star's hand did not have
clearly defined tentacles like those of the creatures still
wandering the room, but there were whorls of greater and

lesser intensity within its membranous boundaries. Samlor was determined not to scream and slap at the glow which he needed in this place, but the instinct to do so was very strong.

The lid did not rise under gentle pressure from his left thumb. There was no visible catch or keyhole, but the little object had to be a box—it didn't weigh enough for a block of solid ivory. Samlor put his dagger down on the desk to free his right hand—

And read the superscription on the piece of parchment there, a letter barely begun:

> *To Master Samlor hil Samt*
> *If you are well, it is good. I also am well.*
> *I enclose w*

The script was Cirdonian, and the final letter trailed off in a sweep of ink across the parchment. Following the curve of that motion, Samlor saw a delicate silver pen on the marble floor a few feet to the side of the desk.

Samlor set down the ivory box, and he very deliberately kept the weapon in his hand. From the look of matters, Setios might have been better off if he'd been holding a blade and not a pen a week or so earlier. Instinctively, the caravan master's left arm encircled Star, locating the child while he turned and said, "Khamwas. This is important. I think I've been doing Setios an injustice, thinking he'd ducked out to avoid me."

The other man was so still that not even his chest moved with the process of breathing. The absolute stillness was camouflaged for a moment by the fact that the octopuses threw slow, vague shadows as they circled the room. The manikin on Khamwas' shoulder was executing some sort of awkward dance with his legs stiff and his arms akimbo.

"Khamwas!" the caravan master repeated sharply. "I think we need to get outa here *now*."

Tjainufi said, "Do not say, 'I will undertake the matter,' if you will not."

Almost simultaneously, the Napatan shook himself like a diver surfacing after a deep plunge. He opened his eyes and stood, wobbling a little and using the staff for support. His face broadened with a smile of bright relief.

"Samlor," he said, obviously ignorant of anything that had happened around him since he dropped into a trance. "I've found it—or at least, we need to go down."

"We need to—" began the caravan master angrily. Tjainufi was watching him. The manikin's features were too small to have readable expression in this light, but the creature must think that—"

"Look," Samlor resumed, speaking to—at—Tjainufi, "I don't mean I want to get out because we found what *I* wanted, I mean—"

"Oh!" said Star. There was a mild implosion, air rushing to fill a small void. "There's nothing inside."

She'd opened the box, Samlor saw as he turned. His emotions had gone flat—they'd only be in the way just now—and his senses gave him frozen images of his surroundings in greater detail than he would be able to imagine when he wasn't geared to kill or run.

A narrow plate on the front of the ivory box slid sideways to expose a spring catch. When the child pressed that—the scale of the mechanism was so small that Samlor would have had to work it with a knifepoint—the lid popped up.

To display the inner surfaces of the ivory as highly polished as the exterior; and nothing whatever within.

Star was looking up at him with a pout of disappointment. She held the box in both hands and the ball of light, detached from her palm, was shrinking in on itself and dimming as its color slipped down through the spectrum.

For an instant—for a timeless period, because the vision was unreal and therefore nothing his eyes could have taken in—Samlor saw blue-white light through a gap in the cosmos where the whorl of white hair on Star's head should have been. It was like looking into the heart of the thunderbolt—

And it wasn't there, in the room or his daughter's face— for Star was his daughter, damn Samlane as she surely *was* damned—or even as an afterimage on Samlor's retinas when he blinked. So it hadn't really been there, and the caravan master was back in the world where he had promised to help Khamwas find a stele in exchange for help locating Star's legacy.

Which it appeared they had yet to do, but he'd fulfill his obligations to the Napatan. He shouldn't have needed a reminder from Tjainufi of that.

"Friend Khamwas," Samlor said, "we'll go downstairs if you want that. But—" his left index finger made an arc from the parchment toward the fallen silver pen "—something took Setios away real sudden, and I wouldn't bet it's not still here."

Khamwas caught his lower lip between his front teeth. He was wearing his cape again, but the caravan master remembered how frail the Napatan had looked without it.

"The man who looks in front of him does not stumble and fall," said the manikin with his usual preternatural clarity of voice.

"Samlor," said the Napatan. "I appreciate what you say . . . but what I seek is here, and I've made a very long—"

"Sure," the caravan master interrupted. "I just mean we be careful, all right?"

"And you, child," Samlor added in a voice as soft as a cat's claws extending. He knelt so that Star could meet his eyes without looking up. "You don't touch anything, do anything. Do you understand? Because if the only way to keep you safe is to tie you up and carry you like a sack of flour—that's what I'll do."

Star nodded, her face scrunched up on the verge of tears. The drifting glows dwindled noticeably.

"Everything's going to be fine, dearest," the caravan master said, giving the child an affectionate pat as he rose.

It bothered him to have to scare his niece in order to get her to obey—while she remembered—but she scared *him* every time she did something innocently dangerous, like opening the ivory box. Better she be frightened than that she swing from his arm, trussed like a hog.

Because Samlor didn't threaten in bluff.

Khamwas said something under his breath. His staff clothed itself in the bluish phosphorescence it held when the caravan master first met him in an alley. With the staff's

unshod ferule, the Napatan prodded the study door, lifting
the bronze latch. When nothing further happened, he pulled
the door open with his free hand and preceded Samlor and
Star into the hall beyond.

Samlor touched the latch as he stepped past it. Not a
particularly sturdy piece—typical for an inside door, when
the occupant is more concerned with privacy than protection. But it *had* been locked, which meant somebody had
paused in the hallway to do so with a key after he closed the
door.

Otherwise, it would have to have been locked from the
inside by somebody who wasn't there anymore.

In the old Ilsigi fashion, a balustraded hallway encircled a
reception room which pierced the second floor. There was a
solid roof overhead rather than the skylight which would
have graced a Rankan dwelling of similar quality.

The stairwell to the ground floor was in the corner to the
left of the study door. Khamwas' staff, pale enough to be a
revenant floating at its own direction, swirled that way.

"The, ah," Samlor said, trying to look all around him
and unable to see anything more than a few inches beyond
the phosphorescent staff. "The doorkeeper. It's
not . . . ?"

"We wouldn't meet it even if we opened the front door
from within," said Khamwas as he stepped briskly down
the helical staircase. "It isn't, you see, a *thing*. It's a set of
circumstances which have to fit as precisely as the wards of
a lock.

"Though it wouldn't," he added a few steps later, "be a
good idea for anyone to force the door from the outside.
Even if they were a much greater scholar than I. Ah, Setios
collected some—artifacts—that he might more wisely have
left behind."

CHAPTER 6

THE RECEPTION ROOM was chilly. Samlor thought it might have something to do with the glass-smooth ornamental pond in the middle of the room. He tested the water with his boot toe and found it, as expected, no more than an inch deep. It would be fed by rainwater piped from the roof gutters. Barely visible in the shadow beneath the coaming were the flat slots from which overflow drained in turn into a cistern.

Except for the pond, the big room was antiseptically bare. The walls between top- and bottom-moldings were painted in vertical pastel waves reminiscent of a kelp forest, and the floor was a geometric pattern in varicolored marble.

"Well, which way now?" the caravan master demanded brusquely, his eyes on the door to the rear half of the house. Star was shivering despite wrapping her cloak tighter with both hands, and Samlor didn't like the feel of the room either.

"Down still," said Khamwas in puzzlement. He rapped the ferule of his staff on the floor, a sharp sound that contained no information useful—at least to the caravan master. Perhaps it just seemed like the right thing to do.

"There'll be a cistern below," said Samlor, gesturing with a dripping boot toe toward the pond. "The access hatch'd be in the kitchen, most likely. Not in this room."

He started for a door, ill at ease and angry at himself for

67

that feeling of undirected fear. Part of his mind yammered that the Napatan was a fool who again mistook a direction for a pathway . . . and Samlor had to avoid that, avoid picking excuses to snarl at those closest to him in order to conceal fears he was embarrassed to admit.

Star poked a hand between the edges of her cloak. She did not look up; but when her fingers cocked, a bright spark swam rapidly from it and began coasting the lower wall moldings.

"D-dearest," said the caravan master, glancing at the withdrawn, miserable-looking face of his niece, then back to the light source. Star said nothing.

The droplet of light was white and intense by contrast with the vague glows that both—he had to admit the fact—magicians had created earlier in the evening. It might even have looked bright beside a candle, but Samlor had difficulty remembering anything as normal as candlelight while he stood in this chill stone room.

Pulse and pause; pulse and pause; pulse. . . . He'd thought that the creature of light was a minnow, or perhaps no more than a daub of illumination, a cold flame that did not counterfeit life.

But it surely did. A squid rather than a fish, too small to see but identifiable from the way it jetted forward with rhythmic contractions of its mantle.

The marble floor was so highly polished that it mirrored the creature's passage with nearly perfect fidelity, catching even the wispy shadows between the tightly-clasped tentacles of light trailing behind. The colors and patterning of the stone segments created the illusion that the reflection really swam through water.

"*Star*," the caravan master demanded in a restrained voice. "Why are you—"

The reflection blurred into a soft ball of light on a slab of black marble, though the tiny creature jetted above it in crystalline purity. The squid pulsed forward and hung momentarily over a wedge of travertine whose dark bands seemed to enfold the sharp outline.

Then source and reflection disappeared as abruptly as they had spurted from the child's gesture.

"What?" said Star, shivering fiercely. She scrunched her eyes shut so that her uncle thought she was about to cry. "What *happened*?"

Samlor patted her, blinking both at the sudden return of darkness and his realization of what he had just seen. Star might not know what she had done or why, but the caravan master did.

"Khamwas, come over here, will you?" he said, amused at the elation he heard in his voice as he strode to the sidewall where the thing of light had disappeared. "You know, I'd about decided we were going t' have t' give up or come back with a real wrecking crew."

"A hundred men are slain through one moment of discouragement," said the manikin on Khamwas' shoulder.

"In this town," the caravan master responded sourly, "you can be slain for less reason 'n that."

"I, ah," said the Napatan scholar. "What would you like me to do?"

"Star, come closer, sweetest," Samlor cajoled when he realized his niece had not followed him. Something was wrong with her, or else she was reacting strongly to the malaise of this house—which affected even the relatively insensitive caravan master.

She obeyed his voice with the halting nervousness of a frequently-whipped dog. Her hands were hidden again within her cloak.

Samlor put his arm around her shoulders, all he could do until they'd *left* this accursed place, and said to the other man, "Can you make it lighter down here? By the wall?"

Khamwas squatted and held his staff parallel with the edge molding. The phosphorescence was scarcely any light at all to eyes which had adapted to the spark from Star's finger, but it was sufficient to distinguish the square of black marble from the pieces of travertine to either side of it in the intaglio flooring.

Samlor could not discern a difference in the polish of the black marble from that of the rest, but the way it blurred the light which the others had mirrored proved what would have been uncertain under any other conditions.

He tried the stone with the tip of his right little finger; the

rest of the hand continued to grip the hilt of his long knife.
The block didn't give to light pressure, neither downward
nor on either of its horizontal axes, but it didn't seem to be
as solid as stone cemented to a firm base ought to be.

"Is there something the matter with the floor, here?"
asked Khamwas, resting easily on his haunches.

Samlor would rather that the Napatan keep an eye out
behind them, but perhaps he couldn't do that and also hold
the staff where it was useful. The glow was better than
nothing.

Besides, he doubted that any danger they faced would be
as simple as a man creeping upon them from the darkness.

"This block doesn't have the same sheen as the others,"
explained Samlor as he stood up slowly. "It's not on any
path, particularly, so maybe it's been sliding or, well,
something different to the rest."

He stepped gingerly on the block, which was only
slightly longer in either dimension than his foot. By shifting
his weight from toes to heel and then to the edge of his boot,
the caravan master hoped he could induce the marble to
pivot on a hidden pin. He was poised to jump clear at the
first sign of movement.

There was none.

Well, then . . . if he pressed the block toward the
wall—

Samlor's hobnails skidded, then bit into the marble
enough to grip as he increased the weight on them. The
black stone slipped under the molding with the silent grace
of mercury flowing.

There was a sigh from behind them. The two men jerked
around and saw that the ornamental pond was lifting onto
one end. The water, which had dampened Samlor's boot a
moment before, did not spill though it hung on edge in the
air.

There was a ladder leading down into the opening the
pond had covered.

"Collector, you called him," said the caravan master
grimly as he watched his reflection in the vertical sheet of
water.

"A good trick," responded Khamwas, nettled at the

hinted contrast of his knowledge against that of the missing Setios.

The Napatan stood and began muttering in earnest concentration to his staff. Samlor assumed the incantation must have some direct connection with their task and their safety.

When the phosphorescent staff floated out of Khamwas' hands, dipping but not quite falling to the ground, the Cirdonian realized that it was merely a trick—a demonstration to prove that Khamwas was no less of a magician than the owner of the house.

It was the sort of boyish silliness that got people killed when things were as tense as they were just now.

Apparently Tjainufi thought the same thing, because he turned and said acidly into the scholar's ear, "There is a running to which sitting is preferable."

Star's hands wavered briefly from the folds of her cloak; Samlor could not be sure whether or not the child mumbled something as well. Flecks of light shot from her fingers. They grew as they shimmered around the room, gaining definition while they lost intensity—jellyfish of pastel light, and one mauve sea urchin, picking its glowing, transparent way spine by spine across a 'bottom' two feet above the marble floor.

The staff clattered and lost its phosphorescence as it fell. Samlor snatched it before it came to rest on the stone. He handed it back to his male companion. "Let's take a look, shall we?" he said, nodding to the ladder. "Guess I'll go first."

"No, I think I should lead," said Khamwas. "I—"

He met the caravan master's eyes. "Master Samlor, I apologize. It'll be safer for me to go first, and I'll spend my efforts on making it safe."

The multi-colored jellyfish made the reception room look as if it were being illuminated through stained glass. The sea urchin trundled its way forward to the opening in the middle of the floor, then continued downward at the same staccato pace as if the plane on which its spines rested lay in a universe where sideways was up.

That might be the case.

The two men walked to the opening and looked down while Star hugged herself in silence.

The room beneath the floor was a cube or something near it, ten feet in each dimension. Mauve light filled the volume surprisingly well, though the simulated urchin did not itself seem bright enough to do so. The floor shone with a sullen lambency.

The furnishings were simple. A metal reading stand, high enough for use by a standing man and empty now, waited near the center of the room.

To its right stood an elaborate bronze firebox on four clawed legs, a censer rather than a heating device. The flat sides of the box were covered by columns of incised swirls, more likely a script unknown to the caravan master than mere decoration. The top was smooth except for a trio of depressions—an inch, three inches, and six inches in diameter. Aromatics could be placed there to be released by the heat of charcoal burning in the firebox beneath.

At each corner of the top was a decorative casting. They were miniature beasts of the sort which in larger scale could have modeled the censer's terrible clawed legs. The creatures had catlike heads, the bodies of toads with triangular plates rising along the spine for protection, and the forelegs of birds of prey. Serpent tails curled up behind them, suggesting the creatures were intended as handles for the censer; but anyone who attempted to put them to that purpose would have his hands pierced by the hair-thin spikes with which the tails ended.

There was no other furniture in the room, but a pentacle several feet in diameter was painted or inlaid on the concrete floor to the reading stand's left. It was empty. The floor and white-stuccoed walls were otherwise unmarked.

Khamwas' lips pursed.

"Go ahead," said Samlor with a shrug. "Maybe your stone's on the ceiling where we can't see it."

"Yes," said the Napatan, though there was doubt rather than hope in his tone.

Khamwas thrust his staff as far into the mauve light as it would go while his hand on the tip remained above floor level.

Nothing happened, but Samlor was not fool enough to think it had been a pointless exercise. His companion was doing what he had promised, concentrating his talents—better, his knowledge—on the task at hand.

Still holding out the staff in his direction of travel, Khamwas backed awkwardly down the ladder. The ferule banged accidentally on the censer as he turned. It made Khamwas jump back but did not concern Samlor, who saw what was about to happen.

The crash and shattering glass from upstairs spun the caravan master, his teeth bared and his left hand groping for the throwing knife in his boot sheath.

"The wind," murmured Star, the first words she had spoken since the trap door rose. She wasn't looking at her uncle or at anything in particular.

But she was right. A door banged shut, muting a further tinkle of glass. One of the window sashes had not been secured properly. A gust had slammed it fiercely enough to shatter the glass.

"Are you all right?" called Khamwas.

The question impressed Samlor, for it sounded sincere—and in similar circumstances, he would have been worried more about his own situation than that of his companions.

"We're going to get drenched when we leave here," the caravan master said. "Leaving 'll still feel good. Any luck yourself?"

The Napatan grimaced. "The room's empty," he said. "The brazier's as clean as if it was never used. I'm not sure it's here at all."

"Do not ask advice of a god and then ignore what he says," snapped Tjainufi. He was rubbing his tiny face on his shoulder like a bird preening.

"Step back," said Samlor. "I'm coming down."

He turned to his niece and said, "Star, dearest? Honey? Will you be all right for a minute?"

She nodded, though nothing in her face suggested that she was listening.

The quicker they found what Khamwas needed, the quicker they—Samlor—could sort out his niece's problem.

He jumped into the cubical room without touching the ladder.

Samlor landed in perfect balance, feet spread and his left hand extended slightly farther than the right so that leverage matched the weight of his long dagger. Despite Samlor's care, his hobnails skidded and might have let him fall if Khamwas hadn't clutched the Cirdonian's shoulder. The floor was dusted with sparkly stuff, almost as slick as a coat of oil.

Jumping might not have been the brightest notion, but the caravan master hadn't liked the idea of doing exactly what an intruder was expected to do.

The concealed room had an underwater ambiance which wasn't wholly an effect of the glowing sea urchin trundling across an invisible bottom at waist height. The mauve light rippled, but neither the furniture nor the two men cast distinct shadows on the walls.

"What does your—" Samlor said, making a left-handed gesture to indicate either Khamwas' staff or nothing at all "—your friend say about what you're looking for?"

"That I've found it," Khamwas replied, turning his head to view surroundings which were no less void on this perusal than on earlier ones.

Samlor stamped his foot. Sparkling dust quivered, but the concrete was as solid as the bedrock on which it was probably laid.

Then he kicked the nearest wall.

Stucco blasted away as the hobnails raked four short, parallel paths and squealed on the stone beneath.

"Well, I think we know where t' look," said the Cirdonian in satisfaction.

The stucco his boot had scraped was covering two distinct blocks of stone—a slab of polished red granite and another of marble shadowed with faint streaks of gray. Both stones were inscribed, though on the softer marble the markings had been weathered and further defaced by Samlor's boot.

He brushed at the stucco with his left hand, flaking away a patch his kick had loosened. The writing on the granite slab was Rankan but of a form so old that the doubled consonants and variant orthography made all but a few words unintelligible to the caravan master.

"Why, this is wonderful, my friend," said the Napatan with a smile brighter than the mauve glow as he bent over the cleared patch.

Tjainufi beamed and added, "There is no good deed save a good deed done for one who has need of it."

"We're not outa the woods yet," said Samlor with a dour glance at the walls around them. If they had to clear all the stucco, or even half, if their luck were average (which it probably wouldn't be), it was going to take a lot longer than the caravan master wanted to spend in this place.

"No, that's all right," explained the Napatan with the uneasy hint of mindreading which he had displayed before. "I'll use a spell of release and the covering will come away at once. He must use the ancient writings because they focus the power with which the years have embued them."

Maybe that was what Setios used to do with them, Samlor thought as his companion knelt before his upright staff again, but he'd bet Setios hadn't much use for them or anything else in the world just now.

Khamwas was whispering to himself and his gods. Samlor looked at him, looked at the dagger—saw that the watered steel blade was only that, only metal; probably all it ever was, except in his mind.

"Star?" he called toward the rectangular opening. "You all right, sweetest?"

He could barely hear the reply, ". . . all right . . . ," but a couple of the pastel jellyfish were drifting over him in placid unconcern. She'd be fine, Star would.

If any of them were, she'd be fine.

Samlor squatted and squeezed up dust from the floor on the tip of his left index finger. It was colorless (save for the mauve light it reflected) and much too finely ground for him to be able to tell the shape of the individual crystals.

A caravan master has plenty of opportunity to examine decorative stones, jewels and bits of glass cut and stained to look like jewels in the dim light of a bazaar. The dust could be anything, powdered diamond even; but most likely quartz, spread in a smooth layer across all the flat surfaces in the room.

Except for streaks—shadows, almost—stretching from the reading stand and the legs of the bronze censer. The dust seemed to have been sprayed violently from the direction of the pentacle in which Khamwas was almost standing.

"K—" Samlor began in sudden surmise.

The Napatan had been whispering, but now his voice rose in a crescendo. Khamwas' eyes lifted also; they were wide open but obviously not fixed on anything in the room.

Stucco shattered away on all sides, raining over Khamwas and the caravan master who reached for the ladder with his left hand and swung his blade at anything which might have slipped behind him as he crouched.

Nothing had. The choking flood of sand and lime-dust filling the air as the walls cleared themselves made Samlor pause where the attack he feared would only have driven him to swifter motion.

The slow tumble of the mauve light-source continued, though the mineral-laden air absorbed the illumination. A ball a few feet in diameter glowed in place of the urchin's sharply limned spines and carapace. As dust settled out, the glow spread and paled while the features of the source at its heart slowly regained definition.

"Khamwas," said the caravan master. His eyes were slitted and a fold of his cloak covered his mouth and nose, a response made reflexive by years of dry storms whipping across his caravan routes. "*Where* did Setios keep his demon in a crystal bottle?"

"The gods preserve me from such knowledge, friend!" said the Napatan as his eyes swept the upper levels of the walls which could already be viewed with sufficient clarity. He filtered the air through his cape; a desert-dweller himself, Khamwas must have more experience with dust storms than Samlor did. "Believe me, Setios was mad to keep such a thing by him, and you and I would be even madder to carry it off ourselves."

"That's not what I mean," the caravan master said. He raised his voice, so that it could be heard through the muffling cloth and because he was at a desperate loss to know what he should do next. He would have climbed out of this place at once, except for his fear of what might follow him to where Star stood shivering.

No wonder the child had been terrified into a near coma. She must have known. . . .

"Here it is!" cried Khamwas, brushing the reading stand as he swept closer to a wall. "*Here* it is!" he repeated, then sneezed.

The wails of the sunken room were formed entirely of inscribed stones, but the pieces had little commonality beyond that. Some were squared columns, set with one face flush and the other three hidden even now that the stucco had fallen away.

A few bore symbols which were not writing at all. One of them was a small block of peridotite, polished smooth before a single diagonal was cut across its coarse crystals. The block had marked the victim's place in a temple of Dyareela. Samlor could not imagine anyone removing it from its original location—or being willing to have it close to him thereafter.

The Napatan was brushing his left palm across the face of a slab of gray granite, cleaning it of dust that had settled there after the spell of release. The stele was about three feet high and half that across. Figures—presumably gods— filled the upper portion, and there were about twenty vertical lines of script beneath them.

"To the blessings of Harsaphes," Khamwas said, his index finger pausing midway down one of the later columns. "*Harsaphes*, not Somptu as I'd always assumed, and the ruins of the temple of Har—"

"Khamwas, *listen* to me!" Samlor shouted. He gripped the scholar with his left hand, though that meant dropping his cloak while there was still dust in the air. "You say something happened to magic a little bit ago. Would that have broken the crystal that held Setios' demon?"

"The townsman," said the manikin who was not in the least affected by the chokng atmosphere, "is not the one who is eaten by the crocodile."

And men who leave magic alone, translated Samlor as he

whirled toward glimpsed motion, aren't destroyed by its creatures.

A hand was emerging from a slab of limestone on the far wall. It was tenuous enough that the settling dust coexisted with the limb, which was so thin that it would have been skeletal were it not for the gleam of a scaly integument.

The three fingers each bore a claw an inch long and sharp as shattered glass.

"Get up the ladder!" Samlor shouted as he leaped for the apparition behind the watered steel blade of his dagger. The hilt was adequate for his big hand when he slashed with it, though it was shaped wrong and would have been uncomfortably short had he chosen to thrust—

Which would have done as much good; as much, and no more.

The clawed hand twisted to grip the blade while an arm as wire-thin as the hand continued to extend from the wall. Steel parted the limb like smoke, and the claw slipped through the whisking dagger as if it in turn had no substance.

Another hand was reaching through the stone beside the first. The blur above and between them was growing into a narrow reptilian face.

"Get *out*!" the caravan master shouted again when a glance toward the ladder showed him that Khamwas stood where he had. He had crossed the top of his staff with his left forearm.

"No, run!" Khamwas replied. He had been chanting under his breath, and his face spasmed with the effort of breaking back into normal speech. "I released it again, but I can hold it for long enough."

The demon's head and torso had emerged from the wall. One leg was striding forward in slow motion. The creature was half again as tall as Samlor, and it was thinner than anything could be and live.

One hand shot out and snatched the sea urchin which shattered beneath the claws into a cascade of mauve sparks. As the demon's arm withdrew, the sparks formed again into their original shape. The creature of light continued to pick its way through the air.

Samlor was quite sure that if the claws closed on his niece, their effect would be permanent.

"*Run Star!*" he shouted, afraid to turn from the demon. It continued to pull itself from the stone.

Khamwas hadn't moved, though his mouth resumed its unheard chanting. Maybe Samlor could jump for the ladder himself since the fool Napatan refused to do so. Slam the lid back over this hellish room—if the lid would close without a search for another mechanism. Run out the front door with Star in his arms, praying that he could work the bolts swiftly enough . . . praying that the doorkeeper would ignore them as they left, the way Khamwas had said it would. . . .

Samlor stepped forward and swung at the demon again. He wasn't going to abandon Khamwas to the creature unless there were no other choice.

He chopped for a wrist. Instead of slipping through like light in mist, the caravan master's steel clanged as numbingly as if he had slashed an anvil. The demon seized the blade and began to chitter in high-pitched laughter.

All of the demon but its right leg had pulled free of the wall. That leg was still smokily insubstantial, but the claws of the left foot cut triple furrows in the concrete as they strained to drag the creature wholly out of the stone. The left hand—forepaw—was reaching for Samlor's face while the right gripped his knife.

Samlor's mouth had dropped open as he breathed through it, oblivious of the dust that would have made him cough another time. He jerked straight down on the dagger hilt, ducking from the swipe that started slowly as a boulder rolling, but completed its arc at blinding speed.

The blade screeched clear. If a man held it, his fingers would have been on the floor or dangling from twists of skin.

The demon's paw was uninjured, and its claws had streaked the flat of the blade against which they were set.

Samlor caught the throatclasp of his cloak. He could throw the garment like a net over the creature and—

—and watch the claws shred it as the demon, steel strong and more than iron hard, leaped free to dispose of the men before it. The creature's eyes had no pupils and glowed orange, a color which owned nothing to the urchin which still tumbled innocently around the room.

"*Khamwas!*" the caravan master shouted, because the demon was already in the air and perhaps Khamwas could get up the ladder while the Cirdonian occupied the creature with the process of being slaughtered. . . .

The demon halted in midair, its left foot above the concrete and its right leg, spindly and terrible as that of a giant spider, lifting to deliver a kick that would disembowel Samlor. Dust settled and the urchin of light rolled jerkily forward, one spine at a time. The demon hung frozen like an idol of ravening destruction.

Its eyes were as bright as tunnels to Hell.

Samlor started another cut at the demon. Light reflecting from the triple scratch on his blade reminded him how useless that would be, so he turned instead to Khamwas.

Who had not moved since last Samlor had leisure to glance at him.

Khamwas hunched slightly forward, his left forearm crossing the top of his staff and his eyes fixed on the demon with a reptile's intensity. Tjainufi still perched on his shoulder.

The Napatan's lips had been moving soundlessly, but now he said in a cracked whisper, "Go on . . . quickly."

The demon was not quite frozen. The movements the creature began before Khamwas' spell took effect were still going on. The leg that stretched toward Samlor at a glacial pace quickened noticeably when the Napatan spoke, and the demon's mouth gaped slowly to display interlocked arrays of teeth like needles in the upper and lower jaws.

"But how can you," the caravan master began as he slipped a step back, beyond the present arc of the claws. The demon bent at its girl-slim waist as it leaped, because otherwise its flat skull would have banged the ten-foot ceiling.

"Samlor," said the Napatan scholar, "get *out*! I brought you here!"

The demon had trembled back to near stasis for a moment. Now it lurched far enough forward in its unsup-

ported motion that it was clear one hand was reaching for
Khamwas' head even as the kick extended toward the
Cirdonian.

"There is none who abandons his travelling companion
whom the gods do not call to account for it," said Tjainufi.

"Fuck your gods," said Samlor, who was already sliding
the knife back under his belt to free his hands. He encircled
the Napatan's waist, underneath the cape for a firmer grip,
with his left arm.

"No" said Khamwas desperately.

"Do your *job*," Samlor snarled back as he lifted the
smaller man. The air swirled with the demon's renewed
movement, but the claws now behind the caravan master
did not rend him as he stepped with regal determination to
the ladder.

Focusing on the creature from the stone was for Khamwas. Samlor hil Samt had the responsibility of getting them
both back up the ladder while his companion *did* that job,
eyes, arm and staff locked into their duty.

Khamwas' body was muscular, but weight wasn't the
problem. Carrying him upright while Samlor's right hand
needed to grip the ladder for balance was brutal punishment, and it reminded him of how badly he had strained
himself getting into this *damned* house.

One foot above the other, each step a deliberate one
because a jolt at the wrong time might break Khamwas'
concentration irrevocably. No way to tell what was happening behind him, and nothing to do about it if things weren't
well. One foot and then the other.

A gust of wind shocked Samlor as his head lifted above
the floor of the reception hall. Fabric, a curtain or a
counterpane, had been snatched from a room on the upper
floor and was flapping from the railing.

Star was calm as molten glass as she watched her uncle
struggle up the ladder with the other man clamped to his
side. At his first wild glance, Samlor thought the whorl
of white on the child's temple was one of the creatures of
light which pulsed through the reception hall. It was so
bright. . . .

He couldn't bend over to balance with his palm on the

floor as he neared the top of the ladder, so the caravan master mounted the last three rungs at a quickened pace. Toppling backwards would mean the floor killed them if the demon didn't, but if Samlor sprawled on his face the result would be no better. He'd seen the creature start to move; it would be on them in an instant if Khamwas were flung out of his concentration.

Samlor stepped from the top rung to the marble floor, sucking in his lips as he strove to move as smoothly as a duck gliding on water. He set the Napatan down, conscious of the man's weight only after he was free of it, and with same motion strode for the wall and the latch mechanism.

Khamwas' voice was audible again, breaking with strain as he chanted over and over again a dozen or so words. Sweat from the Napatan's face had splashed Samlor's left forearm as he climbed.

The caravan master's boot skidded when he tried to slide back the piece of marble which was half withdrawn beneath the molding. Instead of trying again with his hobnails, Samlor knelt and scrabbled at the black stone with both sweaty palms. It moved into position with the same greasy certainty with which it had opened.

The pond of mirror-smooth water slipped down to cover the demon soundlessly.

Samlor skidded as he ran from the sidewall to the front door. Hobnails weren't the footgear for these polished stones . . . and this house wasn't a place for humans. Not now, and probably not before Setios' pet got loose.

There was no inside door latch.

"You didn't let them out, Master Khamwas," said Star, patting the hand of the scholar who had knelt and was sobbing with exhaustion. "They're playing with us."

"Come on," Samlor shouted. There was certainly a way to open the inner and outer doors from here, but he didn't have time to fool with it. "We're leaving the way we came!"

"There's six of them, Uncle Samlor," said Star. "They're playing with us."

Something emerged from the pilaster beside the stairs to the second floor. It was a clawed hand like that of the demon below. Instead of streaming like smoke from the stone, it broke free as a chick emerges from an egg. Rock shattered away from the groping limb, and a section of the wall started to lift.

Khamwas rose to his feet. His face was blank and his body swayed with fatigue. He crossed his arm over the staff again and began a whispered chant.

The wall from which the demon crashed, already formed, was load-bearing. Tortured roofbeams squealed as plaster in chunks of up to a hundred pounds broke away. A big piece hit the center of the pond and blasted water out across the reception hall.

Samlor caught his niece with one arm and Khamwas with the other. He flung them, all three together, to the floor against the nearer sidewall. A block of stone, notched for the butt of a crossbeam, tumbled from the roof to the rail of the second-floor walkway. It caromed to the floor in a shower of dust and chips.

"We'll get out through the back!" said the caravan master who doubted that they would. The wall beside where they hunched under cover of the walkway was crumbling as gray claws harder than the stone emerged from it.

Across the reception room, the other sidewall was disintegrating into bits and blocks. They hid but did not disguise the cause of the destruction. One of the demons was clasping a dismembered human leg. Samlor figured he knew where Setios and his servants had gone.

Six of 'em, Star'd said. Likely five more than they'd need, but you didn't quit just because you couldn't win. . . .

The three humans rose and scuttled for the room's back wall and the door there. They were bent over because the walkway's partial roof was no protection against blocks bouncing from the floor at crazy angles.

The front half of the house staggered forward into the street with a roar that was not loud until Samlor realized that he could not shout with enough volume to be heard by the two companions he had dragged with him into the temporary safety of the door alcove.

Skeletal, inhumanly tall figures minced toward the trio,

shrugging off the tons of rubble that had thundered down on them. There were four, and the mound of stone and timber covering what had been the floor of the reception room heaved as the creature in the room beneath rejoined its fellows.

Sheets of pain flapped across Samlor's body from a center where his right hip had blocked a ricocheting chunk of stone that weighed as much as he did. The crosswall dividing the house was built as solidly as the exterior. It remained essentially undisturbed when the emerging demons had shattered the front of the house. That portion of the building had demolished itself as brittle stone shifted in a vain attempt to find new foundations.

The door in front of Samlor was locked or possibly jammed when ruin made the house twist, but the panel was only thin wood inlaid with horn and ivory in patterns which were probably significant as well as decorative. Khamwas pounded it with the ferule of his staff, breaking off scales of ivory without doing anything to get them through the doorway.

Samlor would have kicked the latchplate, but he was pretty sure that his right hip would neither support him alone nor lift his boot high enough for the purpose. Wondering how many seconds they had before a demon lunged onto them, he rotated on his left heel and grabbed a torso-sized block from the wreckage that had spilled inward during the collapse.

The demons were advancing with tiny steps, chittering in self-satisfaction. When they chose to, they picked their way over the piled rubble, but one of the four figures strode through the tons of jumbled rock like a man wading in the surf. The fifth of the creatures heaved itself into sight with the ease of a toadstool bursting pavement to reach the open air.

"Care—" cried Samlor, turning with the block in his hands. The movement was so painful that he could feel only his scalp, his palms, and the ball of his left foot.

"—ful!"

The stone splintered the door and carried on, crashing on the floor of the hallway beyond and then bouncing harmlessly from the legs of the sixth demon poised there with its arms spread across the passage.

The air was dead still. The caravan master turned again, no more conscious of his pain than a fox is conscious of the way its lungs burn from running when the hounds encircle it for the last time.

"The sky," Khamwas said hoarsely. "*Look.*"

Samlor drew the long dagger from his belt and lifted Star to his chest with his free arm. The semicircle of demons waited, crouching slightly, with their spindly, steel-strong arms interlocked. They were close enough that if one of the creatures leaned forward, it could rip the caravan master's face away in its pointed teeth.

"*Look!*" Khamwas screamed, and even so his voice was smothered by a sound like the scream of a giant snake.

Samlor looked up. He could see almost a mile into the sky, up the lightning-lit throat of a descending tornado funnel.

The lower end was shaggy with tentacles of water vapor condensing in the lowered pressure surrounding six separate suction vortices. They extended toward the ruined house.

"Down!" cried the caravan master, but Star twisted like an eel from his arms and stood while the two men tried to flatten themselves.

One of the demons leaped away, covering twenty feet of the distance toward the street before being caught by a suction vortex. The creature reeled upward into the main funnel, like a crab being lifted into an octopus's crushing beak. Blue-white lightning licked soundlessly but with coronal radiance from one side of the void to the other.

The funnel hovered at the level of what remained of Setios' roof. A miniature vortex snaked past Star's erect head, so close that it should have touched her hair but didn't. It was no more than the diameter of a wine jar, spinning widdershins though the main cloud rotated with the sun.

Samlor lay on his back, clutching the medallion of Heqt in his left hand as he watched transfixed. The broken door panel exploded into splinters. They cleared themselves up the shaft of the screaming vortex. The demon flashed out in the grip of the wind, upright and battling momentarily while its hind claws gouged pieces the size of a man's fist from the stone of the doorjambs. Then the creature was gone, falling upward into the sky in a helix so tight that its limbs had been plucked from its body before it disappeared into the tunnel of lightning.

The tornado was lifting and folding in on itself like a purse whose drawstrings were being tightened. Samlor hadn't seen what happened to the four remaining demons, but they had vanished when he knelt to look around.

"If you are not slack," said Tjainufi in a perfectly audible voice, "then your god will be active for you."

Samlor uncurled his fingers from the amulet of Heqt; but it had not been to the toad goddess that he screamed his prayers in the last instants—

"I thought Mummie's box was empty," said Star as her eyes met the caravan master's. "But it wasn't."

The tornado funnel flattened into the overcast almost a mile above Sanctuary. Only then did the normal wind return, a huge gust of it, and with it the start of a cold downpour. It was as dark again as the inside of a tomb.

But the whorl of hair on Star's temple burned for a moment like the lightning's heart.

CHAPTER 7

THERE WERE OIL lamps in the caravansary, but they could not compete with the blaze of lightning through the clerestory windows beneath the great vaulted roof. Unlike the sun by day, the storm's harsh illumination blasted from any direction—and sometimes from every direction at once. Thunder shook the building and filled its hollows so thoroughly that there was no question of trying to speak except between the echoing peals.

Star murmured in her sleep, burrowing deeper into her uncle's cloak as he stroked her shoulder.

"Did you hear the watchman at the gate below as he let us in?" Khamwas asked Samlor. "He looked at the sky and muttered. 'He's back.' I wonder who the fellow meant?"

Samlor shrugged at his companion whose face, lighted for the moment by a blue-white flash, had an inhuman intensity. "All the 'back' I care about is getting myself and Star back out of this hellhole. That'll wait till dawn—but only because they won't open the city gates till then."

"Be gentle and patient," said Tjainufi, sprawled at his miniature leisure on Khamwas' shoulder. "that your soul may become beautiful."

Samlor was relaxed as well—he was alive, after all, and that was better than he'd expected for several recent hours. "I'm very gentle and patient, little one," he said, "which is how I'm able to keep from hurling you through a stone wall.

Indeed, it may be that when I've been apart from you for a few years I'll find I miss your comments."

"Ah, Master Samlor," said Khamwas diffidently. "That raises a matter that I'd like to discuss with you."

Fresh thunder silenced the Napatan and left Samlor with time to consider his answer to the question he knew was coming. He was sick with anger—at Khamwas, for preparing to make a reasonable request, and at himself for putting so much emotional weight on what should have been a business proposition to which he would decide yea or nay.

The caravansary was built in two levels. Below, rooms opened onto the hollow interior. These were for merchants to store the goods they brought to Sanctuary behind heavy, bolted doors.

The rooms in which the merchants slept were on the level above, each chamber separate from the rest. Access was by ladder through the strongroom beneath. When the ladder was drawn up, as now, the occupants were as safe as men could be in Sanctuary.

After a night of terror like the one he had just survived, all Samlor wanted was safety.

And Khamwas was about to ask him to take further risks.

Star's hand, tiny and white, patted her uncle's scarred, wind-roughened, knuckles.

"You've done me great service tonight, Master Samlor." Khamwas continued when the echoes let him speak. "Helped me find the information I needed—you cannot imagine the importance of those few words—and brought me out alive."

"We're quits, then." said Samlor, his voice a tiger's growl like the muted thunderclap in the background. "You helped me to what I was looking for too . . . and as for getting out alive, I don't know that either of us had a great deal to do with that."

"I—" Khamwas began.

"Besides," Samlor continued deliberately. "I don't count myself safe until we're back in Cirdon. Which is where I'm headed now with Star."

"When you have delivered your niece to a place of safety," said Khamwas, "I wish to hire you as my

companion for the journey I have next to make. You are
experienced as a traveller and—" he met and held Samlor's
eyes. Blue lightning fingered across them in token of the
coming thunder. "And there may be danger, physical
dangers, of the sort you proved tonight that you are
experienced with also. I will pay you well."

"Give one loaf to your laborer" said Tjainufi with a
sardonic smile. "Receive two from the work of his hands."

"I don't *claim* to be a charity, Master Samlor." Khamwas
retorted sharply, as if the caravan master and not the
manikin had spoken. "I need a man like you; and, having
seen you in operation, I cannot imagine that anyone else
would be more than a pale echo."

There was a deafening crash, and for a moment light
sizzled and cracked from all the bolt-heads projecting
downward from the roof trusses. Animals stabled in the
adjacent courtyard blatted or whinnied.

"Do you think flattery will help you?" Samlor demanded. But of course it would, and the statement was no
more than the truth. That wouldn't have been enough by
itself to cause Samlor to change his plans, but—

But the stranger from Napata had proved he was willing
to sacrifice himself to permit Samlor and Star to escape.
How could Samlor refuse to help a man as honorable as
that? As honorable as himself.

"Star'll be back in Cirdon," said Samlor loudly, muting
his voice as the child stirred restively on his lap. "Back with
my parents. With the servants, at least, who know who
they'll answer to if anything harms the child while I'm
away. There'll be no magic if you hire me, only a man who
knows camels and donkeys."

"And the end of a knife that cuts," murmured Khamwas.
"Yes, I understand that, Master Samlor."

He paused for long enough that Samlor hoped he was
rethinking, preparing to change his mind. Instead Khamwas
said, "I wouldn't permit Star to come with us now. Her
powers are—" he shrugged "—I can't even guess how
great. I'm only a scholar, and she. . . ."

He shrugged again. "But for all that, she's a child the age
of my own daughter—at least if she's still alive, my

daughter Serpot and Pemu her brother. And this will not be work for children."

Samlor gave Star a hug, controlled against his fierce desire to squeeze the child until their two forms merged. She could be safe then because he would always be there to guard her. . . . Detaching himself carefully, Samlor left Star curled on the couch while he strolled to the barred windows overlooking the interior of the caravansary.

Travellers too poor to hire strongrooms huddled on the floor in informal groups about cooking fires. A few sang or played stringed instruments—despite the thunder, or because of it.

"If you're expecting real trouble," said Samlor with his face to the bars, "there's others you could hire. Soldiers, men with proper armor, swords. Nobody hires me to fight. I just run caravans the easiest way I can."

Tjainufi said, "The hissing of the snake is more effective than the braying of the donkey." The thunderclap that began a moment behind him did not drown out his voice.

"Master Samlor," said Khamwas, meeting Samlor with quiet eyes when the caravan master turned from the window. "There may be bandits on our path. Surely there will be cases where the presence of a man of your—strength and demeanor—will prevent trouble that might otherwise arise."

The copper bowls of the lamps rattled against the chains by which they hung, counterpointing the violence of a nearby stroke.

"But the real risks," Khamwas continued as though there had been no interruption, "are of a different nature, and I must face them myself."

He waved a hand. "Yes, of course I could hire wizards as easily as I could hire soldiers . . . and perhaps no less reliable ones. But the business is a family one, in this— era—and in past time as well. If it's to be accomplished, I must do so myself.

"I would be. . . ." Khamwas went on. His eyes and voice dropped in sudden diffidence before he said; "I'd just like to have a friend at hand, Samlor. Not so much for what you'd do, but for the sake of a trustworthy presence."

Samlor utterly refused to acknowledge the admission—and offer—the other man had just made. "You say you'll pay," he said in grumbling harshness. "How much then? And for what?"

"A daily sum," Khamwas responded, emotionless again now that his emotions had been spurned, "equal to your hire for managing a forty-camel caravan. Two Rankan goldpieces."

Samlor nodded. It was interesting to learn that Khamwas, though—"scattered" was a far better description than "unworldly"—had at his fingertips a datum of Samlor's own trade.

"We will be travelling the Napata," Khamwas went on, "but not—initially, at least—to the capital. We will investigate a temple and tomb, I hope a tomb, near a village named Qui. It's some distance south of Napata City, on the river but upstream. I estimate that it will take us two months, but you will know better than I."

"Longer," Samlor said. "We'll be leaving from Cirdon, remember." He sat down on the couch. Star burrowed toward him in her sleep. "If *we*."

"After that," said Khamwas with a nod of agreement, "I will examine the tomb and remove from it the object which I. . . ."

His voice and expression lost their coolness, and he choked momentarily before he continued. "There's a book in the tomb, if I'm right. I've been searching for it as long as . . . as long as I have conscious memory."

The storm had almost played itself out with the last shattering discharges, but a series of muted rumbles now gave Khamwas an opportunity to clear his throat and both men to break eye contact. At last Khamwas said, "There may be danger when I remove the book. Certainly for me, perhaps also for you. I can't claim that any pay would adequately compensate you, Master Samlor, if the risk is yours as well. But—"

The Napatan's mouth broadened in a cool, knowing grin. "If I succeed," he continued, "I will become King of Napata. And that is the very least of what the book will make available to me. You will be well compensated, I assure you. You'll have your heart's desire."

Samlor's mouth quirked in a smile which was either wistful or mocking, depending on how the shadows fell across the harsh planes of his face. "Before you offer me that," he said softly, "you'll have to tell me what it is."

The three of them waited unmoving while the storm rumbled its way toward silence. Star was asleep, and Khamwas looked toward the barred window, wise enough to know not to push his companion—patient enough to follow the path of wisdom.

Samlor mused, dark thoughts sometimes rolling volcanically brighter with moments of rage and frustration. He had every confidence in himself, absolute certainty that he could get what he wanted.

But he didn't know what that was. His words to Khamwas had not been any sort of joke.

Moving slowly enough that it was not a threat, Samlor drew the coffin-hilted dagger from his belt. He held it point high, an edge toward him and one of the flats of scribbled metal facing the Napatan scholar.

"Master Khamwas," Samlor said, "how do you like this dagger? The pattern in the iron?"

Khamwas shrugged. "Very pretty," he said. Innate good manners saved him, barely, from snapping at the frivolity.

"What d'ye suppose it'd tell me I should do if I looked at it now?"

"Pardon?" said Khamwas. This time the question didn't seem frivolous, but it was completely unintelligible to him. Either Samlor had a fund of knowledge closed to his companion, or Samlor was going mad.

The Cirdonian caravan master was not acting particularly like a man with special knowledge.

"Well, it doesn't really matter," said Samlor in a bantering voice. He slipped his dagger carefully under his belt again. "I've already decided I'm going along with you. After all, that way one of us is going to know what he wants."

"I'm very glad to hear that," said Khamwas. He stood up

and clasped Samlor's hand in token of the bargain they had just struck.

Khamwas didn't have the faintest notion of what had gone through Samlor's mind in the past few minutes, but neither did he care. Khamwas knew exactly what he wanted, just as Samlor implied.

It didn't occur to him that he might be mistaken in his desire.

And he certainly didn't understand what Tjainufi meant when the manikin chirped, "A remedy is effective only through the hand of its physician."

CHAPTER 8

THE WIND WAS hot and charged with sand. Though it swept for hundreds of miles up the valley of the River Napata, the shimmering air brought no hint of moisture with it to the nostrils of Khamwas and Samlor.

"This is the place," Khamwas croaked to his companion. He turned as he started to speak and, convinced of his inattention, the camel on which he rode snaked its head around to bite.

"Child of *Hell*," Khamwas snarled as he kicked the beast's muzzle. The motion had become almost instinctive through long practice on the road from Cirdon. The beast gave an angry bleat, not so much pained by the boot sole as frustrated at its failure to clamp its square yellow teeth on its rider's calf.

Samlor was logy with the motion of his own beast. He had reined to a halt when his companion did, but it was a moment before Khamwas' words had any more meaning than did the rasping wind that surrounded them. The camel's shambling pace did not rock a man drowsy but rather hammered him to semi-consciousness. Being familiar with the process, as Samlor had been now for decades, did not change it from the physical punishment it had been the first time he rode one of the beasts.

Children of Hell indeed.

Coughing to clear his throat before he ventured a reply,
Samlor said, "The temple we're looking for? Where then?"

Instead of giving an immediate response, Khamwas
began to dismount with the care required by stiff muscles
and a camel whose ill will had been demonstrated over
several hundred miles of travel. Samlor remained where he
was, taking advantage of the saddle's height to survey their
surroundings.

There was nothing very prepossessing about them.

The journey from Sanctuary to Cirdon had been along a
regular caravan route—an easy trip for Samlor and not
overly grueling for Star and Khamwas.

They'd placed Star in the hands of family retainers—as
safe as she could be away from Samlor and probably safer
than anyone else was around a child with the powers Star
controlled. Then Samlor began really to earn his fee.

He and Khamwas followed the east bank of the River
Napata for a hundred miles that seemed an eternity. A reef
of hard sandstone cut across the desert on a course nearly
parallel to that of the river. Where rock finally met water
here, it formed a bluff sixty feet high.

The path had risen for a mile or more, but the ascent was
so gradual that Samlor had been unaware of it until now
when he found that by looking to his left he could see well
past the other bank. The river's course was brown, golden
where the sun reflected from it and gleamingly muddy to
either side. The hills in the distance were dark brown, and
the plains they enclosed were dun except where green
marked village plots, irrigated with water lifted by water-
wheel from the river below.

Even the foliage was dulled by dust.

There was a village nearby on their side of the river as
well, indicated by the tops of date palms a quarter mile
ahead. Nothing could be grown on the sandstone, but
beyond it there must be a fold of earth suitable for
irrigation.

"Yeah, hasn't been so very bad a way," said Samlor,
thinking back on the completed journey with already a
touch of longing. He had liked working for Khamwas,
being responsible for carrying out tasks in the best way

possible—but letting somebody else decide what those tasks should be. Khamwas knew what he wanted. . . .

And Khamwas was a good man with whom to share a journey. Not especially skilled, but willing and intelligent. Cheerful within reason, but not a maniac who redoubled the unpleasantness of storm or baking heat with bright chatter.

Not so very bad a journey though, now it had ended.

"It is on the road that a man finds a companion," said Tjainufi. In dim light the manikin was more visible than he should have been. Conversely, the sunlight that flooded the travellers now blurred around Tjainufi so that the manikin seemed to have been molded from translucent wax. His voice was no less wingedly clear at one time of day or another.

Khamwas ignored Tjainufi. He bent at the waist and twisted, legs spread and tense as he tried to work the cramps from his muscles.

"We should have hired a boat and crew as soon as we reached the river," he said. His reproach was made impersonal by the fact that he did not turn to face his companion as he spoke. "We would have been here as soon, and been in better shape."

Convinced at last they had arrived, Samlor lifted himself from the saddle of his own camel and dropped heavily to the ground. He could have alighted more gently, or even forced his beast to kneel and halve the distance; but that would have added insult to Khamwas, who already felt injured by the choice of conveyance on which the caravan master had insisted.

"The wind's been in our face all the way down the river," said Samlor, loosening the rust from both mind and tongue as he fitted them to the thought. "A boat couldn't drift against it, not as sluggish as the current is. We'd still be a hundred miles upstream. Not as stiff, mayhap. But not in very good humor by now, I'd judge."

"That's very unusual," said Khamwas as he walked to the edge of the bank. From cracks in the sandstone grew bushes, low and seemingly as dry as the rock and sand around them. They were attractive enough to the camels that both began to browse instead of bolting or making further attempts to use their teeth on their riders.

"I don't trust the weather, ever," said Samlor. "And I don't know enough about boats to feel comfortable about it." He grinned and squeezed his companion's biceps. "I'm responsible for getting you here, remember? And, unusual wind or not, we've gotten here, haven't we?"

Khamwas grinned back though there was a gray tinge of fatigue behind his expression. "So we have," he agreed. "What do you think of them?"

He gestured downward, over the bank. Samlor stepped forward and followed the gesture with his eyes.

"Heqt and her waters!" he blurted, realizing for the first time that there was something here to see.

The river had cut a scallop in millennia of battering against the sandstone reef. Human labor had then modified the smooth, water-sculpted, curve into an array of huge statues.

Samlor looked down at four of them, their feet half buried by sand that drifted over the escarpment to fill again the cavities that men had carved away.

There was little to tell of the subjects from this angle, but at the further horn of sandstone was another quartet of statues. They were perhaps smaller than those immediately beneath Samlor, but they were not hidden by sand or the angle.

They were monsters of a sort that the Cirdonian hoped were wholly mythical.

All were human in some portion of their physiognomy. The nearest had a woman's head beneath a crescent helmet. She snarled, leaning forward over the river on doglike legs and a hairy body that was more like a bear's than that of any other creature with which Samlor was familiar. The statue was cut into the living rock of the bluff, but it—all four of them—were in such high relief that only their heads and feet remained in contact with the stone of which they were a part.

The statue on the opposite end of the relief bore a man's head, but in no other way was it the male counterpart of the first. The creature's torso was that of a lizard with traces of

blue paint remaining in the crevices between its belly plates.
Eight legs that could have graced a spider or a crab splayed
outward from the shoulder area, gripping the pilasters to
either side with clawed feet.

In the center of the array of statues was a doorway cut
through a pilaster of double width. It was only by measuring
by eye the bluff's height above the river that Samlor could
estimate that what seemed to be a low door was really ten
feet high—though only a quarter the height of the statues.

The pair of reliefs immediately flanking the doorway
were not without human attributes, which made them the
more monstrous. A cobra head, its hood flared, watched
coldly from above the body of a grasshopper—from which
dangled a human phallus and scrotum. The composite
creature stood upright, but its limbs were those of a bull.

On the other side of the door, a fish head gaped from a
feathered torso with vestigial wings and bare, human
breasts. Gnarled, hairy legs, those of a troll or a great ape,
completed the grotesque ensemble.

"That's pretty impressive, Khamwas," Samlor said with
all emotion purged from his tone. It embarrassed him that
shapes in stone could affect him with disgust and more than
a touch of fear.

"All things are in the hands of fate and of god," said
Tjainufi.

Samlor glanced at the manikin. Tjainufi's features displayed nothing beyond bland indifference. The comment
didn't mean anything, so far as Samlor could see . . .
which, he had learned, might mean there was something
important that he didn't see.

"They're paired temples, you see," said Khamwas as he
peered with satisfaction down at the statues cut from the
face of the bank directly beneath them. "Harsaphes and
Somptu, this is Harsaphes under us here. There's always
been a belief that Nanefer was buried with his book on the
site—others have been searching for the book a thousand
years before *I* was born. But it seemed he was in the Temple
of Somptu, because the reference in the carving from the
Old Palace was to 'a tomb in the smaller temple.'"

Khamwas gestured across the curving rock face toward

the grotesque reliefs—a temple?—facing them. As he did, the door in the center of the design disappeared into deeper shadow. Samlor blinked at the illusion, then realized that the panel had been opened inward.

A hunched figure stepped into the light. It looked mouse-sized at the feet of the rock-carved monsters, but it was certainly human—a small man, stooping, dressed in a robe of black or sooty brown. The hatred in his glance was palpable, even over a distance far too great for Samlor to discern his features.

"But that must have been a mistake. Or perhaps a deliberate deception," said Khamwas, returning his attention to the figures beneath him. At least from this angle they appeared to be a quartet of seated men, monstrous only in that they were even larger than the reliefs on the opposite horn of rock. Sand drifting over the escarpment had covered one figure waist high, lying across the feet of the next and the threshold of the door set between pairs of figures.

"We've got company, Khamwas," said Samlor, touching his companion's arm and nodding toward the distant figure. "Across the way."

"Oh, yes, him," Khamwas replied unconcernedly. "He's been here since, well, long before the first time I came here to examine the temples. The Priest of the Rock, the local villagers call him, some sort of holy man. He actually lives in the Temple of Somptu, praying, I suppose, and the villagers support him with little offerings. Not that his needs are very great."

Khamwas paused, then rubbed his hands together and said, "Well, we'd best look the place over, hadn't we? I've examined the temple before, of course. But it's very different now that I *know* Prince Nanefer is buried here."

"A moment, friend," said Samlor, checking Khamwas with a touch. "We'll need food, the camels'll need fodder—and I think we'd best take care of those things at the village—" he nodded in the direction of the palm fronds and squealing water wheels "—before we settle in here."

"Just a look—"

"It's waited a thousand years, you tell me," said the

caravan master with a tight grin. "It'll wait for tomorrow better'n dealing with the—living surroundings—will."

"Well, I rather thought you'd, ah, take care of such things without my presence," said Khamwas. His expression was hooded and his voice careful, because he didn't understand why he had to state the obvious. Samlor was not only competent to deal with mundane cares of food and campsite, those were the reasons the Napatan scholar had hired him.

"I can take care of that, sure," said Samlor gently. "But I can't do that and watch you at the same time . . . which is why you hired me."

Khamwas blinked, suddenly aware of parallel truths, his and his companion's.

"The fellow down there," Samlor continued. "He doesn't like us a bit, and he may have friends who feel the same way. I'm not leaving you here alone."

"The Priest?" Khamwas said. He straightened and faced the distant figure, arms akimbo. The men were scarcely more than blobs of color to one another, but the challenge was as obvious as a slap in the face. "He's harmless."

The Priest of the Rock turned and disappeared within his shadowed doorway like a sow bug scurrying back beneath a rotting log. The panel closed behind him. It was so massive that the curving rock brought the sound of the door slamming all the way to the men watching it close.

"He's old," said Khamwas. "He lives in the temple and he'd like to think he owns it, owns them both. But he knows he's there on sufferance of the crown of Napata. All the ancient monuments are property of the state. If a peasant like him ever interferes with visitors, he'll die chained to a water wheel on a prison farm."

"Honor the old men in your heart," said Tjainufi, his posture matching the stiff arrogance of the man on whose shoulder he stood, "and you will be honored in the hearts of all men."

Khamwas jerked his head around, though the manikin must have been too close for his eyes to focus on it.

"This is far too important for the wishes of some mud-dwelling hermit to be consulted," Khamwas snapped. For the first time since Samlor had met them, he saw the scholar angry at Tjainufi. "I did him no harm when I was here before, unless you call clearing away the filth in which he lived harm. I'll do him no harm now. But he will *not* keep me away from this prize because he doesn't like other men examining these temples!"

Tjainufi did not speak or change his stance. After a moment, Khamwas turned his head away.

Samlor looked at the facing reliefs, grimaced, and looked down at the temple his companion intended now to explore. It must be cut back into the rock directly under them—a vaguely unsettling notion, though the footing here was certainly more secure than that of an ordinary building's floor. They would have to reach the temple door by the sand slope to the left, awkward going down and damned difficult coming up. Maybe he could rig a knotted rope as an aid. . . .

"I'm going to go down to the temple," said Khamwas, transferring the angry challenge in his voice from the manikin to Samlor. "You may leave or stay as you choose."

"Always true," agreed the caravan master with a smile which threatened more than the words did. Khamwas read the expression correctly and paused.

Idly, half pretending that he wasn't doing what he knew full well he was, Samlor slid the coffin-hilted dagger from its new sheath. The bright sun bathed the whole blade in a shimmering surface reflection which had no color or form but that of white light. But turn the flat slightly, and there crawled the whorls and quavers of black metal on white, a meaningless design—

Which spelled SAFE for a moment before becoming iron again and alloys of iron rippling coolly with reflected light.

"That is—" began Khamwas, abashed.

Samlor sheathed the weapon. Not that he trusted it, but . . . Khamwas ought to be able to handle himself against one old man, even without his magic. He knew the place, had been here before, after all.

"No, that's fine," said Samlor. "I was just letting my imagination go, that's all. Foolish. I'll off-load the camels and take one to see about supplies."

Khamwas relaxed visibly and nodded. Tjainufi mimicked the Napatan's motions, but Khamwas either did not notice or refused to notice.

"Hey, but look," Samlor added. He glanced away, embarrassed at what he was about to say and uncertain whether he could control his expression when he said it. "Ah. Don't—you know, don't do anything, you know, major, while I'm gone, will you? I don't know that I'd be a lot of help with, you know, magic. But if I'm supposed to be supporting you in this whole business, then . . . well, you're paying me to be around."

"Thank you," said Khamwas. "Friend. I know how much you dislike the idea of my scholarship."

He cleared his throat before he continued. Neither man was looking at the other. "But no, nothing significant will happen while you're gone—even if I intended it. A few minor location spells, perhaps. That didn't help me before, but now that I *know* the general whereabouts of the tomb, I'm sure the rest will follow.

"But nothing important will happen. I promise you."

CHAPTER 9

THE MOST IMPORTANT thing that happened in the next three days was that Samlor shaved the price of millet by a couple coppers per peck. The villagers were beginning to treat the newcomers as long-term residents, not travellers.

Samlor didn't consider that good news. As for Khamwas, natural gentility kept his frustration from blazing out—but his mild personality was growing spines beneath the veneer.

The caravan master paused at the temple entrance and rubbed his palms against one another to clear them of fragments of the coarse rope by which he had descended the slope. The four reliefs ignored him, staring southward across the river and the horizon. The figures were of seated men—or rather, a man, thick-featured and facing stiffly forward. The four copies were distinguished from one another only by the degree to which sand swirling off the escarpment had worn them.

Frowning at his own hesitation to look, Samlor glanced over his shoulder toward the other rock-cut temple. The monstrous carvings did not face him directly but the Priest of the Rock, a smudge in the angle of the doorway, did. He squatted there, scarcely visible in the distance, during every daylight moment that Samlor chanced to look in that direction.

The priest was harmless. He was accomplishing as little as Khamwas was.

Samlor stepped into the temple, rubbing his eyes to ease the shock of stepping from sunlight into darkness almost as solid as the rock above.

The temple's extent had surprised Samlor when he first entered it, expecting a low adyton and nothing beyond except a cult statue or—since they were searching for a tomb—a sarcophagus.

Instead, the central corridor of the temple was cut more than a hundred yards into the interior of the outcrop. Two large halls broadened from the main corridor, peopled with statues which would have been colossal were it not for the much greater reliefs on the temple facade. The walls and ceilings—twenty feet high in the first hall, fifteen feet in the second—were covered with incised writing and low reliefs of pomp and battle. Each relief was complex by itself and, considered as parts of a whole, staggeringly beyond the ability of a man to comprehend.

Besides the main halls, there were ten or a dozen obvious side chambers, some of them five yards by twenty in size. All were covered with their own carvings. Several of the chambers had been sealed with slabs of stone mortised so neatly that they appeared to be part of the living rock. The slabs had been broken out in the ancient past by men searching for treasure or the treasure of wisdom.

But there could be no assurance that *all* of the hidden chambers had been opened.

Samlor's hobnails sparked as he strode through the darkness of the great hall. The doorway cut sunlight into rigid edges which rolled across the dark stone like a knife cutting cloth. Perhaps—and probably only for minutes, one day a year—the sun stabbed to the further end of the central corridor, illuminating the altar and painted reliefs there in a dazzling triumph of astrology and engineering.

But for most of the year, the halls were barely relieved by scattered reflection and the side chambers were as dark as if they had never been excavated from the stone.

There was a glimmer of light through the opening into the second side chamber. Samlor stepped between a pair of lowering, kingly figures who helped support the ceiling on their ornate headdresses. They were set far enough in from the wall that the carved script behind them could have been read under the proper conditions. Samlor had neither the light, the knowledge nor the interest to do so.

He ducked his head—even a shorter man would have had to do so—to enter the smaller chamber at right angles to the hall. It smelled of burned oil. Though the atmosphere was breathable, it made Samlor's stomach roil after the clean, hot air of the escarpment and the central corridor.

Khamwas sat cross-legged in the center of the floor, his face toward the doorway but his eyes unfocused until Samlor stepped into view. A tripod of reeds tied with bast held a lamp near the ten-foot ceiling; the flame illuminated the reliefs there, but the poor-quality oil cast a permanent sooty shadow across them as well.

"I'm no closer than I was this morning," said Khamwas in a flat voice. "I'm not sure that I'm any closer than I was twenty . . . three years ago, when I first came here."

Samlor shrugged. He didn't need words to understand what Khamwas' face had made evident. "I've bought supplies," he said. "No fresh vegetables, I'm afraid, but I think I'll be able to get a flitch of bacon soon. Be a nice change from the fish."

He bobbed his head toward the lamp above them.

"Want me to add some oil to your lamp? Move it?"

Khamwas shook his head sharply, then relaxed the angry moue into which his lips had pursed themselves. "Sorry," he said, apologizing for the retort he had not spoken. "It's beginning to seem pointless. I find *no* reference to a tomb of Nanefer. . . . And others who've gone over *all* the reliefs here in past years, past *centuries*, none of them found anything either."

"I sort of thought," said Samlor carefully, dropping into a squat himself so that their eyes were nearly at a level, "that you'd be using your magic to locate the tomb." He nodded toward the staff lying beside Khamwas and felt rather pleased with himself that he had kept his voice from trembling when he made the suggestion.

"My servant is useless if he does not do my work," chirped Tjainufi in obvious agreement.

Khamwas nodded. "I'd expected that, too. Location

should have been relatively easy, even though I hadn't had
any success when I was here before."

"You've sharpened your skills," said the caravan master
approvingly. His belly was flip-flopping at the possibility
Khamwas meant instead that he had come to new arrangements with those who could grant such powers. Nothing
came without cost.

"Yes," agreed Khamwas, too calm to have been aware of
any other possibility. "But mostly because I *know* the tomb
is here, and that assurance gives me a, a base to probe more
precisely than I could otherwise."

He paused. "Except," he said, "I'm losing my assurance. If the tomb were within a *mile* of this temple, I should
have a hint of it. But there's nothing."

"Look," said Samlor, surprised at the way his voice
echoed here when anger raised and whetted it. "We didn't
go through that in Sanctuary for a no-show. You *found* what
you needed. By Heqt and all the gods, you're going to learn
to use what you got if it takes till we're both old and gray!"

Khamwas blinked, his face turned upward. Only then did
Samlor realize he was standing again.

Tjainufi was nodding. "It is in battle that a man finds a
brother," he said.

"Dunno that this is exactly a battle," said Samlor wryly,
embarrassed at the way he'd spoken out. He hadn't been
shouting, had he?

"In any case . . ." said Khamwas, accepting the hand
Samlor offered as he started to rise. "In any case, you're
acting as a brother. No, I'm not—we're not—going to give
up. There's something odd about the results of my location
spells. It's as though the tomb didn't exist at all."

Samlor cocked an eyebrow.

Khamwas shook his head forcefully. "No, there's no
question whatever of Nanefer's death and burial. He might
not be *in* the tomb, but the *tomb* exists."

He bent and retrieved his staff from the floor. "I think I'll
learn why that's happening."

The lamp was guttering near the end of its oil. Samlor
nodded toward it and asked, "Are you coming out? Or do
you want me to fill it?" His greater strength and dexterity

made it easier for him to collapse and lower the tripod without disaster.

"Neither, I think," said the Napatan with a smile. "The darkness may prove a benefit."

Samlor ducked his way into the great hall and strode past the royal caryatids. They had stern, solemn features now that his eyes were adapted to the amount of light spilling through the doorway.

Outside he sneezed, even though his eyes were slitted. He slid his cornel-wood staff from his belt to give his hands something to do. Probably he ought to busy himself with meal preparations, but there was no way to judge how long Khamwas would want to remain in the temple. Good that he had his enthusiasm back. Without it they were—

Well, not lost. But Samlor certainly didn't want to spend the rest of his life in a place where he, at least, had nothing in particular to do.

The sun was low, hammering a golden oval across the brown river. The landscape was almost as bright as that of noon, but there would be no twilight to separate it from the darkness to come.

Samlor walked slowly cross the great facade of the temple. Sand blown around the cliff stung his cheeks and the back of his hands. His eyes had readjusted to the light, but now he slitted them against the grit.

Shadows thrown by the low sun gave texture to what seemed smooth surfaces earlier in the day. The sandslope which had drifted across the feet, then knees, of the eastern pair of reliefs provided the path to the top of the escarpment. Samlor toiled up to it, more hindered by the soft footing than the gentle angle.

There was a slight swale in the sand beside him, next to the stone.

Samlor paused, his left hand on the knotted rope which took enough of his weight that his feet didn't slide him back toward the river. Pursing his lips as he wondered what he was trying to accomplish, Samlor reached across his body with the wand in his right hand and probed the swale.

The iron ferule slipped through drifted sand, then scraped to a halt a foot or so beneath the surface. A pock in the stone, reasonable enough and of no interest . . . but Samlor shifted his stance slightly, wiggling the slender staff; and, when he put his weight on it again, the tip slid until Samlor's hand touched the sand.

Samlor withdrew the wand so that the black handle stood out against the gold sand while he considered the situation. If there were a hole that deep in the rock face, it wasn't natural. Nor was it very large, because his probe had wedged against the side until he shifted it to get the angle just right. Unless—

The caravan master grasped his wand again and this time tried to work it down in a sawing motion as if cutting a vertical line in the rock face. The sand resisted, shifting like a heavy fluid away from the thrust of the wood. Occasionally the ferule scraped rock, but only sand hindered the general downward motion of the wand.

Samlor had found a crack in the rock, and it was damned likely that he had broken their impasse as well.

Leaving his wand as a stark marker, Samlor slid the twenty feet back down the slope at a rate controlled only by his willingness to kick his feet forward more quickly than his body's impetus could topple him head over heels. Sand and gritty dust sprayed in a dry parody of a duck landing on the water.

"Khamwas!" he shouted, even before he reached the entrance. "Khamwas. Come here!"

The Priest of the Rock was no longer huddled in his doorway. Samlor blinked when he noticed that. It should have been good news—in a small way—because of the way the priest bothered him.

Somehow it didn't seem good, though.

He had to stop when he plunged into the hall of the temple. He was too excited to trust himself to run through the darkness when a misstep into a caryatid would batter him as thoroughly as running into the cliff from which the statue was carved.

"Khamwas!" Samlor bellowed and began to shuffle forward, his hands stretched before him.

"Samlor!" bellowed Khamwas, so shockingly close that Samlor's hand cleared his fighting knife by instinct. "I've found it! It's east of the main temple just a little ways."

"Buggered Heqt," muttered Samlor under his breath. In a more normal voice, he said, "Yeah, I found it too—on the ground. Let's go take a look.'"

He tried to sheathe his dagger, but the darkness and the way adrenalin made him tremble prevented him. After he pricked his left index finger twice while it tried to steady the mouth of the sheath, he lowered the blade instead so that a flat was along his right thigh.

Khamwas had the advantage of seeing Samlor against the lighted doorway, so he had been able to dodge from the collision course the two of them were otherwise following. He put his hand on Samlor's shoulder and guided or directed his companion outside with him.

"All that it took," Khamwas bubbled happily, "is one more try. If you hadn't braced me, my friend, we'd. . . ."

"It's up the slope," said Samlor, pausing briefly to put his weapon back where it belonged when talking to his friend and employer. In slightly different circumstances, that reflex could have caused a very nasty incident indeed.

"Oh," he added, pointing across the curve of the cliff to the smaller temple. "Our friend's finally gone away."

Khamwas, already grasping the rope as he strode slushily up the slope, glanced in the direction of Samlor's gesture. As a result, they were both looking toward the relief when the spider-limbed monster shuddered away from it. The movement came a fraction of a second before the echoing crackle of rock breaking.

"Earthquake!" cried Samlor. He turned to be sure the escarpment and carvings towering beside them were not also toppling to crush them across the sand and into the nearby river.

The cliff above was as solid as it had ever been. The river was a brown stream. It was vaguely streaked by its current, but it had not become a mass of whitecaps dancing to the rhythm of the underlying strata.

The monster had not fallen from the other relief. It had walked. And it was walking toward Samlor and his companion.

Khamwas slid back to firmer footing, where sunbaked mud cemented the sand into a narrow shoreline around the face of the cliff. "Don't worry," he said with structured calm. "I'll stop it."

He braced his staff and crossed his left arm over the end as he had done in the crypt beneath Setios' house.

The relief with a woman's head and a bear's body also began to stretch itself shatteringly away from the cliff of which it had been part.

The spider/lizard/man-thing moved with the awkwardness of a knuckle-bone bouncing in slow motion. Its legs splayed so broadly—thirty feet or more—that the four of them on the outside roiled and gurgled well out into the stream.

"I can't hold two of—" Khamwas began.

A third creature, the fish-headed one, shifted in a patter of gravel.

Samlor crouched. "We've got to—"

"Run," he had been about to say, but he was quite certain that the progress of the stone creatures was faster than he could manage for more than an hour.

Saddle a camel? The animals would have broken their hobbles and run by now, as surely as the fourth beast-thing was tearing itself from the facade.

Gods! but he wished Star were here.

While his mind echoed with that thought which he would rather have died than entertained, Samlor drew his coffin-hilted dagger. His body was cold with awareness that he'd been willing to risk the child's life because he wasn't man enough to live without her to save him.

At least he could die fighting.

DISTRACT HIM said the blade of the dagger as it flicked through the periphery of Samlor's vision. His mind was so focused on the next minutes—which he expected to be his last—that the words did not register until he was three shuffling steps past the desperately chanting Khamwas.

Were the stone joints of the leading creature softer than the shanks, the way those of a normal crab would be?

Would a twelve-inch blade penetrate—if it could penetrate—deeply enough to injure creatures the size of these coming on?

The woman-headed monster was beginning to clamber over the thing with a man's head and arthropod legs. It had frozen again, two of its pincered feet raised as the river lapped close to the plates of its lizard belly.

"Distract him!" Samlor cried as he skidded to a stop. He turned, wolfish joy on his broad, worn face. "That's it. *Distract* him, Khamwas!"

"I can't distract them!" the Napatan cried in frustration.

The man-headed thing profited from Khamwas' broken concentration to lurch forward again, half-carrying the creature which had started to climb over him. The other two statues continued to trundle along behind, laughably clumsy on troll legs and bull legs—except that those legs spanned four human paces at a stride.

"*Him*, you idiot!" Samlor screamed. "Distract the fucking priest!"

Then he turned again and sprinted toward monsters and the other temple. If Khamwas couldn't understand—or couldn't perform—they were both dead very soon. It was as simple as that, and therefore Samlor had to proceed on the assumption that his companion would carry his load.

The woman-headed thing had pushed the creature on eight legs farther away from the cliff face so that the two of them advanced in tandem. The river was low at this time of year, but the strand between the rock and water was so narrow that the monster with the head of a man was forced almost completely into the water.

The male head growled like millstones grating. When the female mouth opened to snarl back, it displayed a maw of hooked teeth like a shark's.

Samlor was twenty feet from the leading monsters when a pair of crows swept past him, cawing angrily and slapping their pinions at one another.

The woman-headed creature swatted at the birds with a blunt-clawed forepaw. The motion was swift and precise, eliminating Samlor's faint hope that the monsters of stone would prove too awkward to catch him as he dodged between their legs.

The doglike paw hit the noisy birds. They flowed through the stone with a green flash and continued to clatter their swift course toward the smaller temple. One or both the trailing monsters clawed and bit at the crows as they passed, with no greater effect.

"All *right*, you bastards," Samlor whispered, pausing in a crouch for an instant. His left hand was empty and spread wide, while his right was cocked to hold the knife in position for a disemboweling stroke. His body faked to the right, toward the man-headed creature which reached forward with a pair of limbs. Their pincers sprang open like shears.

There was a distant flicker of green, visible only because the closed doors of the lesser temple were in such deep shadow. The female head turned snarling toward the creature beside it whose eagerness to get at Samlor was crowding her/it against the cliff.

All four of the monsters set into place like the statues they had been moments before, though their poses were now contorted by recent motion.

Samlor sprinted, ducking his head beneath one of the gaping pincers. The shadow cooled his skin and froze his soul.

The legs of the two leading monsters had splayed across one another as they struggled for position. Samlor laid his hand on one of the arthropod limbs to swing himself through the maze without slowing. It was warm and gritty to the touch, the feel of sun-struck stone and not that of anything which could have been alive.

There was room to pass between the third creature and the cliff without touching either, but as Samlor did so, the feathered body moved and the grotesque stone breasts swayed above his head.

He pushed off from the wall. The change of direction and the sudden impetus it gave him saved Samlor from being crushed. A limb, shaped like a bull's foreleg and the size of a large tree, stamped an impression six inches deep in the hard ground.

Samlor dived beneath the grasshopper body that wobbled between the bovine hind legs, rolled, and came up running while the creature turned, froze, and started to move again in jerky fashion. Stone ground on stone as others of the creatures shifted and fouled one another like storm-tossed boats in a narrow harbor.

Running on foot wasn't a particular talent of Samlor's, but he had the lungs and leg muscles to pound toward the

smaller temple fast enough to pull him away from most
human pursuers.

These pursuers weren't human.

Wind in his ears and the pounding of his blood cloaked
the noisy movements of Samlor's opponents behind him.
Stone hit stone with hollow echoes, like those of great fish
sounding. There was a hiss as loud as steam venting through
a geyser.

He didn't glance behind him to see whether or not the
stone monsters were tangled with one another because of
the distraction Khamwas had supplied. He could only hope
that they were—

And that the discomfort of lungs burning with exertion
quelled fear of what was about to happen to him. He'd
noticed before that aggravating discomfort was the best
antidote to panic. . . .

The door leaves had long since disappeared from the
larger temple. Samlor assumed the panels closing the
temple in which the Priest of the Rock lived were wooden,
sun-dried and flood-warped—vulnerable to the fury and
determination of a man as strong as Samlor hil Samt.

It was a shock when he realized that the double doors set
into the stripped facade were of the same fine-grained
sandstone as the cliffs around them.

Samlor slapped one leaf with the flat of his left hand,
more to bring himself to a halt than from any expectation
that the doors would fly open. The stone panels rattled the
wooden bar within which held them closed, but there was
no hint of real weakness.

The ground trembled as one or more of the carved
monsters began to stagger back toward Samlor.

The doors rotated on pins carved from the upper and
lower edges of both panels. They were sheathed in bronze
and set in massive bronze sockets inlet into the transom and
threshold of the temple. The metal was verdigrised and
worn. It almost certainly dated from the original construction of the temple a millennium before.

But the pivots weren't going to break under any stress
Samlor could bring against them without a stone-cutter's
maul.

The crows cawed and clashed with beaks and pinions

from the interior of the temple. Their racket came not through the thick stone panels but around them: use of rock in this way required that moving parts be fitted more coarsely than would be needful with material which was easily worked.

It was incredible that the Priest of the Rock could concentrate amid the racket the birds made, but the slow, thudding footsteps from behind proved the bastard could.

Sometimes you met somebody who was just too good for you.

And sometimes, that was the last fellow you met.

Samlor put his mouth to the crack between the door leaves and bellowed, hoping to startle the priest within. There was enough gap between the panels to squeeze in the first joint of his little finger, but the stone plates were four inches thick. Not even a wrecking bar would give him enough leverage to shatter a pivot with side thrust.

But the blade of his dagger would slide all the way through.

"We *got* you, fucker!" Samlor shouted at the door as he slipped the long, watered blade through the crack between the leaves. He would have explained that he was still trying to distract the man inside, but mostly it was just animal triumph finding a vocal outlet.

And, partly, it was a prayer that he *had* triumphed.

The bar closing the door crossed the gap at waist height. The edge of the dagger met it as Samlor drew the blade up through the crack. If the bar were pinned or run through staples, they were still dead, but—

The blade continued to lift, against the weight of the bar but without any suggestion that the bar was locked into place.

Samlor moved convulsively, gripping the dagger hilt with both hands and jerking the blade upward with all his strength. The bar flipped out of the shallow troughs in which it was laid and fell loudly against a wall, then the floor.

The stone troll's hand reaching for Samlor missed him because he dived into the temple as the doors swung away from his thrusting shoulder.

The room in which Samlor rolled back to his feet, fatigue forgotten, was scarcely half the size of the first hall of the greater temple. Its low ceiling was supported on square-section pillars instead of regal caryatids.

And it stank.

If Khamwas had cleared the chamber many years before while he searched for the Tomb of Nanefer, then that had been the room's last cleaning. The Priest of the Rock used the interior for all his bodily functions. Air blown from the desert desiccated the result, but it could not remove the effluvium.

The priest sat now in the center of the chamber: ankles crossed beneath his thighs, head bowed, and seemingly oblivious to the pair of crows which cawed and yammered in tight circles around his head.

The room darkened as the cobra-headed thing knelt and tried to grip Samlor with a hairy, knotted hand. The creature blocked much of the sunlight flooding through the doorway, but the intruder was beyond its grasp.

Samlor reached the priest in two quick strides. He lifted the old man by the woolen shawl that was his only covering. Even for the caravan master's left hand alone, the priest was an insignificant burden.

"Quit it!" Samlor shouted, giving the priest a shake to reinforce the demand. "You've lost! Don't make me kill you."

The priest's eyes were the only smooth surfaces in the chamber. They reflected the light. His mouth was open but toothless as well as speechless.

The crows vanished abruptly.

"There," said Samlor, sure that he was being obeyed. Deep breaths and the harsh necessity of taking them made the stench bearable but not unnoticed. "We're not going to hurt you or the temples either. We're—"

The interior was suddenly brighter again. That was good in itself, but it meant that the creatures outside had not returned to being sandstone carvings. Samlor glanced around.

The cobra-headed thing had moved out of the doorway so that the man-creature could reach inside with one of its longer, arthropod arms.

Samlor's right hand and left moved together like a pair of pruning shears, the one anchoring the priest against the other and the dagger blade that swept across the wizened neck.

The vertebrae resisted more like cartilage than bone as Samlor drove his steel in a berserk determination to finish the business once and for all.

The priest's head fell away and powdered when it hit the stone, like a seashell burned to lime but able to retain its shape until it receives a shock. The body slumped but did not thrash in the shawl which confined it. An arm slipped to the floor, separated when the elbow joint crumbled. No other part of the Priest of the Rock retained its shape.

Samlor flung the garment toward a far corner in the kind of convulsive motion a man makes when he finds something loathsome crawling on his hand. The shawl flapped open in a cloud of dust and bone splinters. They settled into a lighter-colored blotch on the filthy floor.

Samlor moved toward the door, shaky with reaction and the fatigue poisons in all his muscles. Some of the dust from—from the shawl, leave it at that—some of the dust was still drifting in the air. Samlor wanted very badly to get out of the temple before he drew in another breath.

He had to crawl through the doorway because of the long, pincered arm reaching through it and the sculptured human face bent close as if its blank stone eye were trying to look into the temple.

Khamwas caught Samlor by the wrist and shoulder at the entrance to the lesser temple. The knife still in the caravan master's hand almost gashed Khamwas, who seemed untroubled in his enthusiasm to hug Samlor.

"I was sure you were, well. . . ." Khamwas said to his companion's shoulder. "I prayed for you. There didn't seem to be any use for the, for the crows after you were inside yourself. So there wasn't anything I could do to help."

"Do not weary of calling to the gods," said Tjainufi sharply. "They have their hour for hearing petitions."

Samlor squeezed the Napatan firmly, then stepped away and straightened. He ducked his head again immediately because the lizard belly of the thing which clawed into the temple was still above them like a low roof.

"Let's get away from here, huh?" he said, muttering so that the queasiness he suddenly felt would not be evident in his voice.

When the damned things were threatening his life, he'd had no time to be disturbed at their supernatural provenance.

The reliefs, now free-standing statutes, were scattered between the entrances to the two temples. The woman-headed monster was a hump on the riverbank where it had toppled when the Priest of the Rock tried to regain control of his creatures. The other three were immediate obstacles as the two men began to walk toward the larger temple.

Light was pouring toward the West like blood into a sacrificial bowl.

"Hey, look," Samlor said quietly. He was glad that the shadows, deepening with every step the men took, hid his face. "Maybe I said some things when it got tense, you know. I don't remember. But I wouldn't be here if I didn't, you know, respect you."

"My brother is useless," said—replied?—Tjainufi, "if he doesn't take care of me."

"I don't remember anything either," said Khamwas. Then—not that there was any doubt that he *did* remember—he added, "There wasn't time to stand on ceremony, while you were saving both our lives that way."

"*I* save?" Samlor jeered. "Never thought I'd be so glad to see a couple birds, buddy."

It was becoming so dark that Samlor began to fear that he would be unable to distinguish the fallen monster from shadows when they reached it. Nobody alive would be amused if he managed to break his nose on a pile of stones after coming through the past crisis with nothing worse than a few scrapes and strains.

In a similar frame of mind, Khamwas extended his staff before them and clothed it with phosphorescence so pale that it was more identification than illumination.

"Ah, I suppose you'll want to get started clearing sand from the tomb entrance?" the caravan master said. "I'll round up a crew from the village with scoops and torches. They probably won't want to come out in the dark, but we can make it worth their while.

"And—and it might be as well they didn't see what the statues there look like until they'd been on the job for a bit. Could be they wouldn't react real good to that."

"I'll take care of the sand myself, Samlor," said the Napatan scholar. "The Priest of the Rock was blocking me—that's why I wasn't able to locate the tomb before. But it'll be all right now."

"There isn't any body, you know," said Samlor to the darkness. "He. . . He fell apart, or. . . ."

"Someone left to watch," Khamwas said reassuringly. The fallen statue loomed ahead of them, visible after all. The female head had broken away from the bulbous hairy body.

"A priest," Khamwas continued as they skirted the rubble, leaving deep prints in the soft margin of the river. "But human, and alive. He was just older than we thought. Even older."

"Everything's relative, I guess," Samlor remarked with studied calm. He resisted the urge to grind sand between his palms in order to clean them of any trace of the Priest of the Rock.

Samlor paused at the lower end of the rope. "I'll get a lamp," he said. "I suppose you'll want light while you, while you work?"

Khamwas smiled broadly in the dim light of his staff. "What I really want, I think," he said—and *I think* had the weight of genuine consideration in its syllables—"is a good night's sleep, for a change. After a hot meal. Would that—" he gestured at the darkness "—be possible now?"

"Just watch me," said Samlor with a smile as wide as his companion's. He began to mount the slope briskly, lifting himself hand over hand along the rope.

He much preferred daylight for whatever it was Khamwas intended to do.

CHAPTER 10

BY DAYLIGHT FROM the escarpment, the lesser temple looked like the wreckage of time rather than of an evening. The man-headed thing lay in a hundred pieces. Its spider legs had proved unequal to their task without the support of the cliff face as well. When one leg gave way, the others followed with a suddenness which reduced the carving to rubble.

Near it were the toppled forms of the other pair of composite creatures. They had been in balance when night fell like an axe blade. The muddy ground let them tilt. Without life or its counterfeit to right them, the statues crashed down and broke under their own weight.

Spring floods would roll the fragments against one another. In a few years the small bits would be gravel and the large ones indistinguishable lumps of sandstone with no signs of human working.

Samlor had never liked ruins. They reminded him that very soon his own bones would bleach or feed desert mice.

But this particular ruin was an impressive monument to the fact that he'd done his job very damned well.

On the slope below the caravan master, Khamwas cried out.

Samlor's face went blank. If he used the rope to support him, he would have come down on top of Khamwas, who was kneeling at the spot marked by the cornelwood wand.

Instead Samlor slid down on a parallel course, braking himself with boots and his left hand.

His right hand did not touch the slope. It held his dagger ready for any problem that steel and ruthlessness could solve.

Khamwas didn't look at him, despite the cloud of dust and sand which Samlor sprayed before him. The Napatan was chanting. He held his staff between the palms of his hands, rotating it slowly back and forth on its axis. Every time the direction of rotation changed, he gave a yelp in a high falsetto, and it was this which Samlor had mistaken for a cry of alarm.

As soon as Samlor understood the situation, he tried to slow himself. He still couldn't halt before he was on a level with his companion, halfway down the slope. Much good he'd have been if there really were a problem. He worried too much.

Tjainufi turned around to face the caravan master instead of the slowly-turning staff. "He who scorns matters too often," he said in a tone of reminder. "will die of it."

Samlor smiled but did not reply lest the conversation distract Khamwas. Though Khamwas appeared to be as surely set in his course as the sun ascending the sky. The Napatan scholar had since dawn been kneeling in the sand, muttering to himself, his staff, or his gods.

Now something seemed to have answered him.

The staff began to spin faster and in one direction, blurring itself into the smooth brown ideal of a staff. All its individuality of grain and usage melted together. Khamwas was no longer chanting or holding the staff, though its ferule was several inches above the ground.

The spin accelerated. Khamwas stepped back. A line of dust rose beside the cornelwood marker. The dust paused, spread a hand's breadth at the top, like a cobra lifting itself from a conjurer's basket. Then it shot upward faster than Samlor could have thrown a rock, roaring and expanding into a whirlwind with uneasy similarities to the tornado which had cleansed Setios' house of its demons.

Khamwas bent and plucked Samlor's wand out of the way a moment before it would have been lost in the funnel. His own staff continued to spin—in the direction opposite to that of the whirlwind.

"The cosmos abhors imbalance," murmured Khamwas as he walked to his companion. Soft sand flooded over his feet and at every step poured back past the straps of his sandals. He handed the cornelwood wand to Samlor.

The point it had marked was a dip in the slope. It was not yet a cavity because sand refilled it, oozing from all sides like viscous oil.

The whirlwind lifted its load twenty feet in the air in a brown column as thick as Samlor's chest. At its peak, the column disintegrated in a plume driven by the breeze over the escarpment. The heavier particles settled out further down the slope, but the lightest of the dust drifted over the river and marked the opposite bank with a yellow stain.

"That's . . . quite a job, you know," said Samlor while his eyes continued to track the dust plume.

Khamwas nodded with satisfaction. "I was at a disadvantage in Sanctuary," he said, rubbing his hands in a physical memory of the task they had just performed. "Several disadvantages. But here—"

He lifted his jaw as he surveyed the river and the irrigated fields beyond it. "This is *my* land, my friend. By right, and by the right of the book's power when I hold it."

He met Samlor's eyes with a gaze as imperious as that of an eagle. "I swore that the day my brothers sold me as a slave," he added.

"Huh?"

Khamwas smiled. His face fell back into the familiar lines of humor and placid determination. "It doesn't matter now," he said, clapping his companion on the shoulder. The stone-chiseled visage was back for an instant. "But soon it will matter to my brothers. Very much."

Samlor raised an eyebrow, then chuckled. "A guy never knows what he's signed on for, does he?" he said.

Khamwas looked at the caravan master sharply and said, "Your commitment's ended. You promised me nothing beyond getting me to—" he pointed at the whirlwind "—*this* point."

"Sure I did," Samlor replied. He hooked his thumbs in

his belt and kept his eyes on the column of sand. "Anyhow, I didn't say I was complaining."

The slopes had flattened near the tip of the funnel. Though a little sand still trickled in, it could no longer hide the square stone door in the cliff face. The whirlwind's color faded to a gauzy white now that it was no longer charged to opacity with sand.

Samlor eyed the portal through the wavering column of air. "We'll have to break it down," he said in professional appraisal. "They'll have set wedges t' fall when they slid the door down the last time."

"Wait and watch," replied Khamwas with his old smile. "The door couldn't fit tightly enough in its grooves to keep sand from seeping through over the ages and filling the passageway beyond."

"You want the villagers with baskets after all . . . ?" Samlor asked in puzzlement, trying to follow the other's train of thought. "Or—"

He blinked and glanced up at the sky, visualizing a thunderbolt from its pale transparency striking the stone door and blasting it to shards.

Khamwas shook his head gently and pointed toward the door again.

The staff had seemed to be slowing its rotation; certainly it had dipped an inch or two nearer the ground. Now it rose and accelerated again.

The tip of the little whirlwind twisted like an elephant's trunk and explored the edge of the stone door. The panel quivered. As Khamwas had said, the grooves in the cliff face in which it slid had to have considerable play. Tiny grit with the persistence of time was certain to have free access through the cracks.

The trunk of moving air sharpened itself wire thin. It was black again with whirling sand. It began to scream with the fury of a saw cutting far faster than a stonecutter's arms could drive it.

The speed of the whirlwind increased by the square of the lessened diameter. The tip was now moving so fast that it would have been opaque even if it were only air.

The sand which it dragged from the interior of the tomb

blasted against the edges of the door and the cliff, grinding them back to the sand from which they had been formed beneath the sea in past eons. The mating surfaces eroded in a black line climbing upward as the whirlwind followed the same pattern a human sawyer would have used.

The dust that reached the upper funnel was so finely divided that it gave a saffron, almost golden, cast to the trembling air.

Khamwas looked at Samlor with quiet pride. Samlor squeezed his companion's shoulder again.

"The wealth of a craftsman," said Tjainufi in what might have been intended as a gibe, "is in his equipment." His voice had almost the same timbre as the wind howling as it ate rock, but his words were nonetheless quite audible.

As the line of black—shadow replacing what had been rocky substance—coursed along the upper edge of the door, the panel began to shift. A handful of gravel-sized hunks flew out and pitched into the river loudly, fragments of a stone wedge.

The whole door, a slab six inches thick, fell out on its face with the heavy finality of a man stabbed to the heart.

Instantly, uninstructed by Khamwas, the tip broadened. The funnel blurred brown with the sand it sucked from the passageway beyond. The sound of the wind lowered into a drumnote instead of the high keening with which it had carved solid stone. Sorted by weight, the debris dropped again far beyond the cavity from which it had come.

The passageway was square and polished smooth. It was easily big enough for a man, but he would have to crawl on his hands and knees. Samlor had been in tighter places, but the one certainty about this one was that there wouldn't be another way out.

Khamwas must have been thinking the same thing, because he said, "I'll leave my staff at the entrance. It will prevent problems like . . . the slab—" he gestured at what had been the door "—rising up and wedging itself into the tunnel again. For instance."

Samlor raised an eyebrow. "You expect that?" he asked.

"Not if I leave my staff at the entrance," Khamwas answered calmly.

The whirlwind had been clearing gradually until only the inevitable dust motes danced in it. Khamwas' staff dropped to the ground so abruptly that its ferule thrust an inch or two into the soft sand. Khamwas' hand snatched the instrument while it was still wobbling upright.

A breeze fanned Samlor hard enough to slap the dagger-sheath against him. The whirlwind dissipated by flinging itself outward. Nothing of it remained but a dry odor and the passageway it had uncovered. The whole shape of the sandslope had been changed by the removal of what must have been hundreds of tons of material.

"Well," said Samlor carelessly. "Don't guess there's much left but for me to get a lamp and lead the way in. Be interesting to see what we find."

Khamwas quirked the left side of his face up in something like a smile. "Nothing inside will have a knife, my friend," he said. "Get the lamp, but I'll be going first."

Samlor nodded curtly and gripped the rope for what had suddenly become a steep climb to the top of the escarpment. There was a touch on his arm. He turned and met his companion's eyes.

"There's no need for you to come into the tomb with me," Khamwas said. "You'd really be no more than a, than a. . . . Well. Any real use you'd be could be performed if you wait out here by the entrance."

"Balls," said Samlor without emotion.

He turned his face away and cleared his throat before he continued in the same flat tone. "I'll be back with a lamp. Maybe we can rig it to the end of my wand so I can hold it in front of you. Leave your hands free for whatever business you've got. Right?"

"Right, my friend," said Khamwas softly.

As Samlor began to climb the rope, finding footholds on the rock which sand no longer covered, he heard Tjainufi below him saying, "A man's character is his destiny."

It didn't strike Samlor as a particularly reassuring comment.

CHAPTER 11

THE PASSAGEWAY SLANTED upward at a scarcely perceptible angle. The rise was enough to have trapped entering sand fairly close to the entrance. The floor and a slanting line down both sidewalls had been polished by the grit to a finish much smoother than that which the workmen had left.

That circumstance, brought out by the way light reflected from stone as the lamp wobbled forward, made Samlor feel the age of this tomb as nothing else had done.

He almost bumped Khamwas again—and almost cursed aloud. The Napatan scholar shuffled forward at an irregular pace—halting repeatedly for no reason Samlor could discern, and then sliding on another ten feet or more as blithely as if his only concern were the strait surroundings.

Khamwas knew what he was doing—Samlor had accepted that as an article of faith when he agreed to enter the tomb. *Samlor* didn't know what his companion was doing, though. It made it a bitch of a job to follow closely enough to keep the lamp bobbing ahead of them and still to avoid stumbling into the man in the lead.

He should have found a larger pole on which to hang the lamp, so that he needn't stick so close to the Napatan. He should have stayed back at the entrance. He should have stayed in Cirdon and gotten on with his own life.

And he really shouldn't think about what was waiting at the far end of this passage. The little quibbling frustrations, about the way Khamwas moved and about how hard the stone was on his knees, were just what Samlor needed to keep in a state of murderous readiness without dwelling on the sort of major threats that could make him panic. He knew how to handle himself from having spent most of his life in the business.

The business of taking damn-fool risks for no good reason.

"There. . . ," said Khamwas in a tone of wonder and satisfaction. He had stopped again.

Samlor grimaced and leaned to peer past Tjainufi on his companion's shoulder.

The lamplight wavered over the intricately painted wall of a room. They'd reached the end of the passageway at last.

Samlor held his breath, fearful of disturbing his companion.

Instead of going through an involved procedure—a chanted spell, a progressive unveiling of some amulet or talisman—Khamwas stepped directly into the tomb chamber. There, where there was enough room to stand upright, he shrugged his shoulders and straightened the folds of his cloak. It was the sort of motion a man makes before he has an important interview.

With a superior.

"Put your trust in god," said Tjainufi, looking back at Samlor still hunched in the passageway.

"Bloody well have, haven't I?" muttered the caravan master. "Coming *this* far?" But he twisted himself upright in the painted chamber, the lamp bobbing on the end of the wand in his left hand.

His right fist was empty, for he would have looked a fool to threaten supernatural opponents with a knife. . . .

But the hilt of the long dagger wasn't far from his hand either.

Samlor's first thought was that he'd misunderstood. They were in a temple, not a tomb, with a man-sized idol seated across from them.

The walls were covered with a brilliantly white plaster which brightened the chamber beyond what Samlor thought was the ability of a single-wick oil lamp. The plaster had been used as the base for frescoes whose bright primary colors had been achieved with pigments of cinnabar, lapis lazuli and finely-divided gold.

The paints showed men and women carrying out all the ordinary tasks of a village or a great household: food production and preparation; weaving and building construction; unfamiliar sports and war in unfamiliar armor and chariots. Each scene was labeled in delicate script which was as unintelligible to Samlor as the paintings were obvious without it.

The entrance was in one of the longer walls. Large storage jars were lined up along it. Samlor dipped his hand into the nearest, brushing aside the lid whose wax seal had crumbled with time. The jar was filled with millet which still looked and felt wholesome.

"Heqt!" Samlor blurted as his eyes glanced over the furniture aligned with the other wall. His eyes jerked back to the cult statue in the center of the array. "That's a *body*."

"This is Nanefer," said Khamwas.

Samlor couldn't tell if the statement were agreement or correction.

There was no smell of death in the chamber; only of dryness and a memory of incense too faint to have been noticed under any other circumstances. Khamwas was waiting as if he expected to be summoned. Samlor swallowed his questions and his nervousness, examining the seated corpse as carefully as he could without going closer.

Nanefer had been a man of average height and slight build in life. His frame was particularly obvious now that desiccation had drawn the skin back against all of his bones, including the ribs which were not covered by the linen kirtle hung from the left shoulder. The garment was cinched with a wide sash of gold brocade, while the straps of the sandals—

"*Heqt!*"

Samlor didn't recognize the corpse's face, since its skin was sunken in and darkened to the color of fire-hardened wood even though age had not brought decay. But the clothes he did recognize.

They'd been on the stranger who attacked him in the Vulgar Unicorn.

Samlor had the watered-steel blade of his dagger half clear of its sheath before he remembered just where that blade had come from. He shot the weapon home again as if it were red hot. For a moment, he stood so still that no further motion disturbed the regular swinging of the wand and lamp which he held.

Finally, he let his body slip back, not to relaxation but at least to a state of loose watchfulness. Besides the coffin-hilted knife, he had the choice of the boot knife or the push dagger at the back of his collar.

The right choice was to leave his weapons where they were. But locking up like that was a real good way to get killed.

One of the real good ways. Getting neck deep in wizards was even better.

Nanefer's black, wizened hands were crossed in his lap over a parcel wrapped in red cloth. Khamwas looked at it, pursing his lips as he came to a decision.

He stepped forward slowly.

Ten feet, the width of the room, separated Nanefer's corpse from the men who had just entered. The floor was covered with the same dazzling plaster as the walls and ceiling, and there were no frescoes to dim its fire.

When whorls of blue sparks appeared in the center of the room, their reflection from the floor doubled their angry intensity.

Khamwas halted in mid-step, then backed in a perfect reversal of his previous motion. He squared his shoulders and bobbed his chin up and down as if to be sure that it was set in the correct position, firm but not outthrust in challenge.

Samlor was worried about position also. He stooped, setting the lamp on the floor with a delicacy which belied the fact that he never took his eyes off the sparks which grew and, with their afterimages, were beginning to sketch a figure. When the earthenware lamp-bowl was safely

down, Samlor dropped the wand also and rose with his boot
knife half-concealed by his palm and thigh.

It was something to throw for a distraction. By now he
had enough data to know that they might want a distraction
which permitted them to get out of the chamber again.

Fast.

The sparks hissed like hot grease as they spread in tight
arcs which wove into surfaces. They were not forming a
figure but rather two figures; a slender, imperious woman
and the babe in her arms nuzzling her bare right breast.

The woman was dressed in much the same fashion as
Nanefer's corpse, and her features were similar to those of
the stranger in the Vulgar Unicorn.

Similar also to those of Khamwas.

"You cannot prevent me, Ahwere," Khamwas said in a
clear voice that bespoke enormous control. "Your fate is
accomplished."

The popping griddle sound ceased, but the silence which
replaced it was unnatural. When the woman began to speak,
her voice did not echo. It was as if they all stood on a
mighty plain instead of in a stone chamber from which
sound dissipated only after hundreds of reverberations.

"Go back, man of my house," she said. She was a statue
of blue fire whose face alone moved as she spoke. The
infant squirmed against her and began to cry in a thin,
hopeless voice. "The price of what you seek is too high."

"Your fate is accomplished, Ahwere," Khamwas repeated gently. "The price you paid is no part of me. You
must stand aside."

He made no attempt to step forward.

Ahwere, who would have been attractive if she were a
woman and alive, laughed. The sound began as something
nearly human and ended in a clucking, like arpeggios
played on dried vertebrae. "You do not think the price is for
you to pay, oh man of my house? But nevertheless, you
must learn just what the price is, mustn't you?"

Her mouth opened, wide and then wider than life or
protoplasm would allow. "*Watch!*" screamed a voice from
the cavern that was enveloping the world. . . .

CHAPTER 12

"DON'T STAND THERE with yer bleedin' thumb up, Ipis!" screamed Shay, the bosun, to the sailor at the bow line. "*Belay* the bloody line!"

Shay glanced with a subservient expression toward the woman beside him and the man who Samlor now was. "Beggin' yer pardon sir, madam." he muttered perfunctorily. Then the bosun's face reformed itself into a snarl as he bellowed, "And *you* lot! *Lower* the bleedin' mast, don't drop it through the bleedin' bilges!"

At the mainsheets, six squat crewmen—naked except for their breechclouts—hunched themselves against the weight they were supporting. They had furled the sail against the upper yard as the richly-appointed craft neared the quay. The fitful breeze was still making it hard enough to dock that Shay decided to lower the twin-pole mast as well. One of the temple servants on the quay had managed to get a line aboard, but the boat was drifting outward despite the efforts of the three oarsmen at either gunwale.

The baby at Ahwere's breast began to squall because of the shouting. She crooned to comfort the child; and Samlor—whose body knew he was named Nanefer, and which acted outside the control of his Samlor mind—stepped closer and put an arm around both his wife and his son.

Sailors and men on the shore began to haul the vessel firmly to its berth.

The quay was stone-built, not wooden. Though unoccupied at present, it projected far enough into the river to dock a pair of vessels the length of Samlor's on either side. A causeway, also stone, led a hundred feet inland to the walled courtyard and temple which stood on the firmer ground at that distance from the riverbank. Drums were beating in the courtyard, and already a group of regally-garbed priests were hurrying to join the handful of servants on the quay.

The vessel edged against the downstream side of the dock. Sailors snubbed it while Shay bawled orders and horrible threats.

"Hush, dearest," murmured Ahwere. "Hush, sweetness. Soon it will stop."

The bank to either side of the stream was a rich green backdrop of palmettoes and reeds in their Spring colors, before the sun and the lowering river dried them golden. The temple's extensive fields were hidden behind the screen of natural vegetation.

Not far upstream from the quay was a massive wall built against the bank for no evident purpose. Like the temple and its outworks, the wall was stone: but the blocks comprising it were cyclopean and of immense age. In the center of the wall—a dam backed against a section of riverbank no different from those to either side of it—was a bas-relief which seemed to be a stylized face, though mud from recent flooding and the patina of age made it impossible to be sure.

A gaggle of musicians had run to the dock with the priests. A plump man with an image of the god Tatenen on his breast gestured to them. They broke into a flute-and-drum tattoo whose timing suffered from the fact most of the performers were panting from the haste with which they'd run from the temple enclosure.

The priest shut them off with another gesture and an angry glare which smoothed to buttery slickness as he turned and bowed toward Samlor. "Prince Nanefer," he said. "Princess Ahwere, little prince Merib—come ashore, please. I am Tekhao the chief priest, and I offer you the full hospitality of the Temple of Tatenen."

Six other priests with scarlet sashes—Tekhao's whole tunic was dyed red—bowed in shaky unison behind their chief.

Samlor nodded to them and handed his wife to the rail ahead of him. Temple servants steadied her as she stepped to the dock, though the babe in her arms and the servants' determined obsequiousness made the job even more awkward than it needed to be.

Takhao himself offered Samlor a hand as he followed Ahwere. "Your father is well, Prince Nanefer?" he asked.

"Certainly, very well," Samlor responded. His current body did not have the aches which had accumulated with the years in his own form, though they were noticeable only now that he lived in their absence. On the other hand, stepping up to the dock was an unexpected effort: Samlor/Nanefer wasn't fat, but neither was he used to efforts more strenuous than strolling through the gardens of his palace.

He was only socially truthful, also. King Merneb hadn't been at all well when they sailed from the capital . . . but that was no business of a temple functionary.

Besides, the king would cheer up as soon as they returned. His present state was mostly because of his concern about his only son and daughter, and their child, his grandson. Samlor was utterly sure that his knowledge was equal to this undertaking, but his father, King Merneb, refused to believe that.

The musicians resumed playing as the party walked toward the temple. "The banquet we have—" Tekhao began.

"And have you assembled the quantity of wax I require?" said Samlor, at close enough to the same time that both men could pretend the prince had not broken in to silence a yammering priest.

"Why yes, your highness," said Tekhao without dropping a beat. "That is to say, most of it is on hand at this moment, and the rest should arrive by—" he glanced at the sun, a finger's length above the reedtops "—well, by early tomorrow at the latest. You must realize that the, ah, the size of the levy was unexpected, though of course the Temple of Tatenen never hesitates to carry out the desires of the King."

"Yes, you've done quite well, then," said Samlor with an attempt to make the words sound appreciative rather than ironic. Tekhao was a toady, but he *had* carried out a difficult task in a short time.

They stepped beneath the arch into the temple enclosure. Two-story buildings were built along the right and left sides of the courtyard, while the facade of the temple closed the end facing the gate and the river beyond. Four caryatids representing aspects of Tatenen, the Creator, supported the temple pediment whose reliefs showed the Court of Heaven over which Tatenen presided.

The courtyard was crowded with folk ranging from those who cultivated the temple fields to priests' wives garbed as richly as the functionaries themselves. They began to cheer when Samlor and his family entered the enclosure.

"Ah, your highness," Tekhao murmured with his lips to Samlor's ear. "It's our understanding that the temple's contribution to the royal granary this year will be reduced by the value of the wax. May we assume that the wax will be valued at the rate prevailing in the capital on the date contributions are due?"

Merib, startled by the cheering crowd, began to wail again, but his cries were lost in the enthusiasm.

"You may assume that the affairs of scribes will be handled by scribes," Samlor retorted loudly enough that he did not need to bend close to the chief priest. "No doubt they will be aware that goods turned over to the king are valued at the place where they come into the hands of the royal agents."

"Of course, Prince Nanefer, of course," boomed Tekhao, smiling so that all his subordinates could see how well he was getting along with the king's son. "We'll conduct you to your chambers, now, and perhaps at the banquet later we can discuss some of the special problems with which a temple estate in this district must deal."

"Of course," said Samlor, irriated at having been so tart a moment before.

The crowd cheered, and Ahwere glanced at her husband across the crying visage of their son.

CHAPTER 13

"WE'RE SO HONORED by the presence of your highness," said Tekhao's wife—for at least the third time during the course of the banquet—while her beaming husband served Samlor the dessert, a compote of limes and white grapes, with his own hands. The other priests, temple administrators, and wives watched the two couples at the high table with expressions of awe and envy as their temperaments dictated.

"Perhaps you can tell me, Tekhao," said Ahwere as she accepted the ladleful of fruit the chief priest was offering. "There's an odd-looking wall next to the dock. Well, near it. What do you use that for?"

Tekhao sat down and filled his own cup from the serving bowl. "An involved question, your highness," he answered with a smirk in his voice. "In a manner of speaking, we don't use it; but in another way it is the reason a temple of Tatenen is located here."

He had forgotten to serve his own wife. Her scowl was one that would wake thunder later when the couple was alone, but now she said sweetly to Samlor, "A child is always such a responsibility, Prince Nanefer, and for you, knowing that your lovely boy will succeed you as king, well. . . . The State is fortunate that such a responsibility is in hands so capable."

Samlor managed a smile. His mouth was full of fruit and

135

his attention was focused on the explanation the priest was
giving Ahwere.

"You see, your highness," Tekhao said, "we didn't build
the wall. That is, human beings didn't. It was placed on
Earth by Tatenen himself when he created the cosmos."

Tekhao permitted himself a brief smile to indicate to his
visitors that he was too sophisticated to believe such a
myth—if they were—but without committing himself to
heresy if Ahwere and her husband took a rigidly accepting
approach to their religion.

Ahwere's nod was no certain indication either way, so the
chief priest went on in factual neutrality. "The wall is only a
hundred feet long, to be sure, but the stones in its fabric are
of exceptional size. There are a few buildings in the capital
as massively constructed, but nothing whatever here on the
Lower River. And even in Napata, the close fit between the
individual stones would be considered remarkable. It is—"

Tekhao paused to consider his words. "It is said," he
continued, "that Tatenen made the stones soft for a moment
after he put them in place, so that the surfaces flowed
together. Despite weathering, there is no place in the wall
that a knife will slip further than a fingertip between the
layers."

"But there's a face on it, isn't there?" Ahwere asked.
"Was that always there?"

Samlor couldn't tell whether Ahwere were just making
conversation, or if she had a suspicion of what he
intended—but would not ask her husband directly.

"Yes indeed, your highness," Tekhao said. "The face of
Tatenen himself, ah—it is said. Stamped onto the stone with
his, ah, seal ring as his final act of creation."

The chief priest's wife stood up and stumped heavily
across the front of the table to reach the fruit compote. One
of the servants standing behind the diners' chairs would
have served her had she flicked a finger toward him—but
that wouldn't have given her the opportunity to glare
straight into her husband's eyes.

"There was once a ceremony," continued Tekhao. Only a
tic of his right cheek betrayed his awareness of his wife's
displeasure. "The Cleansing of the Face, it was called.

Every year the nearby villages brought offerings which they cast into the river, and they scrubbed the face clean. Horrible waste. Ah, the offerings, that is."

"Now the ceremony is held here in the temple," said Tekhao's wife brightly, joining the conversation as a better way of getting attention than glowering from her end of the table. "It's *much* nicer. Though still very colorful, of course."

"Ah, yes," agreed Tekhao with a hint of well-deserved embarrassment. "It seemed more fitting that the ceremony be held here in the temple enclosure. Of course, we know that Tatenen is everywhere, not in an idol or a, or a face on a wall. But it makes it easier for the common villagers to carry out their duties to the god if they associate him with the, ah, house where their offerings are deposited."

"The wall," said Samlor, "is thought to be the dam which Tatenen built to separate the realm of men from the realm of gods."

Tekhao blinked and turned to face Samlor. "Yes, your highness," he said. "That is said. Though—" his round face became as neutral as an expanse of flooring "—nothing is behind the stone except earth. There have been, ah, examinations. Muddy earth."

Samlor nodded calmly.

Ahwere was looking at him past the chief priest's head. Her face was gray with fear.

CHAPTER 14

MERIB WAS ASLEEP, but they could hear the nurse singing to him in the room beyond the doorway screened by reed matting.

Ahwere began to cry softly.

Samlor touched her shoulders from behind, then began to massage them gently as he moved closer.

She turned, throwing her arms around him and burying her face against his chest. "Oh, Nanefer," she said through her sobs. "My prince, my brother, my only love. . . ."

"Don't be afraid," Samlor whispered, bending to kiss her forehead and eyelid. "There isn't anything to fear."

"We're going to enter the realm of the gods, aren't we?" she said, looking up at him. Her eyes, her jewels, and the tears on her cheeks were all that was visible in the screened moonlight.

"Yes," said Samlor simply. "I am. There's no need for you to go with me, though. Shay will do as I order, and—"

"Would you leave me behind then?" Ahwere demanded fiercely. "Watch you go off to die and never return? Is that what you want?" Fresh tears were welling up even though she was so angry that Samlor thought she might strike him.

"I'm not going to die, my darling," he said, trying to ease her close to him again. She resisted only for a moment. "I'm going to come back with the Book of Tatenen. I just don't want to force you to help me in this if you'd rather not."

"Rather leave you?" Ahwere said, but this time with a lilt of joyous remembrance in her voice. "The way I left you when our father would have married you to a governor's daughter and me to a general?"

Samlor smiled and quoted King Merneb, " 'Shall I marry my son to my daughter and risk all my happiness at once? No, I don't dare risk the gods' envy that way.' "

"And it was I who made him change his mind," said Ahwere, "so that you and I could find happiness with the only souls on earth who could make us happy. I will not leave you now."

They kissed. Lips still joined, they moved toward the bed, shedding their clothes with increasing urgency.

CHAPTER 15

SAMLOR WAS SO engrossed that he did not notice when Ahwere entered his work area, the flat roof of one of the temple buildings—now screened so that direct sun would not melt the hard yellow wax. He had shaped a section of the bow and was reaching for another block of material when he realized that his wife was watching him with a slight smile.

He started, dropping the baton with which he formed the wax into a perfect simulacrum of a wood surface.

Ahwere's face clouded. "I'm sorry," she blurted, turning toward the stairs again. "I didn't mean—"

Samlor caught her in his arms. "No," he said, "don't go. You *should* see this, if you want to. I was just—concentrating on what I was doing."

The smile that returned was shaky, but Ahwere allowed herself to be drawn close to what Samlor was constructing.

It was a boat, small but otherwise similar to the vessel which was docked at the temple quay—except that this one was built of wax. Samlor had fitted the flat bottom, shaping the pyramidal cakes of wax into a perfect duplicate of irregular, pegged-together planks of sycamore wood. Now he was raising the slanting wales, starting from the bow.

Ahwere stretched out her finger but did not touch the "planks" until her husband had nodded approval. The material had the grain of wood, but it retained the feel of wax as well as its yellow translucence.

"Watch," he said, anticipating the question she might not have been willing to ask. He picked up his baton, a section of hollow reed the length of his forearm, and took a fresh block of wax which he held against the end of one of the blanks.

When Samlor drew the baton across it, the wax flowed like paint before a brushstroke. Instead of taking the texture of the baton, it formed another "plank"—perfect in its irregularities, even to the trenails pinning it to the pieces it abutted.

Samlor smiled to Ahwere, but he could feel the sweat of concentration on his brow.

"Shay came to tell you that the fittings have been removed from our ship," she said, nodding toward the edge of the roof. The vessel on which the royal party arrived was just visible past the line of the dock, riding on its cables. "He says they'll begin loading the sand after midday. But—"

Ahwere frowned. "But *why*, my husband? Why don't we just use the real ship instead of—" she gestured. "Though it's very wonderful, what you're doing."

Samlor smiled so that the implication of danger wouldn't be the first answer his wife received. "The real boat might be able to—enter the realm where we'll find the book," he explained. "But nothing alive could travel with it for the entire distance. We'll be perfectly safe in this vessel—" he patted the waxen side, without quite touching it "—and the other will carry the equipment we need."

Ahwere hugged him but would not meet his eyes as she said, "Well, I shouldn't have disturbed you. I'll go now."

"You don't disturb me," Samlor said.

Ahwere started to turn away. Samlor seized her and said fiercely, "My love, I *need* you! You don't disturb me. And you mustn't worry."

She nodded, her face against his chest, but Samlor was sure he heard her sobbing as she climbed back down the stairs.

He took another block of wax, set it in place, and began to shape it. His princely face was as calm as the wax itself, but his mind was filled with images of fire and terror.

After he finished the boat, he would form the six oarsmen to drive it. . . .

CHAPTER 16

SHAY CARRIED A rope knout as he oversaw the transport of the wax boat to the water, but he repeatedly slapped his own thigh with it instead of the workmen.

The wax vessel was a light burden for so many hands, temple servants as well as Nanefer's sailors, but it was also fragile. The bosun had no intention of making someone stumble with a flick of the rope-end—and Samlor would have flayed Shay if he *had* taken that risk.

"Easy, then," the bosun ordered, stepping backward ahead of the procession.

Rather than use the stone quay, Samlor had ordered the priests to build a temporary ramp of bundled reeds across the swampy stretch and down into the river. At first the end of the new ramp floated. The reeds undulated down into the muck as they took Shay's weight. The team of men and the boat they carried would submerge the ramp, permitting the vessel to bob in the water without the risk of damage that any other launch would entail.

Beside Samlor stood Ahwere. Her bright smile could have been sculpted in stone for any movement it had shown. He touched her hand and realized the grin he flashed her was almost as false.

"Come on, come *on*, ye buggers!" roared Shay. "Are ye afraid the fishies'll eat yer bollocks?" The bosun was in knee-high water, but the loaded men behind him were driving the ramp deeper even though they were nearer the bank.

"Your highness," said Tekhao, rubbing his sweaty hands together. "And you, your highness," he added with a nervous nod to Ahwere. "I trust the arrangements are to your satisfaction?"

Samlor was keyed up to the point that the question, intruding into his imagined future, had the impact of a blow. His face went pale and he opened his mouth to rip out a curse at the fat priest.

Before the words came awareness and contrition. He gripped Tekhao, forearm to forearm as if they were brothers taking leave, and said truthfully, "More than satisfactory, Tekhao, from beginning—" he nodded toward the temple enclosure. Another ramp of reed fascines led down from the roof where Samlor had constructed the wax boat.

"—to now."

"Now *hold* it, ye buggers!" roared Shay, dog-paddling against the sluggish current. "Don't let it float to bugger-all down the bloody river!"

"But now you'll have to excuse me," Samlor continued, "because it's time for my wife and I to—proceed."

"Oh, Prince Nanefer," mumbled the chief priest in a voice thick with emotion. "Oh, your highness. You don't know what that means to me. . . ."

As Samlor and Ahwere strode quickly down to the stone quay, he wondered what sort of man Tekhao would have been if he could give his god the sort of devotion he reserved for human superiors. A saint, very likely.

And very likely a much worse administrator of the temple and the land which it governed on behalf of the king.

Sailors splashed in the water to keep the boat from slamming into the quay. The wax vessel rode higher than a boat of wood, so the breeze was a greater danger than the current near the shore.

By contrast, the royal yacht sagged very low and the men who were swinging its bow to the stern of the wax vessel had to struggle hard. The mast, oars, and all moveable tackle had been stripped from the yacht, but it was now

loaded with loose sand carried from beyond the edge of the
river's annual flooding.

Samlor's armor and weapons lay atop the sand near the
bow along with a bronze shovel. There was no other cargo.

Samlor unlatched the gold pin which bound the ends of
his sash, then handed the garment to a waiting temple
servitor. He pulled his richly-embroidered tunic over his
head and tossed that to the man also before stepping out of
his sandals.

The stone was warm and a welcome reminder of the
cosmos as he walked to the edge of the quay. Ahwere, nude
also and regally beyond self-consciousness, was beside
him.

Shay had pulled himself aboard the royal yacht and was
waiting in the bow with a coiled line. One end of the line
was tied to the support of the forward steering oar. The
bosun was eyeing the sternpost of the other craft doubtfully,
since it too was made of wax.

Samlor stepped down into the wax boat, supporting his
weight on his arms as long as possible so that his feet
touched rather than slammed the planking. The wax slipped
beneath the pressure of his toes. The men treading water to
keep boat and dock from smashing together cursed as the
hull wobbled and thrust them beneath the surface.

Ahwere followed with the natural grace of a gull banking
through the air. Samlor reached a hand out to her, but he
found the best help he could provide was to lean toward the
other side of the high-floating vessel so that it did not tilt so
much.

"Nanefer, are you sure . . . ?" called Shay from the
bow of the other vessel. The bosun's concern for the
situation had driven normal honorifics from his vocabulary.

"Yes, yes," Samlor agreed, making his way cautiously
to the stern between the lumpish pairs of wax "crewmen"
with fragile oars in their ill-formed hands. The steering
sweep in the stern was becoming increasingly transparent as
full sunlight raked through it, evidence that the wax was
softening and would soon begin to sag.

"Throw me the rope!" Samlor ordered as the bosun
hesitated.

"Sir!" Shay muttered and tossed the hawser expertly to his superior. The coil opened as it flicked across the water, so that Samlor caught only the final loop; just enough to take a turn around the wax sternpost and bind the vessels together.

Ahwere hugged herself, not in modesty but as if she stood naked in a cold rain. The sunstruck hull shifted greasily beneath Samlor's toes. He bound off the hawser with a face as emotionless as the clear sky above them.

"Jump out now, Shay," Samlor called to the man in the other vessel.

"Nanefer, I—"

"Jump out!" Samlor cried in a voice thin with fear. "On your life!"

Shay nodded and obeyed by leaping like a baboon to the quay where sailors fended the vessel from the stone with poles.

The wax boat wobbled. Its sternposts started to give as the current put strain on the hawser. The six wax oarsmen bent forward, then leaned back against the drag of their oars. Ahwere cried out as the vessel surged away from the quay despite the inertia of the sand-laden boat it towed.

The sternpost held. There were real planks beneath Samlor's feet as he took the steering oar.

The oarsmen were no longer crude parodies but humans in all but color and their stony lack of expression. They stroked at a measured rate, plunging their blades so deep in the water that real oars would have fractured under the strain. The wax shafts held, and the waxen torsos bent and lifted, driving the linked vessels against the current.

The oarsmen's faces were turned toward Samlor by necessity of their position, but the blank eyes paid him no attention.

Ahwere stood near the bow, facing her husband. She was afraid but no longer crying. He had thought when he asked her to join him that she would prove steadfast where no one else could be trusted. Now, looking into the love in her eyes, he knew he was right.

The crowd on the quay were watching the vessels, but the few who tried to walk along the bank beside them were

stopped at once by the swamp. Reed bracts waved sluggish-
ly in a breeze that did not touch the sun-hammered surface
of the water.

They had reached midstream. The Wall of Tatenen was a
black stroke between the river and the vegetation beyond it
on the starboard side.

Samlor leaned against the steering oar. The starboard
oarsmen feathered their blades for the space of three
mechanically-powerful strokes by the wax figures on the
port side.

The vessel's bow came around while the towed yacht
eased closer, slackening the hawser between them.

All oars striking together, the wax boat drove for the
bank. The hawser thrummed taut and the yacht unwillingly
obeyed its pull.

Samlor let go of the steering oar, needless now that they
were committed whether he would or no. He walked
forward, between the wax men who cared nothing for him
or for anything, and put his arms around his wife.

The face in the middle of the stone wall was beginning to
blaze. It was already brighter than the sun, and its color was
the blue of lightning crashing in the heart of a storm. The
linked vessels were stroking toward it as fast as a man could
walk on level ground.

Ahwere put her arm around Samlor's waist so that they
stood side by side, watching the visage of Tatenen grow into
a glaring tunnel that pierced the stone and the swamp and all
the universe beyond.

They plunged into the tunnel. Hell roared around them.

Where the wax prow should have flattened on stone,
the vessel bucked. Samlor heard Ahwere murmur, "Nanefer—" and her arm tightened around his bare waist, but
they needed one another for physical support for the
moment. It was no more than that, support, without a hint
of panic.

The blue flames licking from every side were as real as
the angry light they cast, but they spread and dodged away
from an invisible barrier. Neither the wax boat, its crew, nor
the two naked humans clutching one another in the bow
were touched by the snarling blaze.

Samlor glanced behind them. The royal yacht pitched and yawed like a living thing which the flames were tormenting. The railings were beginning to scorch, while the towline blackened except for orange sparks where tufts of rope flashed into miniature fires themselves.

"How long—" Ahwere said, forming great syllables so that they would be heard over the echoing furnace-roar of the flames.

Before she could complete the sentence, the wax vessel lurched again and surged from the tunnel into surroundings which resembled the fire only in that both were hellish.

It was a swamp, but the sky above was so overcast that the noon sun was a red disk. It was nothing like the landscape anywhere along the River Napata.

Ahwere's mouth was open with the words she did not need to speak. The mouth of a beast standing belly-deep in ten feet of muck opened and blatted at them in surprise.

Samlor felt his wife's arm clamp around his waist, but her fear was only reflexive. She thrust her jaw out as she faced the monstrous head that swung closer. Samlor's mind was reminding itself that they could not be harmed—not here, not yet—so long as they remained in the wax boat.

It would have been very easy to hurl himself over the side in a mad attempt to escape. Ahwere's warm presence kept him calm where intellect could only have controlled him.

In size the beast was less like an elephant than a whale roiling the thick waters of a cycad-fringed swamp. Its neck was long and serpentine—slender for the body but still too large for Samlor to have encircled it with both arms.

The head was in scale with the neck. The teeth fringing the jaws were peg-like, not shears. Even so, the bass screech the beast directed at the boat was loud enough to drive the couple in the bow half a step back by its physical impact.

The monster's breath smelled of pinebark and turpentine, pungent but not unpleasant.

The oarsmen continued to stroke, as unaffected by the monster as they had been by the tunnel of flame. The boat's course slid it under the rounded snakelike head. The beast jerked up its neck, then pulled a foreleg from the swamp

and pawed with it. The blunt claws dripped mud and scraps
of vegetation which splashed and streamed away in the air a
few feet over Samlor's head.

The claws themselves hit a barrier there also, though
there was no sound of impact nor did the vessel rock under
the blow.

The monster gave another blat of deafening amazement
and bolted away from the wax ship. Waves the color and
almost the consistency of mud surged across the swamp, but
the oarsmen pulled obliviously and the wax prow slid on
without feeling the shock of the water.

Behind them, the yacht jerked and staggered. Waves
broke over it and streamed away from railings which the
touch of the blue flames had left asmolder.

The monster the boats had startled was threshing toward
the firmer ground in the distance. It sounded like a traveling
waterfall. The volume of viscous muck its legs churned up
was enough to rate a place in the landscape. Another
creature like it roared from somewhere in the haze.

The wax boat bucked, stern down and then rising, as
fiercely as it had when they penetrated the tunnel of flames.
The landscape did not change. Ahwere turned around and
screamed briefly before her own hand clamped over her
mouth.

The monster that had surged away from them was a
creature of imagination only, nightmarish but for that reason
easy to disregard when the nightmare was past. Something
had just crawled half onto the deck of the royal yacht, and it
was a terror familiar to any Napatan.

Only the head and forequarters were visible above the
surface of the reedy water, but they alone were longer than
the full length of the biggest crocodile Samlor had ever
seen. Its jaws opened in laughter or challenge as one of its
eyes glittered at the humans on the wax boat.

The oarsmen continued to stroke, fighting the mass which
held the yacht in its clawed grip, but the hawser between the
vessels was humming with strain.

"Ahwere," Samlor's lips were murmuring. "My love,
my sister, my only love," and he could hear her scarcely-
voiced, "Nanefer . . . ," as well.

The crocodile clawed more of its broad, bone-armored body into the yacht. The over-ballasting of sand was suddenly an advantage, because even a beast the size of this one could not overturn the heavy vessel.

The crocodile got one of its hind legs onto the yacht's rail. Hooked black claws gouged long splinters from the wood.

The mind in which Samlor resided was terrified though steadfast. The caravan master had shut down all his emotions when wax simulacra had begun working as if they were men and more than men. This, though . . . a crocodile, monstrous in size but a natural thing—

It could be fought, even if he couldn't defeat it, and he was wondering what to use for a weapon while the body he did not control crooned to a woman and awaited death.

Streaks of light, unburnt cord were popping out on the surface of the hawser as its skeins stretched under the strain. In a moment they would begin to give way. The rope would part with a crack like stone shearing, and—

The wax boat lurched. In front of them was not swamp but gray waste, a membrane of change through which the bow slipped, the humans and the not-human oarsmen, the sternpost with the stretching hawser—

The crocodile threw itself over the side of the royal yacht. The beast's mouth was open. Past its ragged teeth Samlor could see its corpse-white throat contract as if the crocodile were bellowing at them. No sound penetrated, not even the slap of the waves that the fifty-foot body hurled up as it struck the water and all the landscape disappeared into the gray diaphragm which sealed behind the yacht.

The oarsmen continued to stroke. The vessels moved forward as if the oarblades were not pulling through the air—or something more empty than air.

There was no sky, only stars like needle points, and the horizon was an etched jumble of gray stone against blackness. The wax boat surged ahead, never less than six inches above the surface.

Samlor thought at first that the ground was of finely-divided sand studded with jagged volcanic boulders. By squinting and looking at a point far enough ahead that motion did not blur it, he corrected his error. The ground was glass or glassy slag, and the appearance of sand came from the crazing of the smooth surfaces which threw back light in a myriad of directions.

They were not on a plain but a complex of broad craters, shouldering into one another like the pattern raindrops start to make on a beach. The sharper boulders rimmed craters which had not been battered by latter hammerings. Without guidance or need for a man on the rudder, the wax crewmen slid between these obstacles the way human boatmen would avoid treestumps turning in a flood-swollen river.

The yacht skidded along the ground behind them, grinding away bits of shattered glass which spun and glittered as they fell back. The fragments did not tumble as quickly as they should have, and the pitching of the wooden vessel was of curiously long duration. Laden as it was, the yacht ought to have smashed its hull to splinters each time it hit the ground after bounding over an irregularity.

This was not a place Samlor had ever heard of before.

But then, he shouldn't have expected that it would be.

The wax boat was skirting a crater so fresh and extensive that its rim was a glassy sawblade slashing through half the horizon. They were ascending the slope as they rounded it, though the ultimate direction was confused by the shattered landscape of crater flattening crater in dikes and gulleys.

The sun above had no compromise. Its light fell in knife-edge shadows, though sometimes long cracks drew feathers of illumination through the glassy surface. When Samlor tried to look up at the orb, squinting past the edge of his hand as he would normally do on a bright day, he was almost blinded.

There was no halo round the sun *here*: the sky was either blackness or radiance, with no gradations between.

The rim was close enough to starboard that Samlor thought he could, with care, spit the distance—though perhaps not in this slender royal body.

The crewmen paused. Samlor glanced back at the wax figures, but he could see only their humping shoulders and bull necks. Their faces would have told him nothing about their feelings, their intentions . . . assuming they had either.

The wax boat coasted. The yacht scraped along also, its inertia overcoming friction in this strange land.

The portside oarsmen began to stroke while their fellows held their blades horizontal, bringing the bow around again the same way they had aligned it with the bank of the River Napata a lifetime ago.

This time the vessel was swinging toward a notch in the crater rim which was otherwise a waist-high barrier whose jagged top was sharper than the best steel. They were high enough that when Samlor glanced around him he could see far across a landscape pocked like human skin—but gray and black and the white of surface reflection of the beams of the unforgiving sun.

This was a dead place, and no place for men.

The oarsmen took up the stroke in measured unison, snatching the slack from the hawser and bringing the yacht's bow around in what should have been a squeal of protest—but was soundless here. They drove toward the wall.

CHAPTER 17

THE WAX BOAT slid between edges of glass so close that had the oars been in mid-stroke, the oarblades on both sides would have been sliced away. Ahwere's hand and arm were firm on Samlor's waist, but where their hips pressed together he could feel the rest of her body trembling.

So was his own.

The wax boat and its towed companion had entered a bowl the size of a great city. Its shallow surface was as smooth as warm grease.

The wax boat pulled down the slope at its regular speed. The yacht slid easily behind it.

Something waited at the bottom.

The other craters were broken and leveled by the frequency with which they had been battered by later fellows. Smooth floors shattered; crisp rims pulverized and recongealed into another crater's floor; and the same repeated a hundred times again so that the surfaces had the jumbled formlessness of an ash pit.

The crater which the wax vessel had entered under its own direction was greater than any other in the landscape around it, and no later impact had disturbed its perfection. The floor was marked with pressure waves, undetectable in themselves but marked by the multiple dazzling images of the sun which they reflected.

The thing in the center of the bowl moved restively. Samlor could not be sure of its shape until it raised its head and began slowly to uncoil.

"What. . . ," whispered Ahwere, suppressing the rest of the question and almost the word itself so as not to show fear before her husband.

The mind of Samlor warmed for the first time to this woman who was neither his sister nor his wife. She knew that it was all right to be afraid—but that one must never admit it. . . .

"Only a worm," said the body that was Samlor's for this lifetime. "We'll take the book from it very soon now."

Very soon now.

The distance from the rim to the center of the bowl was deceptive, for there was nothing to provide scale except the worm. Its apparent size increased while the crater rim slowly diminished over the stern of the vessel.

Ahwere took her arm away from her husband and tried to wipe off sweat against her own body. She was not successful, and the absence of her touch chilled Samlor more than did the perspiration evaporating from his suddenly-uncovered skin.

Both ends of the worm's body were briefly visible as coils flowed across one another like quicksilver. They were indistinguishable until the head rose ten feet and the end cocked over at a right angle aligned with the oncoming vessel.

A blue circle glowed where the worm's mouth should have been. Samlor expected to feel something, a blast or a tingling, but the glow only trembled up and down through indigo and colors beyond the spectrum.

"I think," said Ahwere in a voice as emotionless as that of a housewife measuring cloth, "that it must be a hundred feet long, my husband."

Very close, thought Samlor whose mind was jumping with the emotions of a prince who had not faced physical death on a regular basis. And about the diameter of a man's torso—the torso of Samlor hil Samt, and not that of the royal body he rode now.

He wondered what would happen to him when the worm

killed Nanefer. *"There is a price. . . ,"* Ahwere's ghost had warned them in the tomb.

The wax boat swung from its direct course when it was three lengths from the waiting guardian. The worm's head rotated on the column of its smooth, gray neck as it tracked them. Samlor looked back at the blue glow, but the woman kept her eyes straight forward as if she were unaware of the creature sharing this desolation with them. Aloud she said, "If this is the realm of the gods, then. . . ."

The wax oarsmen paused in midstroke. Their backs straightened slowly, the way grass stems return to vertical after being trodden down by a bare foot. The boat drifted to a halt, settling until it rested on the crater floor as if it were no more than it had been—a toy of wax, crewed by waxen lumps.

Behind them, the royal yacht slid to its own resting place. Its greater inertia brought the wooden bowsprit almost into contact with the wax stern.

Samlor hugged his wife, then kissed her fiercely. "Not until I call you," he said. "Don't take any chances until I call you."

As he spoke, Samlor realized what Nanefer had hidden from his wife and suppressed so far below his mind's surface that only now was it clear: Nanefer knew what he needed to gain the book. But he didn't know *why* he was bringing the paraphernalia—and one companion—which were with him now.

The reason for the weapons was clear enough.

Samlor jumped to the ground, then steadied himself on the rail of the wax boat as his bare feet started to slip out from under him. The glass surface forgave no imbalance, and his body did not move as it ought to. He didn't *weigh* what he should, though he hadn't noticed the difference until he left the boat.

The worm watched, rotating its head to follow him as he walked carefully to the yacht and the equipment aboard it. Half the creature's length was in loose coils and the pillared neck, but the rest of the worm was a tight, shimmering mound in the center of the crater.

Samlor hopped aboard the yacht, aided by his lessened

weight (though the change made him clumsy). He began to
don his armor, a task made more difficult by the damage it
had received in the tunnel of fire.

The helmet was now useless. It was a cap of bull's hide,
and the leather had shrunk and warped under the kisses of
the blue flame. Samlor tossed it aside, less regretful than
was the prince whose eyes were for the moment his eyes. It
hadn't been an impressive piece of battle armor to the
caravan master anyway; though Heqt alone knew what
would be useful against the worm.

The shield was a solid piece, though of unfamiliar
construction. The back reinforcement of thin boards had
cracked, but its metal rim continued to stretch the facing of
thick crocodile hide firmly in place. The bony scutes
weren't quite as effective as metal, but Samlor was glad to
heft the shield by its bronze handgrip and measure the worm
again over the rim.

Instead of a sword, he had an axe with a thick crescent
blade, pinned to the shaft at both horns as well as in the
center. The blade was a foot long across the horns, almost
half the total length of the weapon. It didn't balance as well
as a sword of the length and weight, nor did it have the
penetration of a narrow-bladed axe which concentrated its
impact on an edge a few fingers broad. It would have to do.

Or not, as the case might be.

The painted leather over the wooden daggersheath had
emerged black and tattered from the tunnel, but it and the
belt to which it was fastened would serve. Samlor slid the
blade out to check it and be sure that the warped sheath
wasn't binding.

The watered steel blade would have brought a curse to his
lips—if the lips had not been for Nanefer to rule.

Well, it was a good dagger, thought Samlor as his body
buckled the belt around its bare waist and felt its tender skin
protest at the feel of seared leather. Tunics would never have
survived the tunnel, though he would trade the shield now
for a simple linen kirtle. The fact of being clothed might
help him more than the shield's physical protection.

Armed and as prepared as he could be, Samlor turned to
step from the yacht's bow and collided with his wife.

They had spoken normally on the vessel that brought them here, but nowhere else in this desolation was there sound. Ahwere's mouth worked, blurting a tearful apology for being in the way, but the words were only in her eyes and her husband's heart.

Samlor held Ahwere as she backed away, clasping her with his elbows because his hands were filled with weapons. "My love, my—" he murmured, but his voice did not ring even within the chambers of his skull. This *hellish* place!

But he had known it would not be a place for men.

He kissed Ahwere's hair, the lobe of her ear, and last her tear-wet lips.

When he turned again to battle the worm for its hoard, a part of his mind kept remembering that he and his wife could return now with no cost or further danger.

Samlor's own mind and emotions jarred often against those of the royal prince whom he now *was*, but in one respect their personalities were stamped from the same die: they had not come this far in order to turn back.

The worm let him approach, angling its head as he drew nearer. The height of its neck did not change, so that it became a tower threatening him more at every step.

The crater floor felt dry but neither hot nor cold. It was adequate footing so long as he remembered to watch his balance—which not even the gods themselves could do in the midst of battle.

Was the worm a god?

It struck when he was ten feet away from it, so close that Samlor would have begun his rush when his foot next left the ground.

Nanefer's reflexes were not what they should have been, but this *place* permitted him to interpose his unnaturally-light shield to the creature's hammerblow. The blue glow of the worm's snout struck just below the upper rim and clung there like a lodestone to steel. Samlor's legs flew out from under him, but he used the torque of the creature's impact to help swing his own counterblow.

The axe cut helve deep. Samlor felt the crunch of a hard surface, though the worm's body rippled like free-flowing water. When he dragged the blade free, the edges of the long cut sprang away from the wound and made it gape still wider. The interior glistened without color or definite features.

The worm lifted. Samlor had been thrown onto his hips and shoulders, bruised but not seriously injured. His left hand held the shield in a deathgrip so that the creature picked him up as it recovered itself.

A loop of the worm's body wrapped itself about his legs and began to flow upward. The creature was glass-smooth and as powerful as a boulder rolling downhill.

Samlor cut at the worm's neck. His grip on the shield anchored him, but the blow was awkward and crossed the previous wound at a slant. Again the flesh gaped when the axe crushed its way through the surface.

The coil was around his thighs. He felt the flesh tear over the points of his hips. Only the thickness of the worm's body prevented it from crushing his bones. The ring of pressure slipped higher, and a second loop wound itself over Samlor's ankles.

He chopped at the creature's neck with hysterical fury which made up for lack of strength or skill in the physical arts of war. His vision blurred as the upper coil squeezed against his diaphragm, but he did not need to aim the blows. He was swinging at the full length of his arm, and the worm's hold froze it and the man into the same relationship for every stroke.

A jerk of the worm's head snatched the shield away and flung it upward as paired images which merged and spread and merged again while Samlor tried to follow their tumbling arc.

He didn't realize how high he was until the coils dropped him. He was as limp as a sack of millet when he fell, so exhaustion saved him from serious injury when he hit the ground. The worm had lifted him thirty feet in the air—if air was the word—and he would surely have broken bones on the glass surface if he had been tense.

Ahwere's touch more than her strength helped Samlor rise. Her right hand still held the bronze shovel with which she had vainly battered the worm's flank. Her face held no emotion, but that coldness and the fierceness with which she tugged at her husband's shoulders showed that she feared she was trying to lift a corpse.

The worm's body wobbled in curves like those of surf on a low shoreline. Samlor hugged his wife with his free hand as he staggered to his feet. The burning sensation on his left hand meant either blisters or skin stripped when the worm's convulsions tore loose the shield for anything human strength could do.

The creature's head—the first two or three feet of a body which was the same diameter throughout—hung by a thread of glittering skin. It did not move when the body thrashed, and the glow that had licked across the end was gone.

Motioning Ahwere to stay back, Samlor stepped to the worm. He was having trouble breathing because of the way his ribs were bruised, but that was only one more pain in a body which hurt all over. He had open skin on his right elbow and left knee, from friction with the worm's coils or the way he sprawled to the ground.

He heard his blood pounding but not the rasp of air being dragged into his lungs. Everything else about the way he breathed in this place was normal—including the way his chest hurt when he did it—but there *was* no air.

The only thing in this place which mattered was the Book of Tatenen—and the fact that the book's guardian was dead. Samlor stepped close to the worm; paused as he measured the distance; and brought the axe down on the skin which still joined the two sections of the creature.

He used both hands for the blow. Powdered glass and shards of the axeblade sparked away from the impact, numbing Samlor's hands and leaving a white scar on the crater's floor while the worm's motion settled into a gelatinous trembling in both parts of its body.

Ahwere touched his arm from behind. Samlor threw down the useless axe helve before he turned to embrace his wife again.

All he had to do now was to retrieve the book.

When the worm died, its body uncoiled into a sprawl dwarfed by the size of the crater. The rim, jagged as the fangs of a wolf-fish, gleamed beneath the rays of a sun which had remained precisely overhead throughout the battle.

The gray iron box which the worm had encircled until it died was now visible.

Ahwere grabbed Samlor by the arm and turned him with a strength which surprised him as much as *what* she was doing. There was a scream on her face. His eyes were already looking beyond her.

The two pieces of the worm had shivered into contact. A blue glare that hurt Samlor's eyes was spluttering between the ragged edges of the creature's skin. Where the arcs touched, they welded the portions together as if Samlor had not shattered his axe in making sure the separation was complete.

The worm's tail moved in a series of water-smooth curves, covering the box again. The head lifted, its tip glowing lambently as it searched, then focused on the pair of humans.

Samlor drew his dagger with fingers made clumsy by despair, but the instinct with which the prince stabbed hilt deep into the nearest loop of the body was one which the caravan master could applaud. Cutting the head off had done nothing permanent, but perhaps there were vital organs somewhere else in the creature's length.

Not that there was so much as a hope of finding a vital spot in a squirming hundred feet of body.

A loop of the worm knocked Samlor down and slithered across him. The coils couldn't encircle a victim until the head had a grip to anchor them.

Samlor let the creature's own motion draw the blade clear in a long gash. He stabbed again. The steel gleamed with clear ichor. There was no resistance to its passage after the point dimpled the metallic skin.

Samlor pulled himself from beneath the slick weight of the worm's coils and the creature's head slammed onto the ground again. The blue/violet flicker of its snout burned like the heart of a glacier.

The shock left him with no other feeling in the arm he had thrown out to meet the impact. The worm's body cast itself around his ankles with the accuracy of a cattleman's rope.

Blue sparks played dazzlingly across the worm as the long gash began to arc itself closed.

Samlor screamed soundlessly. His weapon tore along the creature's flesh, so deeply the hilt bobbed against the skin like a shearwater's beak scoring the sea.

The blade parted the worm as easily as it would the pulp of a ripe melon—and the top of the cut began to regrow in blue arcs that made the hair stand upon Samlor's head. A loop was crushing his knees together. The touch of the worm's snout drove icy needles through his left arm and into his face and chest.

A coil buffeted Ahwere as she stepped past her trapped husband and poured a shovelful of sand into the cut he had just torn.

Minuscule lightning sealing the wound touched sand and flashed it into glass that spattered volcanically. Instead of healing the cut puckered, then swelled into an abscess boiling with power insulated from its proper use.

The pain in Samlor's legs was momentarily so dizzying that he did not realize the worm had dropped him.

The worm's snout brushed the surface of the abscess. Near the swelling the creature's body spasmed uncontrolled, but the slither of its tail out of its protective coil was deliberate.

The worm had twitched its body a dozen feet from its attacker. Samlor tried to stand but his legs failed him. He slid himself across the crater floor, using his numb left hand as a flipper.

The worm's head twisted from the wound to Samlor. The glow of its snout was still blue but shot through with sparks of sullen red. Samlor twisted his arm. The long blade jutting from the heelside of his fist pointed up, ready to meet the creature if the creature dared to strike.

Ahwere, running up with more sand, flickered in Samlor's peripheral vision. He drove his knife into the worm's side again with a bloody joy that more than balanced the shock of the creature's snout against his unprotected upper chest. The pain shuddering across his nerves ripped the watered steel blade in a jerky zig-zag across the shimmering hide which exploded as Ahwere poured sand into the wound.

This time Samlor's legs worked well enough for him to leap astride the creature as it tried to escape him. He stabbed downward, and the worm's flowing body dragged itself along the pitiless blade of the dagger. The edges of the wound shone like iron as a bellows strokes the hearth, but they did not arc or meld together.

When Ahwere thrust her shovel into the wound, the third load of sand sank through the worm's flesh like lead in hot wax. The creature writhed upward in a great loop that flung Samlor away. As it twisted in the air, the unscarred skin on the underside of its body blackened and sloughed to spray bubbles of molten glass onto the crater floor.

The worm's head and tail were battering the ground. The snout melted a patch of the crater the first time it struck. Then the glow turned inward and the worm's head began to collapse around a bead of orange fire.

Samlor limped over to the worm's body and began methodically to hack it in half. The skin was powdery, and the flesh beneath began to mottle when it was exposed.

The sand which Ahwere shoveled onto her husband's butchery clung to the flesh. There were only a few sparks to fleck the surfaces with glass.

When Samlor finished his work, the two parts of the worm were as still as the sun above. The creature's head had melted several feet back along its body, leaving tarry sludge on the crater floor.

Ahwere held a final shovelful of sand. When she saw that it was needless, she turned the shovel over with royal hauteur, scorning the worm and the glittering crater where it lay dead.

Samlor's dagger was nicked by tiny serrations near the crossguard where the worm's skin had resisted edge-on cutting. They would polish out when he next sharpened the blade, just as his scrapes and bruises would heal and the terrible fatigue-produced trembling would leave his muscles.

The worm's snout had not marked the arm and shoulder

where it gripped him, but there was blue fire deep in his bones in those places.

Samlor walked to the iron box with painful deliberation. Ahwere followed him with the bronze shovel raised like a sceptre. She had understood the use of the shovel and sand when her husband had been too enveloped by the imminence of battle to imagine anything further.

You must have a companion whom you trust to the point of your very life, the spirits he commanded had whispered to him as he made preparations.

He had brought the right companion. He had brought weapons and armor—and a shipload of sand when a basket would have been sufficient.

But nothing is excessive when it results in triumph.

Samlor squatted down before the iron box, a cube whose plain sides were the length of his forearm. It had no lock or hinges, but the mind of Prince Nanefer smiled at it. Samlor's finger traced a sign on the glass of the crater floor while his lips mimed words.

The edges of the box broke apart as cleanly as the sections of an orange pried by careful fingers. One side flopped toward Samlor. When he hopped backward to avoid it, pain blasted both his knees and reminded him of the bruising the worm had given them. He fell to his buttocks on the glass and got up gingerly.

The top of the iron box lay on an inner container of richly-chased copper. Samlor pushed the iron away and squatted to survey the copper. On its sides were engraved hunting scenes—smiling gods striding over cities and fields, lifting men on their tridents like gigged frogs.

Samlor's mind grew cold and Nanefer lost his scornful smile. His finger drew a different glyph between his splayed knees.

A shaving of metal like the waste from a graver's tool began to lift along the upper edge of the copper, at first slowly and then at the speed of flame devouring chaff. The copper was thin as foil, but it would have been proof against material tools—even the watered steel of the dagger which had ripped apart the box's guardian.

The copper twisted as Samlor's spell sheared it into

plates. The face of Tatenen, the Great God, seemed to wink as the front fell to display an inner casket of juniper wood.

Prince Nanefer was wholly sunk into his magic, but Samlor's mind processed differently the data from the senses which they shared. Samlor saw Ahwere standing spearshaft straight beside them, pretending that she did not know what her husband was doing.

There were tears on her cheeks, but to wipe them off would be an admission.

Samlor's finger moved against the ground. The box puffed into smoky fire as enveloping as a wrapping of silk that lifted toward the sun and disappeared in a black train.

The fire ceased as abruptly as it had ignited. The juniper box was wholly consumed, and the box within—for of course there was a box within—was an intarsia of ivory figures on an ebony ground.

The figures were of men and women, carved so perfectly that their features were recognizable even though the panels were less than a foot in either dimension. They were palace functionaries and generals of the Napatan army, and they marched in procession behind the funerary symbols of the royal house. The sarcophagus of King Merneb was being carried at the bottom of the panel.

Samlor drew a glyph and spoke a silent word. His mind put blinders on his eyes so that he could not, *would* not, see if his wife had noticed the design.

The box fell apart, ivory separating from ebony and the whole tumbling to the ground like the sides of a trench cut in sand. Within was a still-smaller casket of silver.

The progress continued in polished figures against an oxidized background. There were two sarcophagi on the silver, clearly identified by the symbols borne high before each. Ahwere and Merib were being carried to their tomb.

The time for doubt is before you start a course of action which has certain death as the price of failure. Nanefer spoke and drew the articles of his spell. Samlor would have done the same if he controlled the body in which his mind now resided.

A litter of previous containers lay where Samlor had been working, plates and parts and ash that his hands swept aside to open the next box. The silver casket did not crumble or fall apart. Instead its surface became translucent, then transparent, and at last wholly insubstantial. It vanished as utterly as if it had never enclosed the box of gold which remained.

There was no need of magic to open the gold casket. Unlike the other containers, this one had a mechanical catch.

Samlor picked up the box, knowing that Ahwere's eyes were on him. The casket was heavy, even in this place.

There were two figures on the box. One was a perfect semblance of Nanefer, molded into the sliding bolt of pure gold. The other shape was the head of a great crocodile covered with lustrous black niello. All he had to do to open the box was to slide the bolt into the jaws of the crocodile.

Ahwere was crying silently. Samlor's hand moved while his mind concentrated on void and the purity of his intention.

He felt the click as the gold disappeared into black jaws. The lid of the box rose by itself.

The sun and stars watched coldly as Samlor lifted the silk-wrapped object from the final box.

It was not precisely a book, though there was no obviously better way to describe it. It was a flat crystal a palm's breadth square on the major surfaces and the thickness of a finger on the sides. The edges looked sharp enough to cut, but they felt safely rounded when Samlor touched them.

He looked up at Ahwere in triumph with the Book of Tatenen in one hand and its red silk wrapper in the other. The grief on her face hardened his visage and brought a flash of anger to his eyes. Even though she was a part of the victory, Ahwere was unwilling to admit that her husband had been right in the course she had opposed from the beginning. . . .

But he was above anger. He had won against the very gods!

Gesturing in brusque command, Samlor led his wife back to the vessel that had brought them here. His weight was normal again, and sound returned—though for the moment it was only the sound of Ahwere's suppressed sniffles.

He squatted to examine the object his courage and learning had gained.

The Book of Tatenen was so clear that Samlor could see the whorls of his hand through it, but there were more fires sparkling in the heart of it than the light of this harsh place should have wakened in a diamond's facets. Samlor raised the dense crystal slowly and held it to his forehead. It was cold, not as the worm's snout had been but rather as one bare hand feels to the other in a winter storm.

He spoke the first Word of Opening which his spirits had taught him back in the realm of men.

It was as if he had stepped from a tomb into a garden on a golden summer day. He was all life in the cosmos, plant as well as animal—and doubtful things he could not describe but which he *was* while the book lay cool against his skin.

All their senses were his senses, all their speech was as clear to him as the voice of Ahwere when they lay together for the first time making love.

There was no confusion. His knowledge was godlike; and, for the time the crystal touched him, Samlor hil Samt was a god.

He lowered the book. Reality shrank back to a glass-floored crater and the wide, wet eyes of his beloved. The blessed wonder of his expression cooled the fear with which she watched her husband, certain of disaster though triumphant by every indicator save instinct.

Samlor lifted the Book of Tatenen and spoke the second Word of Opening.

If the first spell had brought him Summer, the second put him in the heart of clear, dry Winter glittering on an icefield. Every force of the cosmos focused on him, matrices so intricate and perfect that they were beyond understanding.

But he understood.

The injuries his body had sustained while battling the worm—the forces and balances that caused fluids to move or rest, solids to touch but not mingle—were his to know and to change by that knowledge. He knew that his bruises

river. He would never find it again, though he had all the resources of the temple—and the kingdom—with which to dredge and drain. . . .

He did not drop the silk-wrapped crystal.

The wax boat, crushed and already slumping with the sun's heat, began to drift downstream while Shay leaped aboard the yacht and called for more help. His curses at the charring and claw-marks which defaced the vessel were heartfelt.

Tekhao and several other priests were babbling oratorically while servitors offered clothing and refreshments, but Samlor had a mind only for his wife and their infant now nestling again at Ahwere's breast.

He put his arms around them both and said, "This is the beginning of a new age for mankind, and we three are its leaders."

But when the silken parcel in his left hand brushed Merib, the child began to wail.

CHAPTER 18

THE FESTIVAL OF THANKSGIVING going on in the temple courtyard was an enthusiastic background, even in the royal suite facing the river. Rushlights on the roof made the reed tops shimmer and turned the stone causeway into something softly metallic.

A single lamp lighted the room where Samlor made his preparations and Ahwere crooned to Merib in a chair across from her husband.

Samlor brushed the final glyphs onto his parchment with a sure hand. He used sepia, cuttlefish ink, for his medium because its animal nature—and that of the parchment— would add to the virtue of the spell he was creating.

The Book of Tatenen could not be committed to human memory. In use, the mind became a facet of the book instead of the reverse.

But portions of the book could be excerpted by a man of the proper skills and powers; and one portion was enough to safeguard him against attack by men or gods.

"There. . . ," Samlor breathed as he contemplated the page of writing. He felt soggy, weighted down as if he had eaten salty food and drunk heavily. It was merely his reaction to returning to the Realm of Men after another excursion in the dazzling acuity of the Book of Tatenen.

Merib was asleep. Ahwere got up, cradling the infant

with an ease which belied the slenderness of her form. She took the jug of beer from the sideboard and carried it to her husband.

Samlor smiled wanly at her and set the jug on the table beside his brush and parchment. "Next you'll do this, too," he said, reaching up to take her hand.

Ahwere shrugged, resigned and bitter, though she made an effort to pretend otherwise. "You're the scholar, my husband," she said. "I'll never learn—" her chin nodded toward the parchment. "Any more than you'll ever bear a child."

Merib whimpered softly.

Salmor didn't let his face set in anger, but animation of a hard sort prodded through his weariness. "There's no reason you can't learn to read and write," he said. "Just as Merib will. It's very important now."

"Yes, in time," said Ahwere in what a different tone could have made agreement. She walked back to her chair and sat.

Samlor poured beer into the mug which served as the jug's cover. "When I've drunk this," he said, though he had tried to explain the process before, "the spell of protection will be a part of me. Nothing will be able to harm me again."

He rolled the parchment and set it on end in the mug. The pale beer began to darken as it dissolved the ink. Fluid climbed the parchment cylinder slowly by osmosis.

"Yes," said Ahwere. "That must be why everything is out of balance. Because of what we've done."

Samlor turned the rolled document carefully and set it back in the beer with the other end down. The remainder of the symbols added their substance in swirls of color that merged with earlier glyphs and lost definition. The fluid was now the color of the yacht's cedarwood rail after the tunnel had seared it.

"Don't be foolish," he said sharply. "We *are* part of the balance. Nothing's wrong. And you *will* learn the glyphs so that the book protects you as well."

He dropped the soggy parchment on the table. It oozed a

mixture of beer and ink and power. Without looking at his wife, Samlor lifted the mug and drank down its contents.

"Yes, my husband," said Ahwere. "I will learn the glyphs. If there is time."

CHAPTER 19

THERE WERE CLOUDS both on the western horizon and high in the east, but the sky directly above the yacht was clear and perfectly framed by the sunset. The west was a mass of boiling red with only one opening. The beam which escaped through that gap flared in a great keyhole across the opposite cloudbank.

"Unlocking the cosmos," said Samlor cheerfully. Ahwere looked down as if he had slapped her.

Pursing his lips, Samlor got up from his couch and walked to the rail, ducking beneath the deck awning. Merib scooted across the polished planks and caught him by the ankle, gurgling, while Ahwere and the nurse watched cautiously.

Shay stumped toward him from the bow. "Sir," he said, "there'll be a moon t'night less it clouds over. The wind's fair, and anyhow there's no place t' tie up on this stretch as isn't open as a cabin boy's bum. I've said we'll go on s' long as the sky holds, keepin' two men by the sweeps for safety's sake. Ah, with your permission."

Samlor played with Merib's thin hair while the boy pulled himself upright, using his father's leg as a brace. The women, shaded by the awning, were part of the dusk. Muted voices and the odor of leeks drifted back from the crewmen forward.

"All right," said Samlor. "Do as you think fit."

The weight of the crystal wrapped against his bosom concentrated Samlor's awareness. He could use the Book of Tatenen to ensure fair weather; to jerk the sun back in the sky to light their way; to transport himself, those with him, and the very ship to the capital in an instant.

But there was no purpose in any of those things. Nothing, at least, to justify subverting the powers of the cosmos. Now that he had gained his end, Samlor's viewpoint was changing.

His left hand idly fitted and withdrew from the notches across the rail. Samlor was unaware of what he was doing, but Shay followed the action and grimaced.

"Sorry about that, sir," the bosun muttered. "Have t' replace the bloody section, there and farther forrard. Got the bloody sand out and burnished the bloody burn marks out, but them bloody gouges. . . ."

Where the crocodile had clambered aboard the yacht, Samlor realized. Four parallel scratches in the cedar, each of them so broad and deep that his index finger fit loosely within the slot.

"That doesn't matter, bosun," Samlor said sharply. "The boat served its purpose, so the damage is of no account."

He would *not* be chided by a commoner for harming— trivial harm!—a vessel he owned. Just because Shay was responsible for the vessel, that didn't mean the prince its owner could not use it any way he pleased! Why—

The flood of unspoken anger halted. Samlor blinked at himself in amazement. He was as a god in his power, in immortality and in knowledge. But still he thought as the man he had been since birth. Not a bad man, but human, despite the Book of Tatenen carried beneath his girdle.

The yacht rolled so steeply that the rail against which Samlor leaned slapped the water.

Shay was gripping the awning's framework with a sailor's instinct that never left him without a handhold when aboard a vessel. He bellowed, "*Stand to!*" forward to his men, most of whose cries indicated they were as shocked as Samlor was.

When the yacht tilted sideways, Samlor hugged the rail with both arms. His torso hung over what should have been water. Instead, he was looking into the open jaws of a crocodile whose head was longer than Samlor was tall.

The eye turned to him did not wink with pale reflection. It burned blue like the tunnel of flame or the snout of the worm.

Samlor screamed, but his desperate grasp was too late to save Merib. The infant catapulted past his father and wailed as the jaws closed over him.

The crocodile sank as suddenly as it had appeared. When its black claws released the rail, the yacht rolled sharply to the other side, bouncing Ahwere into the covered deck-house again.

"My son!" she cried. "Save my son!"

Samlor had the crystal out of its wrappings even before the vessel had ceased to bob violently back and forth. He spoke the word that found Merib and brought him back to the arms of his mother while the woman cried and sailors shouted in terrified confusion.

But not even the Book of Tatenen could bring the dead to life.

CHAPTER 20

"OH, THIS IS so terrible," muttered Tekhao lugubriously. "He had royal eyes, your highness, *royal* eyes. He would have been a great king."

Then he sneezed echoingly in the tomb chamber.

"My wife and I appreciate your sacrifice, Tekhao," said Samlor, bitterly amused to find that grief had reduced his mind to banalities. "If you would leave us with our—with our. . . . For a mom—"

"But of course, your highness," the chief priest blurted. "Your highness," he added with another bow to be sure that he had not slighted Princess Ahwere.

Tekhao *had* made a sacrifice: his tomb, excavated and lined with red granite brought from desert cliffs south of the capital. It was an exceptionally fine burial place for anyone below royal rank.

And even for a royal infant, if he drowned five hundred miles north of the family tombs across from the capital. The weather was hot and the air at the river's surface almost as humid as the water itself. No type or degree of embalming would permit the tiny corpse to be transported to the capital—except as a mass so putrescent that the bones would slosh within it.

Samlor could not hear Ahwere weeping, but the tear streaks on her face swelled regularly as yet another drop slipped toward her chin. He put his arm around her waist and, with an urging that was barely short of force, he moved her with him to the edge of the bier.

The only lights within the tomb were the blotches of red from the perforated incense burners at each corner. In this enclosure the fumes had a sharpness that would have passed unnoticed in the open air.

Samlor did not need that to remind him of the bitterness of death.

"Farewell, my son," Ahwere whispered.

The lid of the inner wooden casket waited beside the bier. It was painted with a lifelike representation of Merib, a hasty job which spoke well of the skill of the temple craftsmen. The stone sarcophagus was unfinished and far too large for its burden, but there had been no time to carve one to the size of an infant.

Merib's eyelids flickered.

Samlor was sure the motion was a trick of the bad light, but his free hand snatched at the book in his girdle.

The lids opened. Instead of the painted shells which covered the eyeballs and would retain their roundness when protoplasm slumped, Merib stared at the world through blue fire shivering down into the violet. "Do not grieve, my mother," said the lips which were already withering. "Rejoice, for the cosmos is returning to balance."

The eyes closed.

Samlor did not catch his wife when she slumped to the floor, because his own limbs were trembling too badly.

CHAPTER 21

"THERE'S SOMETHING BIG going past on the surface,"
thought the carp as they snuffled the mud near the bank,
"but it doesn't matter to us."

Lesser fish formed lesser thoughts, while birds bouncing
among the reedtops chirped of food and the day's ending.
Lizards stalked insects while a snake moved with glacial
slowness toward a frog.

There were no crocodiles anywhere near the royal yacht.

Samlor lowered the Book of Tatenen with a sigh.

Ahwere had been watching him from her couch. She
touched her husband's hand and smiled, though her expression was almost lost in the dusk. Samlor squeezed her hand
fiercely and kissed her, but he did not put away the crystal.

"I need to talk to Shay," he murmured as he stood and
ducked from beneath the awning. The mast creaked as the
fitful breeze strengthened. Tonight the sky was cloudless
and the wind would stay fair all the way to the capital.

The Book of Tatenen would see to that.

The bosun had been waiting for Samlor. "Ah, didn't
want t' bother you while you was thinkin', sir," he said.
"But I figured we'd tie up along the bank about now." He
would not meet his master's eyes.

"We'll go on," Samlor retorted sharply. "I want to reach
the capital before—" He broke off, unwilling to say,

"Before my father hears of his grandson's death from someone else."

"Yessir, yessir," agreed Shay, bobbing his head. "It was only—the wind what made us heel the other, the other bloody dusk. Didn't know for sure what you'd want."

No one but Samlor had seen the crocodile, not even Ahwere. But his fingers now touched gouges which had not been in the railing when the yacht first sailed back from the Temple of Tatenen. It had not been wind that flung Merib to his death—nor had it been chance.

Shay strode forward, bawling his orders. Still standing, Samlor raised the crystal to his forehead again and became all life in the cosmos as color drained from the sky above the River Napata. There was nothing more dangerous near the yacht than the gnats which twilight drew from the reed beds anywhere. He would continue checking all the way to the capital.

If the gods sent another messenger, Samlor would blast it with enough violence to pay in a small way for what had happened to Merib.

"We'll sail through the night," Samlor said as he seated himself again beside Ahwere. "It'll be safe, and we'll—"

The worm came over the starboard rail behind Ahwere and snatched her into the water before she had time to scream. Samlor screamed instead.

"Oh, she's jumped, she's jumped!" he heard the nurse-maid crying as he commanded the cosmos through the book. "Oh, the grief of her poor darling son!"

All the forces in the cosmos balanced on a point, the Book of Tatenen and the mind of Samlor hil Samt. The currents that rolled Ahwere's body, the gurgle of air still trapped in her lungs—the minuscule scrape of sediment across her sightless eyes—all were his to know and to change.

The worm that seized her with its blue-glowing snout did not exist in the present cosmos.

Ahwere flashed back onto her couch with a slap of sodden garments. Only the dim light and confusion kept her reappearance from throwing the excited crewmen into blind panic.

She stirred, and for a moment Samlor thought he had been mistaken. He embraced Ahwere while the nurse babbled and Shay gave orders to bring the vessel around to where he thought someone was still in the water.

Ahwere's eyes blazed blue when she opened them. Samlor's mouth drew back in a rictus of horror—and hope that still denied reality.

"Rejoice, my husband, my only love," said Ahwere's body. "Soon the cosmos will be in balance again."

"Who's overboard?" Shay demanded. "What's happened?"

A late-returning marsh hawk began to screech in dismal satisfaction.

CHAPTER 22

"SHE DIDN'T KILL herself," Samlor muttered. He had washed his hands a score of times since Ahwere's interment, but his mind told him his skin still was scented with the camphor and incense of her embalming. "They sent the worm to take her. The gods."

"Well," said Shay uncomfortably, "We'll be back soon. The palace should be in sight any time now."

Samlor looked down at the sun-bronzed water curling past their hull. "But I'd *killed* it. Though I suppose it was never alive."

"So it couldn't be killed," said the bosun, making conversation because his master demanded conversation to take his mind off the past—and the future. "Well, the gods set all our terms of life, sir. Yourselves as well as the like of—" he nodded forward "—me 'n the boys."

"Not *me*!" Samlor said, anger breaking through his despair like lightning in storm clouds. "They can't harm me—not since I drank the Spell of Safety."

"Well, I'm sure your father'll be glad to have you safe, at least, sir," Shay said, flicking splinters from the rail with his horny thumb. "He ain't well, I'd heard."

"No, he's not well," agreed Samlor. The blood was draining from his face as he imagined greeting King Merneb in a few more minutes. "Father," he said in his mind, "your daughter is dead, and with her the grandson whom

183

you loved more than life itself. But don't worry: I, who carried them to their deaths, have returned."

"He'll want you to marry again," Shay was saying. "The daughter of one of the neighboring princes, I guess. Well, you may come to love her as much as you did your, well, the Princess Ahwere."

"I can't protect them," Samlor said, his eyes staring at water that they did not see. "I can't protect anyone but myself. A bolt of lightning, the collapse of a building—earthquake. Whoever I marry will die. Perhaps after we have children to take also."

"Well, sir," said the bosun with a strained chuckle. "I can't imagine things are so bad that the whole cosmos is turned to punish one man. Things don't work like that."

"Your highness!" called the lookout at the masthead. "The palace is in sight, and your father's on the wharf to greet us!"

"Go forward, bosun," Samlor ordered curtly. Shay bowed and obeyed.

The stern anchor, its wooden stock reeved through a hole bored in a large stone, hung from the rail opposite the steersman. Its line was bent around a deadeye and tied off. The coffin-hilted dagger which Samlor carried in this life as the other severed the lashings easily.

He sheathed the knife and lifted the anchor from its hooks. The stone felt light—as light as Ahwere the first time he carried her to their couch. He turned around twice so that anchorline wrapped him.

"Your highness!" cried the steersman in horror. "Shay! *Shay!*"

The book was a hard outline clamped against him by his sash. It promised him all the powers in the cosmos.

Except the power of ever again being happy.

Samlor lurched against the rail and went over. The entangling line bound his legs together like a fish's tail, and the stone anchor carried him down as inexorably as a sword stroke.

The last thing he saw was the face of the bosun, staring over the side at him. Shay was smiling.

And his eyes were glowing blue.

CHAPTER 23

THE ANCHOR DRAGGED Samlor head first toward the bottom, but he was standing upright in Nanefer's tomb. The dissonant realities made him flop to the stone floor on all fours.

He bounced to his feet again at once. His skin was aflame with shock and embarrassment. Khamwas swayed but had not fallen.

"You cannot take the book," whispered the ghost of Ahwere. "We have bought it with our lives, all our lives."

The ghost of the infant murmured softly against her.

"I have come for the book, Prince Nanefer," said Khamwas. He held out his hand slowly, though he did not step toward the mummified figure as yet. The tremor in Khamwas' voice assured Samlor that Khamwas too had shared Nanefer's triumph—and its aftermath.

"I would have said the same, Prince Khamwas," said the corpse in a voice like a leather bellows creaking. The withered hands crossed on his lap moved. First tentatively and then with increasing smoothness, they began to unwrap the parcel which lay beneath them.

Samlor was dusting his palms carefully on his tunic. His body had aches and strains in it that Nanefer would never have known in a full, royal, lifetime.

But it was Samlor's body, and he prayed he would never again wear another.

The corpse lifted the crystal from its silken cover. For a moment the Book of Tatenen was dimly outlined by flecks of color in its heart.

Nanefer's thin lips bent in a smile. Light flooded from it with the certainty of the sky brightening at sunrise. The tomb was flooded by it—white and as cold as frozen bone. Ahwere's sparkling ghost drifted or was driven back against a sidewall, so that nothing but bare floor separated the Napatan princes.

Nanefer waved a hand. Samlor's lamp, forgotten in the greater illumination, guttered out in what might have been a stray breeze down the length of the tunnel.

"Will you fight me with magic, Khamwas?" asked the corpse in a wheezingly jocular voice. "Or shall we play a game?"

"You are dead, Nanefer," said Khamwas. "You have no magic and no power to keep the book from me. But—" there was the least quaver in the voice which had been calmly steadfast "—I will play a game with you."

"Then let us play, my kinsman," said the corpse. "Since you have magic and I, who am dead, have none."

Nanefer crooked a blackened index finger toward one corner of the chamber. The table there was set with a crosshatched game board and two bowls of dried beans—black and white. Following the motion of the corpse's finger, the table slid just above the floor in an arc that ended with it resting before Nanefer's throne. The bowl of white beans faced Khamwas.

"I offer you the color of life, kinsman," said the corpse. "Savor it while you can."

Khamwas strode to the game board without glancing aside to see what the ghosts of Nanefer's family were doing. Samlor eyed them, ready to shout a warning if Ahwere attacked Khamwas' back . . . but the veils of blue light that were her figure moved only to pat the insubstantial form of Merib.

Khamwas placed a white bean at an intersection near the center of the board. Nanefer, moving with the assurance of an old man instead of an ancient corpse, set a black piece on an adjacent intersection.

Piece and piece, patterns began to fill the board. Beans clicked softly against the cross-hatched alabaster. None of the adults spoke, but the infant Merib began to whimper again.

The light blazing from the Book of Tatenen was as cold as that which the sun had thrown over the cratered emptiness where the book had been concealed.

Khamwas' face was masked by an expression of controlled emotion. The corpse set a piece and then, instead of withdrawing at once, picked up a quartet of white counters which his pieces had surrounded and captured. Khamwas placed another bean.

Samlor thought his companion was hunching to look shorter. Then he noticed that Khamwas' feet had sunk so that only his ankles showed above the solid concrete.

Nanefer set a counter and swept up more white beans.

The air in the tomb was so dry that sweat droplets sparkled only for a moment on Khamwas' forehead before they disappeared—to be replaced by more sweat. He placed a bean on the alabaster. Khamwas stood bolt upright, and his knees had sunk below the level of the floor.

Under the pitiless glare of the crystal, Samlor noticed a piece shade from white through a dusky gray, then gleam black. Nanefer reached forward with the counter that would close the circle on three more white beans isolated when the one changed color.

"Khamwas!" Samlor shouted. "He's cheating you. They're turning to black, your pieces!"

Khamwas' thighs were sinking into the ground as his opponent scooped up the captured pieces. "*Light*," Khamwas said in a choked voice. "Bring me my staff!"

Samlor plunged down the tunnel on all fours, as heedless of its constraint as a rabbit bolting from a fox. Khamwas was lifting another bean toward the alabaster. From his fixed expression, he seemed to be fighting the necessity of playing out the game to which he had agreed.

The sunlight at the tunnel's end was dim by comparison with the tomb chamber—but the sunlight was warm, and at the touch of it Samlor shuddered with memory of the bone-chilling blaze from the crystal.

Earth tones—brown and ochre and the ruddy sandstone cliffs—stood in welcome contrast to the white ground and primary colors of the tomb. The squall of distant irrigation wheels was an earthly sound and a suddenly blissful one.

Khamwas' staff lay across the tunnel entrance as they had left it. Samlor wondered whether Khamwas thought there was no longer a risk of them being entombed by sand—or whether he was willing to take that risk to keep from slipping into solid concrete first.

Didn't matter. Couldn't matter. Samlor grabbed the staff and twisted himself around in the tunnel. He heard Khamwas scream something from the tomb chamber, but he did not understand the words.

Partly because most of Samlor's mind froze in shocked appreciation of the crocodile filling the tunnel before him.

The beast was not as large as the monster which waddled aboard the yacht in his dreamlife as Nanefer, but it was as large as the stone corridor. The tips of its open jaws touched the floor and ceiling.

Its breath was foul and as cold as Death.

"*Will* you, by Heqt?" Samlor whispered as he drew his dagger again. He could wedge the jaws with the staff, and then the watered steel blade would carve the beast's palate and white gums like cheese—

Or the staff would shatter and the ragged teeth would crush Samlor's armbones as easily as they tore his flesh. But he could not forget the way Merib, his son in all but present reality, had catapulted into waiting jaws like these.

The crocodile dissolved into whorls of blue sparks. They reformed as the wraith of Ahwere, which swept up the tunnel toward the tomb chamber. The air was still and cold, and the ghost's wail was as bitter as the wind over high peaks.

Hunched over—unable to run on all fours because he carried the staff and dagger—Samlor scuttled toward the blazing white square of the tunnel's nether end. He couldn't hear his companion's voice, but the corpse's hacking laughter had the sound of breaking twigs.

"Kham—" Samlor cried as he burst into the chamber. Khamwas had sunk shoulder deep in the floor. He twisted his head despairingly toward the opening, but his arm was reaching up against his will to place another bean on the gameboard.

Samlor slapped the staff into Khamwas' lifted hand. Light from the Book of Tatenen seared through him, making the scarred flesh of the caravan master's fingers translucent so that the bones showed gray against pink encasement.

Ahwere glittered into a tigress and leaped at Samlor. He slashed with the dagger in a frenzy of despair and madness burned into him by the white glare.

Khamwas spoke a word. The stone chamber glowed green like the moss of a woodland at summer noon, when all the light is filtered by leaves above. The tigress disappeared. Ahwere's ghost was a woman weeping as she rocked the babe in her arms.

The crystal was dark. There was nothing white in the tomb except the pieces on the game board, each of which gleamed with the purity of fresh-cut walrus ivory.

Khamwas rose out of the ground as if the staff crosswise in his hand was lifting him. The glow it cast was so uniform that the staff almost disappeared in the perfection of what it created.

"The game is mine, Prince Nanefer," Khamwas said. He struck the board and table aside. The pieces spilled across the floor. All of the beans were white. "Give me the book."

Nanefer did not move or speak.

Khamwas swallowed. He lifted the staff higher, then reached out with his free hand and took the crystal.

Nothing changed, not even the tempo of Ahwere's sobbing.

"We will trouble you no more, great prince," said Khamwas as he backed with formal steps away from the seated corpse. Glancing aside to Samlor, he added, "Precede me. Quickly."

As Samlor scrambled down the tunnel, he heard Ahwere crying, "Our light is gone, our all is gone."

And he thought, though he could not be sure, that he heard Nanefer reply, "Do not grieve, my sister, my love. They will return."

CHAPTER 24

"BACK IN THE, you know," said Samlor as the sun glanced from the polished limestone walls of the outer courtyard of the Palace of Napata. "In the tomb. I thought I wouldn't ever get warm again.

"I suppose," he added, fluffing the sweat-soaked tunic away from his chest, "I'm glad I was wrong."

Khamwas turned, but the hooded cloak he was wearing still covered half his face. He tried to smile, but tension made his expression a frosty one when his intention was warm. "For the way you stood by me then, my friend," he said, "you'll never want for anything. Anything at all."

"I figured you knew what you were doing," Samlor said, looking away. It was easier to tell a half lie than the real truth, that he'd been afraid to think about what he was doing. He'd just plunged ahead on the course he'd set himself when there was time for calm reflection. "Anyway, I told you I'd help."

And that was purely the truth.

Almost no one except Samlor and Khamwas was in the courtyard. The royal levee closed in the hour before noon, and the peddlers who would later turn the courtyard into a fair were held off by the sun though there were no guards to stop them.

There were two guards at the copper-clad doors to the inner palace, but they were more concerned with finding shade in the recessed doorway than they were with loiterers. Samlor avoided staring at them, but he wondered what his companion's next move would be.

Khamwas' face reverted to stony calm. He was too lost in his own plans to care what Samlor had said—or even to have listened to it.

The cloak of a priestly mendicant covered Khamwas to the ankles. It must have been uncomfortable in this heat, but Khamwas noticed discomfort as little as a true religious ascetic would have done. His fingers toyed with the rim of a copper begging bowl which must itself have been hot enough to cook food.

The Book of Tatenen was bound to his bosom, the way Nanefer had carried it when he plunged over the yacht's rail.

A fuzzy glow appeared on Khamwas' shoulder. "If your enemy seeks you," it said clearly in Tjainufi's voice, "do not avoid him." The glow faded as simply as it had appeared.

The copper bowl rang softly as Khamwas tapped it with his fingertips. "*Now* we will see my brothers," he said.

This moment seemed to Samlor the same as any other in the half hour since they first entered the courtyard, but he was glad to be moving again.

The guards straightened as Khamwas and Samlor strode up to them. They carried long-bladed halberds and wore armor of silvered iron scales.

"Admit us," Samlor said as he had been instructed. He spoke with the assurance of authority—which made *him* feel that the guards were going to obey, though he couldn't imagine why. "We have business with the kings."

The guards were taken aback, bracing themselves as they would while being inspected by a superior officer, but their orders were clear. "Audience hours are over for the day, yokel," said the senior man. "Come back at dawn—or before, if you want a real chance of getting in."

"And no weapons," added the other guard, nodding toward Samlor's dagger.

Khamwas tapped his bowl. The doors and the guards' armor rang in sympathy. There were sharp clacking sounds from within the doorleaves as the locking bolts withdrew.

The doors opened inward, carrying the bellowing guards with them. Their body armor was stuck to the metal facing. As the men struggled, their halbards touched the copper also—and stuck as if welded.

Khamwas walked on without glancing to either side. Samlor followed with the caution of uncertainty as to just how long the guards would stay trapped.

Long enough, as it turned out. The doors swung themselves closed and bolted again.

There was another courtyard on the other side of the doors, smaller and shaded by a loggia surrounding it on three sides. A few servants glanced from their own affairs toward the intruders, but the fact that Khamwas and Samlor had come this far implied they were where they should be. None of the servants seemed to want to investigate the commotion beyond the gates.

Arched doorways to the left gave onto a formal audience chamber with frescoed walls and stone pillars cut to resemble shocks of reeds. Khamwas strode on past the empty hall, toward the door directly before them. His fingers drummed at the bowl. This door opened also with a squeal of its metal hinges.

The corridor beyond was high and lighted with clerestory windows. A servant—unarmed, but dressed and adorned in evidence of high rank—lolled in near somnolence on a stool. He lurched to his feet as the intruders approached.

"Who do you think—" he bleated.

"Don't make me hurt you," said Samlor, one finger on his dagger's buttcap.

Khamwas stroked his bowl. "Don't make us hurt you," rang the gold medallion on the servant's chest.

The man screamed and ran down the corridor. Before he ducked into a side door, his arm jerked and flung away the medallion with its broken chain.

A few heads, mostly female, popped out of other doors to see what was going on, but no one else tried to halt Samlor and Khamwas as they strode, side by side, to the gold-plated door at the end.

Samlor was no longer surprised when this door admitted them as the others had done.

There were three men at the table within, all of them in their thirties. The insignia of rank they had put aside—gold-shot shoulder capes and crowns whose bands bore central emeralds carven into reed bracts—left no doubt as to who they were.

"Who's this priest?" one of them demanded with birdlike glances toward his fellows. "Why's he here?"

The door closed behind the intruders, shutting off the growing babble of voices in the corridor.

There were cups on the table, and on the stand beside it was a wine jug with a dipper hanging from its rim. There were no servants present, not even a girl to fill the cups. Khamwas had tramped straight into a private meeting of the joint rulers of Napata.

"Do you recognize me?" he asked in a tone that would have been coquettish in a woman. It was the first time Samlor's companion had spoken since they confronted the guards in the outer court.

"What do you think you're doing, you two?" asked the heavy-set man at the center of the table in a gravelly voice. Formal headgear would have concealed the fact that he was already nearly bald.

Khamwas stroked his begging bowl. The heavy-set man's cup said, "Once there were four brothers—Osorkon, Patjenfi—" all three of the seated men jumped when the cup spoke in plangent tones, then jumped again as their names rolled from its golden tonguelessness "—Pentweret, and Khamwas . . . and Khamwas, who was the eldest, should have reigned when their father died."

While the room still rang with the cup's last word, the crown lying on the table beside the rabbit-featured man who'd first spoken took up the story by saying, "But the other brothers seized Khamwas while he was in the desert searching for inscriptions on ancient monuments. They sold him as a slave to a caravan trading with Ranke—and they stained his cloak with blood to prove to their father that a lion had killed Khamwas."

The man in the center of the table was motionless, but he gripped his mug fiercely enough to blotch his knuckles with strain. The rabbit-featured fellow was staring at his crown.

His mouth opened and shut with little plopping sounds, but he did not speak.

The dagger which the third man had drawn spoke instead. It said, "But the brothers forgot that a slave who has learned certain arts from his studies can find his way to freedom quickly."

The man holding the dagger dropped it onto the table. He flapped his hand through the air as if it had been burned.

All together the mug, crown and dagger chorused, "Khamwas could not return home until he had gained further knowledge, greater powers. But nothing was more certain than that someday he *would* return to confront his brothers—"

Alone, the mug added, "Osorkon."

"Patjenfi," said the crown.

"Pentweret," the dagger concluded.

Khamwas threw back the hood of his cloak.

"We wronged you, my brother," said Osorkon at the center of the table. He was forcing the words through a block of emotions more varied than Samlor could identify.

"Not we, not *me*," babbled Patjenfi, glancing nervously from Khamwas to the brothers with him at the table. "I said—"

"*Fool*," said his crown as Khamwas touched the bowl. Patjenfi fell silent.

"We wronged you," Osorkon repeated. "And it may be that we wronged our father. He would rather—" the bitterness was clear in his rasping voice "—anything in the world than that he lose *you*, my brother. But—"

Osorkon met Khamwas' eyes with a regal glare of his own. "But much as I regret our action, it was necessary. The country would not have survived your kingship, Khamwas."

"After your wife died," said Pentweret, speaking for the first time since Khamwas entered the room, "you didn't care for anything except your stones. Buildings ruined for a thousand *years*. What would have happened to Napata if its king wandered in the desert every day and took no account of the business of state?"

Samlor kept his face emotionless as he looked toward his

companion. Khamwas wore a cool smile which could indicate amusement, or approval—or nothing at all.

"And my children?" asked Khamwas softly. "Didn't I care for them?"

"I misspoke," said Pentweret. "Of course, of course."

"Nobody doubts *that*," insisted Osorkon. "But that wouldn't have kept Napata from fragmenting into as many petty kingdoms as there're villages along the river. And you wouldn't have *cared*. You stopped caring when your wife died!"

"Our father couldn't see that," said Patjenfi, no longer trying to distance himself from his fellows. "Wouldn't see it, I suppose. So what were we to do?" The whine in his voice didn't detract from the sincerity of the question, though it gave it an ugly cast.

"What of my children, then, brothers?" Khamwas said, as gently as a breeze touching the edge of the headsman's axe.

Osorkon blinked. "Pemu and Serpot?" he said. "Oh, they're fine."

"My own are of an age with them," added Patjenfi, "so they're fostered in my apartments. Why—" a look of horror drew across his rabbity visage. "You didn't think we'd have hurt *them*, did you?"

"If you'll give me leave to go to the door," said Pentweret, "I'll summon them. They can be here in a few minutes at most."

Khamwas nodded. His youngest brother slipped past them to the door—which opened to a thrumming of Khamwas' fingers on the bowl. Samlor watched as the man spoke urgently through the opening. Pentweret had been the one to draw a weapon at the first intrusion, and he was wise enough to ask before stepping toward the door.

That meant his instincts were enough like Samlor's that he could be a real problem.

Pentweret seated himself again. He had left the door ajar. Noise from the corridor became a backdrop as omnipresent as the hiss of a waterfall. The crowding servants were nervous, but they were too interested in events to leave unordered.

The noise grew louder until it was cut by a voice of authority. "Your highnesses?" called someone in pear-shaped tones. "The prince and princess are here, as you commanded."

Khamwas turned and snatched the door open with his hand. Samlor glanced from side to side, trying to cover the seated kings as well as whatever waited in the hall. A functionary with gold ornaments, a spotless tunic, and enough fat to prove he did nothing strenuous for a living, waited with a child to either side of him.

Khamwas dropped his bowl with a clang echoed by every metal object in the room and corridor. He knelt and held out his arms to the children.

Their faces blanked. They didn't move.

"Pemu!" Khamwas said. "Serpot! I'm your *father*. I'm Khamwas."

The boy looked to be nine, the girl perhaps seven—the age of Star—though both children had the coppery complexions and straight hair of their father. For a moment they poised, unwilling to trust the news that they weren't orphans after all, living on their cousins' sufferance. Then they ran to the waiting arms, the boy first, sobbing and crying, "Daddy!"

The seated kings looked at one another. Samlor wondered if he ought to clear his knife, but the others were uncomfortable rather than hostile. Osorkon was perspiring freely. He hadn't moved from his chair, but tension was working his muscles hard.

Khamwas turned and stood, holding a child by either hand. His foot thrust out behind him to slam the door closed.

The sound of the door thumping against its jamb—and the fact that it had been closed physically—relaxed the atmosphere within the chamber. Patjenfi looked toward Osorkon and said peevishly, "Well, does that mean he'll be joining us?"

"Don't act like a greater fool than the gods made you," Pentweret snapped from across the table. "If he comes to us this way—" his eyes flicked toward Khamwas and were forced back by conscious effort of will "—he comes as our king."

The only sound in the room was the murmuring of the children as they hugged themselves closer to Khamwas' coarse robe. The three seated men held their breath while they waited for their brother to speak.

Khamwas fluffed his daughter's hair. His fingers paused briefly at the comb of gold filigree at Serpot's temple, then dropped back to her upraised palm. "You saved your lives," he said calmly, "by the way you cared for these while I was—gone."

Samlor could see that Pemu and Serpot didn't understand what was happening, but the tenseness of the situation was clear enough to silence them. Pemu braced himself, threw his chest out toward his uncles and tried to look as much a man as his age permitted.

"And you saved your throne, my brothers," Khamwas continued, "by the way you've ruled Napata since our father died. Together and for the country's good, as you claimed when you sold me into slavery. You've done well. I'm sure you'll continue to do so."

Pentweret's hands began to tremble as his lips stammered through the prayer which his mind had silently rehearsed. Patjenfi tried to jump up, babbling thankfulness, but his legs caught between his chair and the table. Osorkon stared at him disdainfully, until the rabbit-faced man subsided.

"How can you say that," asked Osorkon slowly, "after the way we treated you six years ago?"

Khamwas smiled. "Because you were correct, my brother. I would have been a disastrous king—but I would have demanded my rights as eldest son, because then I would have all the resources of Napata to aid me in my search."

"We never knew just what it was you were looking for," said Pentweret, being as careful as he could to avoid a negative connotation. "We should have tried harder to understand. . . ."

His eyes begged Khamwas for understanding.

"I was looking for the source of all power," Khamwas

replied with a smile that made sense only to Samlor, who had also been Nanefer in another age. "I found it at last."

Khamwas touched the bulge over his heart where the crystal book lay bound, but before he resumed speaking, he gripped Pemu's hand. "I also found that the only power I really wanted, the power of bringing the dead to life . . . is beyond the ability even of the gods."

Again there was silence.

"Well," said Patjenfi at last, "you'll have to live somewhere, if you're back. I think—"

"You'll move into my apartments here in the palace at once," Osorkon interrupted. "I'll leave my servants in place until you can arrange matters to your own satisfaction, elder brother."

"I'll send over clothing from my suite," added Pentweret. "It will fit you, I think." He glanced at the massive Osorkon and grinned coolly. "Again, until you make other arrangements."

"The children will need their things, too," said Patjenfi with a frown. "I do hope that—" He paused, pursing his lips, and finally continued, "Well, if you want to separate them, of course, that's your right, whatever you want. But they've grown up with my three, haven't you, darlings?"

Serpot nodded determinedly. Pemu, less convinced of the question's simplicity, looked from his uncle to his father—who was smiling—and nodded agreement himself.

Khamwas leaned down, kissed each child on his forehead, and said, "Go back and get your things together, darlings," he said as he hugged them. "My brothers and I have one more thing to discuss."

The children went out into the corridor. Before the door closed behind them, Samlor heard Pemu saying in a clear, princely voice, "Take us back to our rooms, Tery. We'll be—"

"One more piece of business," Khamwas paraphrased. As he eyed his brothers, his expression reverted to the icy hardness with which he had first entered the inner palace. Samlor thought of his dagger and thought about the three seated men . . . and wondered what was about to happen.

"Six years ago, my brothers," said Khamwas, "one of

you—let's pretend that I don't remember who—said that if I were killed instead of being sold into slavery, I wouldn't come back later to make trouble."

Samlor now understood the look and the tone.

Patjenfi looked down at his hands, making attempts to smile that each time lapsed into terror. Osorkon met Khamwas' eyes as stolidly as a mirror, but sweat glittered on his high forehead.

Pentweret was looking up also. His eyes were blank and the angle of his chin suggested that he was offering his throat to a slaughterer's blade. His larynx bobbled as he tried to swallow, and bobbled again.

"You didn't take that advice," Khamwas continued, "and perhaps you think you made a mistake."

There had been a tone of playful banter, cat and mouse rather than cat and kitten, in Khamwas' voice. Even that false humor dropped away as he continued, "Don't be certain that I wouldn't have returned, my brothers. I was a scholar even then, though I hadn't a fraction of the powers I have now."

He paused before he concluded, "Believe me, you would be even less pleased to see me now if you had chosen murder."

"Then we can all rejoice to be the men we are," said Osorkon calmly. He stood up and reached across the table to clasp the hand which Khamwas slowly extended to him.

"Welcome home, my brother," Osorkon said. "It's good to have you with us again."

CHAPTER 25

THE WALL OF the terraced garden overlooked the river, but from inside even the enclosure was screened by lush greenery. Expert tending preserved the appearance of untrammeled nature without the dankness and the impossible tangles which "natural" implied in reality.

A fountain played in the near distance, noticeable for its babble and the sheen of mist in the air beyond a border of straight-stemmed bushes with flowers of glowing magenta.

Broad-leafed vines—gourds rather than grapes—had been trained to cover the arbor in which Samlor sat with Khamwas, watching the flock of royal children playing a game with bats and a feather-filled ball on the lawn. Servants stood nearby with refreshments and in case of accident, but the arbor's narrow doorway and curved walls gave it the privacy of a camera obscura.

"I can't offer you more than you've earned already, Samlor," Khamwas said. Both men found it easier to speak when their eyes were on the squealing children than they did while searching each other's expressions. "You'll leave here a rich man—"

"I do all right," Samlor interrupted. "I never doubted you'd keep our bargain—and I've never asked anybody for more 'n that."

Khamwas laid two fingers on Samlor's knee and brought the other man's eyes to meet his.

"You have helped me gain the cosmos," Khamwas said softly. He patted the crystal book beneath his sash, using the same touch with which he had demanded Samlor's attention. "To an extent, I'm wondering what I'll do with the power now that it's mine . . . but don't ever doubt that the power is at your service, or that you've *earned* that service."

"If I need your help, I know it's here," said Samlor as he turned his head again. "You know . . . ," he added.

On the grassy area, Pemu made a goal amid great squealing from the older children.

"You know, it could be that I'd want Star to have a place she could be that wasn't Cirdon. That's a lot—"

"Of course," interrupted Khamwas.

"That's a lot to ask," Samlor repeated sharply. "And it's going to be more as she gets older, the way she, you know, learns things."

"Yes, I do know," Khamwas agreed with a smile. He plucked one of the gourds hanging beside him and turned it in his hands, letting the yellow and green stripes shine alternately in a spike of sunlight through the leaves massed above. "I would be honored."

"You were going to say," remarked Samlor to change the subject—and not to change it— "that you wanted something from me."

"Yes, I was," Khamwas agreed drily. "I was going to ask if you'd stay here with me for a little while, perhaps a month."

"You don't trust your brothers?" Samlor said with mild surprise. He twisted a gourd from its cap also. The rind felt waxy and cool in his hands, artificial rather than alive.

"I *do* trust them," Khamwas corrected, smiling. "And I don't—how shall I say it, fear for my life. But I'd like there to be one person who is—" he looked away, looked back, and smiled again "—my friend, in the next few weeks while I set up my household."

"You can order wax statues to row," said Samlor, picking up a memory the two of them shared from another age. "But you can't tell them how to do it."

"Exactly."

Samlor laughed. "People worry about the gold plate in the strongroom, but they forget about the eggs in the pantry till there's nothing for supper," he said. "Sure, I'll hang around for a while and help you get organized. Anyway, I haven't seen much of your city here."

"I need to get reacquainted myself," Khamwas said. "We'll go out together in the morning."

He rubbed the hidden book with the knuckle of the thumb hooked over the gourd. "It—" he began, then started over with, "We risked much, you and I, to win the book. But despite the difficulties, the dangers, I must admit it was easier than I had expected."

"Don't call your life blessed," said Tjainufi sourly, "until it has ended."

But the men's attention was absorbed by the children, Serpot running toward the arbor in a grass-stained tunic shouting, "Daddy! Daddy! We won!"

CHAPTER 26

"Is THE DISH to your taste, your highness?" said the priest, adding with a nod to Samlor, "Excellency?"

Samlor mumbled agreement while Khamwas continued to peer with rapt attention at the scene in the temple forecourt beneath them.

The bowl of mixed fruit slices had been chilled somehow. At least it felt cool after a day of ambling through Napata with a minimal entourage—Khamwas, Samlor, and the two footmen whom Khamwas' borrowed major domo absolutely insisted must accompany the prince. The inner loggia of the Temple of Tatenen was a good place to rest and view the crowd of late-afternoon customers visiting the expensive shops in the court below.

One thing that Samlor had already decided about Napata was that the religious institutions here continued to do as well as they had in the time of Prince Nanefer. The silver spoon with which he ate his fruit was molded into delicate vine arabesques more estimable than even the metal itself.

"Samlor," Khamwas whispered urgenty. "Do you see her? There, going—"

He pointed. The priest who was acting as personal servant to the temple's guests craned his neck to follow the gesture but fell back two steps in embarrassment when he realized what he was doing.

Samlor leaned against the thick stone rail of the loggia and frowned in concentration at the bustle in the forecourt. A woman wearing a cape and headdress of shimmering red silk had just disappeared into one of the shops, accompanied by several maids. A pair of staff-bearing footmen remained outside, suggesting that they would use force if necessary to prevent their mistress from being jostled within.

"Somebody you know?" Samlor asked, cautious because he could sense Khamwas' agitation. He hadn't seen the woman's face, nor would it have meant anything to him if he had. But his companion had a lifetime of history in Napata, not a few weeks in the desert and two days in the capital. . . .

"I *must* learn who she is," Khamwas said, still whispering. He stared at the foreshortened doorway across the court as if intensity would give him clear vision of what went on inside. One of his hands clasped the rail while the other squeezed Samlor's knee hard enough to be disconcerting.

The whole situation was disconcerting.

"Well," said Samlor, shifting as he set down his bowl; his knee straightened, as if by accident, and flexed out of Khamwas' grip. "I'll go down and see what I can find out." He looked at his companion, waiting for a response to the question his tone had implied.

"Yes . . . ," Khamwas said, focused on the doorway. He turned sharply and added, "But you mustn't disturb her."

Samlor nodded and said with heavy irony, "Oh, you can trust me to handle the business with all the subtlety you would bring to it yourself."

A cloud softened Khamwas' intense features and he stared at the hand which had clasped Samlor so harshly. "I . . . ," he said, looking up again as Samlor rose and shrugged his garments into place. "I'm sorry, my friend. She's very important to me in some way. I'm sure."

"No problem," Samlor grunted as he walked past the priest and lesser servants to the stairs within the temple.

No reason to imagine that it was a problem, and a dead

certainty that Khamwas and the Book of Tatenen could handle any difficulty that arose.

But Samlor kept remembering a grinning crocodile.

The forecourt was busy, though from the height of the loggia it was obvious that there was more empty pavement than there were people. From the pavement itself, nothing but moving walls of people were visible.

Shrugging again—the brocade collar of his new tunic chafed him, though the fabric was soft enough—Samlor strode across the area. As he neared the far side of the court, his eye caught a flash of scarlet: not the woman but her tall headdress, leaving the shop and preparing to enter another one. He started after her, then thought again and stepped into the shop his quarry had just quitted.

The maid who waited while the shopowner wrapped a purchase was dressed even more strikingly than her mistress. Her skirt was of pleated linen, cut to beneath her navel in front but rising almost to shoulderblade level in back. Instead of an ordinary blouse or jacket, she wore the skin of a spotted cat pinned to bare her left shoulder.

The head hung over her right breast. The beast's eyes had been replaced by topazes, and the maid's own irises were of the same tawny lambency.

"The cat won't bite," the woman said drily to Samlor.

He blinked, realized that he had paused with his hand resting on the doorjamb—and then realized that his mouth was open.

"Yes, sir, may I help you?" asked the shopman with a tinge of concern underlying his professional brightness. He was folding the second of a pair of carnelian earrings, elephants astride the globe of the cosmos, into a square of velvet.

"Ah, I—" Samlor said. "Ah, my business is with the lady."

"Is it indeed?" said the woman, giving him a look of appraisal as cool as that of a cook pricing fowls in the market.

"The, ah, the lady who was here a moment ago, in red," he plowed on. "I believe you may know her?"

"Know my mistress?" said the woman. When she smiled, her mouth opened as wide as the cat's. "Yes, I should say I do."

The shopman was listening to his customers in obvious interest. Samlor gave him a look freighted with the frustration he could not let loose on the woman. The man jumped, then trotted to the back of the shop muttering that he needed better ribbon.

Samlor relaxed. The maid was playing a game, flirting at second-hand as it were, and there was no harm in that. He smiled and said, "Milady, a friend of mine—a high-placed friend of mine—noticed your mistress and was curious about who she is. Rather than make a public production of it, he asked me to check quietly."

That was pretty close to the truth, and it conveyed the threat without stating it. Coquetry was very well and good, but this amber-eyed woman had to know where the real power in the discussion lay.

"I'm sure my mistress Tabubu would thank your friend—" her tone made the word 'master' and a slur because Samlor had not used it "—for his solicitude, if he chose to present himself in person," said the maid. "A lady of her position isn't in need of help from others, however highly placed, of course."

She shifted her stance. The false cat eyes winked from her breast.

Samlor raised an eyebrow and one corner of his mouth.

"She is here to make offerings for her father on the seventh anniversary of his death," the maid continued, bowing to the silent goad. "He was the prophet of the god Mnevis.

"I would have thought your highly-placed master would know Tabubu," she added with a tart voice and a flounce of the cat's head. "But—" she smiled again "—her house is in Ankhtawi, across the river, and we don't leave it very often."

"You've been very understanding," said Samlor—an understatement if ever he had made one. "I appreciate it. Perhaps we'll have the opportunity to speak again."

The woman stretched her shoulders back so that her chest arched and the cat slid against her. "And you?" she asked. "Do you have a name, or shall I call you 'Boy'?"

Samlor grinned back, aware of the game she was playing and too controlled to lose at it. "I'm Samlor hil Samt," he said. "But I answer to any name that seems appropriate."

He turned and strode out of the shop, hearing the owner bleat something inconsequential.

The woman called, "My name is Pre," but the words did not bring Samlor back into the shop. He had information to pass on to Khamwas, whose anxious face peered from the loggia opposite.

Besides, Samlor had a nagging fear that if he continued talking to Pre, he would succumb to his growing desire to throw her down on the floor and screw the hell out of her.

"Well, what have you learned?" Khamwas demanded, his discourtesy redeemed only by his obvious agitation. "She'd already left the shop when you went in, you know?"

"Sure, I know," said Samlor, frowning. "Look, you can hire people to snap at. All right?"

Khamwas' left hand touched his sash. His thumb hooked beneath it, toward the Book of Tatenen—but he snatched his hand back as if it burnt, an instant before Samlor would have buried the watered steel blade in his chest, determining for good and all what protection the book afforded.

"My . . . ," said Khamwas, pale with amazement. He reached out and clasped Samlor's hand, drawing him willingly back into his chair by the rail. "Samlor, I don't know why I'm so jumpy. Please forgive me."

The sincerity could not be doubted. "I'm not my best either," said Samlor, apologizing for what he had been ready to do.

"But what *about* her, the woman?" Khamwas went on eagerly. Already he had resumed his appraisal of the crowd below. "There, she's still here!"

"Her name's Tabubu," Samlor reported.

He kept expecting Tjainufi to make a comment, but the

little manikin wasn't on Khamwas' shoulder. Hadn't been
since . . . the day before, in the garden, he thought.

"She's the daughter of the Prophet of Mnevis, and she's
here to make offerings on the anniversary of his death."

"Good, good," said Khamwas, though his enthusiasm
did not cause him to look around at his companion. "That
means she's the head of her household and able to make
decisions for herself."

Samlor was watching the crowd also. The scarlet garments were easy to spot. Now the woman was leaving a
booth selling floral sprays to be laid at the feet of the statues
of gods in memory. She didn't hold the caravan master's
eyes, though. His concentration was on the maid beside her,
as lithe as the cat whose skin she wore.

"Now . . . ," said Khamwas. "I want you to approach
her. Tell her that I'll give her ten gold pieces to spend an
hour with me. Only an hour, and no one will ever know
about it."

Samlor blinked as if Khamwas had just taken his clothes
off and begun to dance on the railing.

"Well?" Khamwas prompted, glancing at his companion
with an incipient scowl.

"Ah," said Samlor. "Ah, Khamwas, I'm not—I wasn't
born here, so I wouldn't know. But this Tabubu—friend, she
doesn't seem to be the kind of woman you'd, you know,
offer money to. Not even her servants. . . ."

He didn't realize at once that he had let his voice trail off.
He was too engrossed in his imagination.

"Yes, yes of course," agreed Khamwas. "Of course. I
told you, I'm not feeling myself today."

He paused, cleared his throat and went on. "She owns
property, so she'll have a lawsuit with a neighbor over
boundaries or irrigation rights. Tell her I'll have it settled in
her favor."

"Ah?"

"Or perhaps she has a complaint over her tax assessment." Khamwas burbled on, oblivious of the wondering
look on his companion's face. "There's nothing simpler. All
she has to do is tell me what the problem is and it's solved.
For just an hour with her."

He beamed.

Samlor shrugged as he got up again. "Well," he said—aloud but speaking to his own doubts, "you're the local. I'll see what I can do."

He might have been more hesitant about his mission were he not looking forward to talking again with Pre. If Khamwas were successful, well—Samlor was going to have an hour to fill also, wasn't he?

CHAPTER 27

PRE CARRIED THE velvet parcel of earrings, but lesser members of the retinue bore the sprays of flowers which would be thrown onto the altar. As they withered, their color and vibrancy would infuse the spirit on whose behalf they were offered.

Tabubu strolled free as a flame, pausing now to examine fabrics racked in an open-fronted shop. Her staff-bearers watched the crowd with their mistress in the corner of their eyes—ready to conform to her movements, protecting her without blundering into her path.

Good men, and they had more than a casual awareness of Samlor hil Samt.

At closer look, Samlor found Tabubu imposing, but the feeling she aroused in him was awe similar to that he felt beneath the gigantic reliefs of the river temple. The red silk of her headdress was diaphanous. Through it he could see that her hair was dressed in multiple braids, each banded at intervals with broad gold rings. Tabubu's bracelets bore complex designs in coral, carnelian and turquoise, all mounted in heavy gold.

The material of her dress was only slightly less transparent than her headgear, and the straps plunged to waist level in front. The pendant dangling across the cleft between her breasts was of metal filigree, gold and electrum—the alloy

210

of gold and silver. It seemed to depict a crocodile swallowing the ball of the world.

Tabubu's eyes glanced across Samlor like sunlight from a glacier. The pendant, rather than the two husky attendants, changed his intention of speaking directly to her. Instead, he approached Pre. She had been watching him with amusement from the moment the caravan master reappeared in the forecourt.

"My friend," said Samlor carefully, using the bustle around them as an active form of privacy, "believes he can be of service to your mistress. It may be that she has a lawsuit that he can have settled to her advantage. Or—"

Pre's eyes had grown as hard as the jewels glaring from the cat on her bosom. "What would your master," she asked, "expect in exchange for these services? If he is merely a generous man, let him help those who have need of it."

"He's a very discreet man," said Samlor, aware that his own desire for discretion had put the situation in the maid's hands. "As discreet as he is powerful."

He could feel Khamwas staring at his back, demanding some indication of success. Damn him, he could handle his own affairs if he was in such a hurry! Where did he get the notion that Samlor was a pimp?

The spotted cat, smaller than an adult leopard, rose and fell with the breasts it covered.

"He would spend an hour with your mistress," Samlor plowed on, proceeding with what he had started, "in the most complete secre—"

"What!" Pre cried, bringing stares from all directions. "Why doesn't he just offer money, then? Does he think my mistress is a whore?"

Samlor trembled. All his emotions were turned to lust for the splendid woman whose harangue was making a public fool of him. He didn't understand it, but he *never* understood much when he was thinking with his dick.

"You there," called Tabubu imperiously. "Samlor. Come here."

Feeling as though he were encased in crystal, Samlor obeyed the scarlet-garbed woman. He remembered that he

had intended to speak with her before, but he could not
imagine how he had presumed so far. Her voice was
contralto, and it reverberated as if it were coming from a hot
furnace.

"If Prince Khamwas has something to tell me," said
Tabubu, "then he can visit me at my home tomorrow."

She was tall to begin with, and the red silk of her
headdress waved above her like the plume of a volcano.
Samlor faced the woman as he had faced death many times
before.

And not even Tabubu's dominating presence could quell
his desire for her maid Pre.

"He should remember," Tabubu added, "that I am a
priest's daughter and not a common prostitute. Not common
at all."

She turned away with a flash of the pendant swinging
between her breasts. The staff bearers moved to block
Samlor if he tried to follow their mistress toward the inner
court of the temple, reserved for religious purposes.

Samlor didn't notice them. For a moment he stood
puzzled, though he knew that Khamwas would begrudge
him every instant until he had reported.

Most people in Napata didn't even realize that Khamwas
was alive, much less that he was accompanied—served, if
you would—by a Cirdonian named Samlor hil Samt.
Tabubu's knowledge was as striking as the woman herself.
It was something for Khamwas to think about before he
decided what he should do next.

As Samlor made his way back across the court, he
thought of Pre clasping her arms around his shoulders and
crossing her legs behind his buttocks as he thrust within her.

CHAPTER 28

THE STATE BARGE was too reminiscent of Nanefer's yacht for Samlor to find the river crossing pleasant, but Khamwas was so abstracted that he did not appear to recall the disastrous journey of his dream.

"Your highness," said the desperately fat, desperately perturbed major domo who had come from Osorkon with the apartment. "There's still time to reconsider, and I can only pray that you will. It simply isn't fitting for a member of the royal house to visit a commoner at home."

Khamwas continued to stare over the bow toward the approaching pier. He said nothing.

"Well, she's a priest's daughter," said Samlor, speaking because the gurgle of water made him jumpy and because he was trying to convince himself that what they were doing was reasonable. "A prophet's, her maid says."

His voice didn't silence the water bulging around the bow, either.

"A commoner," said the major domo flatly.

Pemu and Serpot had woven their father a chaplet of flowers and presented him with it as he boarded the barge. Khamwas' fingers touched the braided stems absently, then stripped the chaplet off and dropped it over the side. The petals had already begun to wilt in the sun.

The major domo sighed and pressed his lips together in an expression of pudgy disapproval.

Ankhtawi, the suburb across the Napata River from the capital, was not heavily populated, but the bank was divided among mansions whose grounds were more extensive than would have been possible on the east side. The barge had struck across the river in a slant that used the current to bring them downstream in the direction which the servants believed Tabubu's house lay. For some minutes the vessel had been coasting past landing stages of greater or lesser ostentation while servants whispered doubtfully among themselves.

The doubt was over. Pre stood in the midst of a group of gorgeously-attired retainers on the nearing dock. Today her breasts were covered by the skin either of a large monitor lizard or of a small crocodile.

"Welcome, Prince Khamwas," she called as crewmen scurried around their oblivious master as they carried out the business of docking. "My mistress Tabubu awaits you."

The major domo was hopping from one foot to the other, afraid that the operation would be marred by curses or a crunch of wood on stone—and horrified that it was taking place at all.

"And welcome also to our entertainment, Samlor hil Samt," Pre went on. Her smile was as wicked as Samlor's thoughts.

The three-rung ladder hooked over the dockside for the guests to ascend was of ebony carved with serpentine patterns and gusseted at the joints with gold. Khamwas climbed it with the clumsy deliberation of a sleepwalker. His fumbling delay forced Samlor to suppress an urge to hurl his friend and companion aside into the water.

He was preventing Samlor from standing again beside Pre.

The major domo and the five lesser servants whom that worthy considered the minimum entourage (since the visit *had* to occur) followed, but Pre left them for the servants of her retinue. The maid strolled through the archway into the mansion's walled garden with Khamwas to one side and Samlor on the other.

Khamwas walked with the fixity of a coursing gazehound, but Pre's presence drew Samlor like an arm around his waist. He wanted to touch her, but he did not dare as yet.

The false amber eyes of what was surely a crocodile grinned as the head wobbled with Pre's breast.

The garden between the house and the river was more formal than that of the royal palace. Four narrow reflecting pools reached like sunrays toward the building, giving different aspects of the pillared facade to those on the central walk. Lilies with broad, blue flowers floated in the water, but at certain angles the distorted reflections of the pillars seemed to engulf the plants.

There were birds, hopping among the mandrakes, oleanders and chrysanthemums, but they rarely chirped.

Beside the house and to the right of the paved walk, another pool was almost hidden by a screen of powder-leafed shrubs—wormwood, closely planted against a bronze fence with inward hooks. There was no sound from the water, but the rank odor warned Samlor of what he would see when he peered over the shrubbery.

A crocodile, its head raised by the haunches of another of the reptiles, stared back at him. The nictitating membrane winked sideways across its eye, occluding but not hiding the slitted amber orb.

Samlor's fingers twitched toward the dagger in his belt; but Pre was striding on, and he followed.

The double doors into the house were of louvered wood, broad and high. They sprang inward as the procession approached, causing Samlor's heart to skip momentarily with a different animal emotion . . . but they were moved by another pair of servants in scarlet livery. Only instinct had suggested otherwise.

Tabubu stood in the doorway. The hall behind her was double height, but a broad staircase curved from the floor to a railed mezzanine on the visitor's right. Tabubu offered her hand to Khamwas and gestured toward the stairs. "Greetings, noble prince," she said. "I have prepared refreshments for you above."

Tabubu was again dressed in scarlet, but the only item of her costume which had not changed since the day before was her breast pendant. A headband and broad coils of gold shaped and confined her hair into a tapering cascade framing both sides of her face.

A round plaque of red glass fused onto gold fastened either tip of the hanging coiffure and lay on the upper curve of Tabubu's breasts, perfectly mirroring her bare, rouged nipples. The straps of her dress crossed her cleavage to support the high-waisted skirt.

The cloth flowed like wine when she moved and, like wine, was translucent.

"There is a table set for your men," said Pre, gesturing to the side room toward which liveried servants were conducting the major domo and his subordinates. He didn't look especially happy, but even he found no additional reason to protest at the circumstances.

Tabubu and Khamwas led the way up the stairs, the woman's fingertips resting on her visitor's hand in a fashion that managed to be both intimate and reserved. How intimate Samlor did not realize until Pre touched his hand and guided him behind Khamwas.

The stair treads were of onyx in an openwork frame of bronze, but they only hinted at the luxury of the floor above. The floor was blue and dazzling, strewn with crushed lapis lazuli and turquoise. Light from the windows opening onto the garden reflected from the stone in a cooling fire.

A circular table stood in the center of the room, between the rails over the entrance hall and the painted wicker screens from which came muted sounds of food preparation, dishes clinking and muttered commands. Braziers released perfumed smoke which the breeze from the wind-catching vents in the ceiling distributed through the air.

There were only two couches at the table, padded and sloped upward so that a diner could recline on his left elbow and eat in comfort.

"Rest here, honored guest," Pre murmured as she handed Samlor onto one of the couches. Tabubu was providing the same service for Khamwas, speaking so softly that only the warmth of her tone was audible across the table.

Servants came out from behind the screens. The two

women took cloths and silver bowls from them, then knelt beside the guests.

"Let me wipe away the stains of travel," said Pre. She dipped the cloth into her bowl of rose-scented water and gently swept it over Samlor's hands and forehead.

The awareness of her fingers burned Samlor through the cooling moisture. He reached toward the woman, but she intercepted him with the cloth and wiped his scarred fingers. "Why, we scarcely know each other," she chided with a lilt that ended in a giggle as she whisked away the cloth and herself.

Across the table, Khamwas tried to embrace Tabubu. She nestled closer to him, then twisted lithely away to hand the bowl and cloth back to a servant. One nipple had left a streak of rouge on Khamwas' cheek. "I told your man," she said mildly, "that I'm not a prostitute."

"I know that, I *know* that," Khamwas said, the words coming out in a series of gasps as though he had been punched in the stomach. "I'll marry you."

"Kh—" Samlor said, starting from his couch. No more of the word came out because Pre seated herself on the cushion so that her hips nestled against the angle of his groin.

"You must be thirsty," she said as she held a cup of wine to Samlor.

He shivered at the contact and touched his lips to the rim. Pre tilted the cup without spilling the rich, undiluted vintage, seemingly unaware of the way Samlor's arm encircled her beneath the crocodile skin and cupped her breast.

Tabubu slipped onto Khamwas' couch in a motion which mirrored that of her maid. Servants passed to and from the screened end of the room carrying dishes, but they were as silent as the breeze and almost as little noticed by the men at the table.

"You'd marry me indeed," said Tabubu with a mixture of scorn and caress in her tone. Carbuncles below the rim of her cup glinted as she held the wine to Khamwas. "And then what, pray tell? As soon as I marry, my father's estate reverts to the Temple of Mnevis and I have nothing."

"But what does that matter?" asked Khamwas dismissively. His arms encircled her, and he added as he nuzzled toward her breast, "I can take care of you. I have everything. . . ."

Tabubu moved only slightly, but her guest's lips touched her pendant instead of her nipple as he intended. "*You* can," she said. "*You* have, no doubt. Well, before you take your pleasure with me, noble prince, you'll have to make over all your property to me in a deed of maintenance."

For a moment her breast lay on Khamwas' cheek. Then, when his arms tightened and relaxed spasmodically, she was on her feet again and slipping away from him.

"Yes, yes, I'll sign the deed!" Khamwas cried hoarsely. He seemed to be trying to get up from the couch, but his legs were tangled. "We'll go to a scribe, we'll go today. But first—"

"More wine," said Pre, ordered Pre, as Samlor started to speak.

It was a heady vintage, but it did not affect him the way the woman's presence did. He tried to grope between her legs but found his hand caught in the many filmy layers of her skirt.

Pre urged her vulva against his touch, through the soft fabric. "Not in front of the mistress," she teased in a whisper. "At least—not until they. . . ."

Her voice dissolved into a giggle as she spun gracefully to her feet, holding the empty wine cup out to the servant waiting to exchange it for a full one.

Tabubu was standing, a statue limned in the fire of her garments. She clapped her hands sharply.

A servant scampered up the stairs, bobbing his head to his mistress.

"Show up the scribe and the witnesses," she ordered.

"Witnesses?" Samlor muttered. He shook his head, trying to clear it of the wine fumes. Pre swayed near the couch, smiling down at him. He started to rise, but it looked as though the maid were going to seat herself beside him again.

The servant returned. Beside him was a man who mounted the stairs with a sprightliness which belied the age which had reduced his hair to a white fringe. He carried a small writing desk folded and a wicker satchel with rolled paper, brushes, and an inkpot. From his chest on a necklace of turquoise hung a roller seal.

"You summoned a scribe?" he said, seating himself on the floor with brusque assurance. He unfolded his writing desk and set it over his crossed legs. "I am Aper. What is the document I am to draft?

Shuffling up the stairs more slowly, their faces set in expressions of disapproval bordering on fury, were Khamwas' three brothers.

"Prince Khamwas will assign all his property to me," said Tabubu imperiously. "His brothers are here to witness the contract."

The scribe noddèd, unrolled a length of well-made paper on his desk, and began writing with quick, practiced brush strokes.

"Khamwas, what *can* you be thinking of?" demanded Osorkon, halting two paces into the room. He swung his head and glared at Samlor as he added, "And you—you're supposed to be his friend, aren't you? How can you let him commit such nonsense?"

"I—" said Samlor.

Pre eased herself down against him, offering wine and the warmth of her body. "Only a fool involves himself in another's family affairs," she whispered.

The softness of her hips reinforced the obvious truth of the statement. Samlor drank as his hand reached under the crocodile skin.

"Brother, we brought your children with us and they're below now," said Patjenfi. "Surely you can't intend to leave Pemu and little Serpot destitute for—" Words failed, so he flicked his hand through the air in the direction of Tabubu, a gesture as scornful as it was angry.

"Pemu?" Khamwas repeated, his head jerking as if his brother had slapped his face. "Yes, th—"

Tabubu smiled down at him and thrust her groin forward suggestively.

"Do you think you can threaten *me*?" Khamwas snarled at Patjenfi. His hand clasped his sash where it bulged over the crystal book. "I'm a god, do you realize? You will do as I command, or—"

He paused. Instead of leaving the threat unspoken, he added in a voice as quiet and cruel as leprosy, "I will blast you as if you never existed, Patjenfi." His gaze swept his brothers. "I will blast you all."

"I didn't—" said Patjenfi.

Pentweret silenced him in a chopping gesture. "You have the right to dispose of your property, my brother," he said in a voice tremulous with emotions and his attempt to control them. "But for your sake as much as for your children, think about what you're doing."

"The document is complete, lady," said the scribe. He held it up to Tabubu along with the ink-charged brush.

Samlor could not recall ever having seen a smile as cruel as that with which Tabubu gave the deed and pen to Khamwas.

Khamwas tried to smile back, but the expression was not successful and the man's hands were quivering so badly that he could scarcely hold the paper he was to sign.

Tabubu leaned over so that her pendant and full breasts wobbled in front of Khamwas. Her fingers rested on his hands, not so much to guide them as to still their trembling.

Khamwas touched the brush to the document and drew his name with the sure strokes of an accomplished scholar. His face had no expression and his eyes did not appear to be focused.

Beneath Samlor's fingers, Pre's breast was as densely fluid as molten lava.

Patjenfi was muttering unintelligibly to himself; Osorkon's broad jaw was set in grim silence; and the curse Pentweret spoke was fully audible.

The scribe rose, holding his desk open with the ink palette upon it. Crushed stone clung in blue shadows on the back of his thighs. His face was professionally bland and perhaps genuinely bored.

Tabubu dropped the executed deed onto the desk and waved the scribe negligently toward Khamwas' brothers. "The witnesses must sign," she said.

Nodding, the scribe held the desk out for Osorkon to use the brush waiting in the hollow of vermilion ink.

"I thought we behaved badly to you six years ago," said Osorkon. He stared at his lounging brother, then scribbled his signature with disdainful haste. The brush, carefully frayed from the reed which formed its stem, flattened under Osorkon's pressure.

"We were models of familial affection," he added, "compared to the way you're treating your children." He turned his back.

Tabubu was standing at an angle to Khamwas, watching Patjenfi take the brush and fastidiously try to straighten its splayed bristles on the flat of the palette. Her fingertips were massaging the front of her dress, working slowly downward from her navel.

"You'll regret this, my brother," said Pentweret as he took the brush in final turn. "But it won't be undone. It can't." He sighed and turned away.

Pre was touching Samlor, rubbing him with feather-light fingers the way Tabubu massaged herself. His vision was blurring. Khamwas's brothers were trudging down the stairs with lowered heads, but reflections from the surface of the wine kept staining their image in Samlor's eyes.

The scribe had squatted again to roll his inked seal behind each signature on the deed.

Tabubu was kneeling beside Khamwas' couch. She allowed him to kiss her as if the prince were a rambunctious puppy whose affections were too cute to be degrading.

"My lady," said the scribe, holding out the completed document.

Tabubu rose as she took it and slapped Khamwas' hand with the rolled paper as he reached for her.

"You *can't* deny me now!" Khamwas bleated. His tone made it obvious that he knew she could—and that he expected her to do so.

"Deny you?" said Tabubu, snapping the scroll open angrily. "It's you who're denying me!"

Samlor had not heard an order to the servants, but they were returning up the stairs with—

"Your children haven't signed this yet!" Tabubu was

saying. Her voice was as cold and hard as the walls of the
crater where Nanefer fought the worm. "Do you think I
don't know what will happen? When you're gone, they'll
take everything away from me."

"Daddy, what—" said Serpot. She took a quick step
toward Khamwas, past a servant whose reaching hand
halted when the child and the child's words stopped at
Tabubu's glare.

Serpot hopped back beside Pemu. The boy was as stiff as
a soldier being cursed by his superior. Tears rolled down
Serpot's cheeks although she tried to hold them back with
closed eyelids.

"You see?" Tabubu hissed. "They'll ignore any agreement you make!"

Samlor kept seeing Star rather than Serpot facing Tabubu
in blind misery. He wanted to get up and hurl a smirking
servant through the window to the crocodile pond beneath. . . . That would show this bitch what the real
power was in this world where women were only toys for
men.

He didn't move though, couldn't move, because Pre had
given the cup to another of the servants. Now, as she
caressed Samlor with one hand, she rubbed her own groin
with the other.

"Tell them they must sign the deed," Tabubu ordered as
she dropped it on the little desk the scribe carried. He bore it
to the children as he had to Khamwas' brothers. His face
showed no more emotion than the paper did.

"Father?" said Pemu. His hands were gripping his thighs
as if to keep themselves from being dragged upward toward
the waiting brush.

"Don't speak, Pemu," Khamwas said. He lay on the
couch with his eyes closed and his fists clenched.

"Tell them they have no inheritance!" Tabubu said. Her
voice was chilled steel, but her belly thrust and withdrew
rhythmically a few inches from Khamwas' face. "Tell them
you have beggared them for life and that they must sign
their agreement to what you've done!"

"Da—" Serpot pleaded.

"I can't bear your voice!" Khamwas screamed in sudden anger. "Sign it! Sign it! Don't make me hear your voice!"

"I will do as you order, Father," said Pemu stiffly. His cheeks were flushed with embarrassment, at the scene and at his father's behavior.

Serpot turned to hide her open blubbering, but a liveried servant stood behind her and she whirled around again. "I can't," she wailed. "I *can't* write, I can't I can't I can't!"

As Ahwere couldn't write the symbols that would have protected her, thought Samlor.

Pemu wrote his name with the careful certainty of a child who is well taught but as yet lacks the practice which makes the motions instinctive.

Prince Nanefer had been a scribe and a scholar without equal in his time, and he was dead as surely as Ahwere. Samlor wanted to say that to Khamwas, but only a sigh of pleasure escaped when he opened his mouth.

"Your brother will sign your name, child," said the bland scribe. "Just make a mark on the paper."

Serpot could not prevent her eyes from dripping as she took the brush from Pemu, but she dabbed the tip against the paper with queenly disdain which belied her sobs of a moment before.

They were good kids, royal in the best sense of the word, but Samlor hil Samt couldn't move a muscle to help them. He was kneading Pre's breasts. The crocodile hide was coarse against the backs of his hands, while the skin beneath was as smooth as finest silk save for the erect nipples.

"My lady," said the scribe coolly as he returned the document to Tabubu after sealing the new signatures also.

Tabubu sat on the couch, her hips to the curve of Khamwas' lap just as the maid sat with Samlor across the table. Her right hand played with Khamwas' hair while the left gently waved the scroll in his face. Khamwas was trying to pull the woman prone onto the couch with him, but only the dimples in the silk beneath his fingers suggested that she resisted him.

Samlor had expected Pemu and Serpot to be led away. They still stood by the window looking doubtful, frightened—and as resolute as children could be in the face of unspoken threats.

"You've really tried to provide for me, dearest, flower of my life," said Tabubu as she leaned slightly closer to Khamwas. Instead of icy hectoring, her tone was a lover's in the moment following a splendid climax.

"But you can't, you see, darling—" her voice was as soft as the breast which dangled just low enough to brush Khamwas' ear "—so long as the brats are alive. *You* saw how your brothers hate me. If you were gone, they'd snatch everything away from me and give it to—"

"But they're my *children*," Khamwas whimpered. His eyes were open, but Tabubu's pendant hung too closely before them for him to be able to focus on it.

"*I* can give you children," Tabubu murmured, "and I can give you much more."

She leaned still further forward. Samlor thought she was whispering into Khamwas' ear, but instead she was nibbling it. Her tongue was very pink against her teeth for an instant. Then she smiled and purred, "Much more, little flower. But first you must kill them."

"*Daddy*," Serpot cried.

"*Silence!*" Khamwas shouted back. His face was livid with strain. "I told you to be silent, didn't I?"

"You see how they obey you," said Tabubu, her lips inches from Khamwas' ear. The words drilled through Samlor's brain, but he did not try to move.

"Do the abomination that you demand, then," Khamwas said past the hand that he had thrown over his eyes.

"N—" Samlor stammered, "N-n—"

"No, heart of hearts," said Tabubu. Her hand touched Khamwas' and softly guided it to her quivering breast. The agony of his uncovered expression smoothed to chalky emptiness. "Your man must do it. Otherwise the act will be laid to me. Order him."

"No," said Samlor. He got to his feet, though he could not feel anything below the pulse throbbing in his groin. "*No.*"

"You heard her," said Khamwas without emotion. Men

in scarlet robes held Pemu and Serpot, but the children refused to demean themselves with vain struggle.

"You can't order me!" Samlor shouted. He had drawn his long dagger. If there had been a servant behind him when he flashed around a fierce glance, the watered steel blade would have disemboweled the man. There was no one.

"Samlor, I beg you," Khamwas whispered. "For our friendship—*please*. You must understand. . . ."

Someone did stand behind Samlor now. His motion as he turned seemed as slow as wax melting in the sun. Pre's hands teased open Samlor's sash. She was nude. Her pubic hair had been hennaed to a startling shade of red.

Pre pressed her body against Samlor and kissed him with her whole naked length. "Now . . . ," she murmured. turning him with her fingertips on his shoulders and the memory of her warmth consuming all choice but obedience to Tabubu's will.

Samlor walked slowly toward the children. He tried to grasp Pemu by the hair, but the boy's head had been shaved to mere fuzz in the fashion of the country. Instead, Samlor closed his hand across the skull with his fingertips on one temple and the pad of his thumb on the other. He turned the boy so that Pemu's tightly-clenched eyes were on him.

The eyelids flew open as Samlor cut the boy's throat from ear to ear. The blade severed all four branches of the carotid artery, bathing both victim and killer in hyphenated spurts of blood. It dripped onto the floor, cratering the lapis lazuli dust and turning it into purple gum.

Pemu's head flopped to the side when the muscles holding it erect were cut, but his eyes were still bright as the servant holding him turned and dropped the dying child out the window. The body splashed in the pool beneath. One, then the other crocodile slammed their jaws on it with a sound like vaults closing. In the room's dead stillness, Samlor could hear the boy's ribs cracking beneath the pressure of ragged yellow teeth.

He looked back at Khamwas. He could feel nothing except Pemu's blood, and that burned like boiling vitrol.

"Go on," Khamwas croaked.

Tabubu's dress lay crumpled beside the couch. She wore nothing but the dangling crocodile pendant toward which she drew Khamwas' face.

Samlor turned. His bloody left hand was a claw poised to wrap itself in Serpot's hair and jerk the child's throat up for his blade.

Her face was already lifted to him. Her eyes were glistening with tears, but they were open and her slender throat bobbled as she swallowed a sob.

"Don't you want me?" Pre breathed in Samlor's ear. She was standing behind him, so close that when she lifted herself on her toes the pressure of her body slid Samlor's tunic up on his hips.

He swung the coffin-hilted knife in a short arc that grated on Serpot's neckbone as it tore through everything else, skin and flesh and the tough cartilage of her windpipe. Her tongue stuck out in final terror as the force of the blow flung her sideways, against the smiling servant holding her.

A voice in Samlor's mind screamed "*Father*!" and his eyes flickered with images of Star, not Serpot, being lifted and hurled through the window to the reptiles waiting below.

His dagger clanged to the floor. There was blood everywhere, ropy trails slung from the blade as it cut clear and great pools splashed on the sparkling dust by the child's jugular emptying her life.

Pre's arms were around Samlor. She kissed him, the touch of her lips beneath his ear drawing his face around to meet them.

"Now," she whispered as she drew Samlor down onto the blood and lapis of the floor with her, "take what you have earned, my hero."

He didn't realize he was tearing the strong linen of his tunic until the fabric ripped. He knelt between Pre's thighs and felt her heels encircle him.

As he thrust forward, her grinning mouth opened wider into bestial jaws . . . a tunnel of blue fire . . . into a screaming void that filled the cosmos. . . .

Samlor was face down on the ground outside the arbor in Khamwas' garden. Khamwas was within, sprawled across the curved wicker bench in a pose that must have been as painful as the way Samlor's knee pressed a knotted root in the turf.

Samlor had cut the neck off a gourd—two gourds, he saw, when Khamwas sat up. His cock was stuck through the hole, and that hurt also.

"What in the name of heaven are you doing?" demanded Osorkon in amazement. Behind stood the palace children, their game forgotten, and the equally frightened servants who had been watching them. "Are you drunk?"

CHAPTER 29

"COVER YOURSELF, FOR pity's sake," said Osorkon scornfully as he stepped past Samlor to the entrance of the arbor.

Samlor turned toward the wall and tried to blank out the memory of childish faces gaping in amazement at him. The rind was tough enough that the edges scraped as he pulled the gourd off him. That pain helped him—not forget, but at least put aside the shock and embarrassment that made his skin burn all over his body.

"Brother," Osorkon said in cold fury as Khamwas disengaged himself from a similar gourd. "If you've returned to degrade yourself and the kingdom, so be it—your family has no power to stop you, you've made that clear. But tell us now so that we can exile ourselves and avoid watching further disgusting exhibitions."

Samlor squeezed the front of his tunic together. He'd torn it all the way to the waist, despite the brocaded hem. It was an impressive feat of strength—for a singularly unworthy purpose.

"Where—" he said, more to get his voice working again than because he understood where the sentence would go next. "H-how long have we been here?"

Osorkon turned. In his face Samlor saw the concern which Osorkon's personality converted to anger before he could openly display it. "Well, some hours," he said. "You were watching the children play, and then you began to behave, well, oddly."

He blinked, trying to drive away the image of just how oddly his brother and Samlor *had* behaved. "They became concerned, and your major domo—" that plump servant, sweating with emotion and the sunlight into which only a crisis had drawn him, attempted a smile of acknowledgement "—thought I should be summoned rather than a doctor at first."

Osorkon looked from Samlor to Khamwas, doubtful but obviously hoping that medical attention would not be necessary.

Samlor's dagger lay in the grass. Its blade was stained with the juice and pulp of the gourd.

Khamwas stepped stiffly out of the arbor. He held the Book of Tatenen in his hand. Lights winked and changed in its crystalline interior, but sunshine on the open lawn did not affect the display.

Samlor said nothing, but his face grew very still. His eyes met Khamwas' when the book glinted between the men in its own rhythm.

"I think. . . ," said Khamwas.

"What is that thing?" demanded Osorkon. "Is it a jewel?"

"Nanefer won't send us a dream next time. We'll really live it," said Samlor, ignoring Osorkon. "And there won't be a damned thing we can do, even knowing it." His groin ached with the abuse he had just given it.

". . . that we'd best return this now," said Khamwas, completing the thought that he did not realize had been interrupted.

"What *are* you talking about?" Osorkon begged, suffused with the fear that his brother was going to break out into aberrant behavior again.

Samlor and Khamwas were walking toward the house, discussing preparations for their formal return to the Tomb of Nanefer.

As they passed the wide-eyed servants and children, they opened their arms. Khamwas strode on, holding his son by the hand, while Samlor carried the little girl who was not Star.

The manikin Tjainufi capered on Khamwas' shoulder, crying, "Happy is the heart of the man who has made a wise decision!"

The sparks in the crystal's heart had muted to warm pink and a yellow the hue of sunshine.

CHAPTER 30

"THE BOOK," TRILLED Ahwere's ghost. Her form shrank and expanded like a doll twisting on the end of a pendulum, now close to Samlor and now farther away. "They've come back with the book."

"Royal prince," intoned Khamwas, "royal princess, we return to you what is yours."

"Royal Prince Merib," Samlor echoed according to the directions his comrade had given him, "we beg forgiveness for having disturbed your rest."

Thirty musicians were playing on a barge on the river outside, and there was a chorus of over a hundred boys on the strand, chanting a hymn of praise to Tatenen. The music had been loud even while Samlor followed Khamwas up the tunnel; but in the tomb chamber, outside sounds vanished as utterly as if they took place in the crater of the worm.

The corpse of Nanefer laughed.

Samlor was sweating and his nostrils were full of the dry, thick odor of incense boiling from the braziers he and Khamwas bore on their heads. There was no real danger that a quick motion would unlatch the perforated lid and pour burning coals down on the wearer—but it was possible, and the crawl through the tunnel was as abject a means of abasement as any Samlor had undertaken.

"Welcome, Prince Khamwas," said the corpse. "Welcome, noble Samlor."

One of Nanefer's dry, blackened hands gestured. Suddenly no heat came through the thick pad protecting Samlor's head from the brazier. The glow of the similar brass censer which Khamwas wore also cooled.

The room brightened with clear light flooding from the Book of Tatenen. It bathed the sparkling, ethereal ghosts of Ahwere and Merib. Instead of washing them away, the light gave substance to the figures, making them appear solid at a glance and warming their skin and clothing with its natural colors.

"Take off your headgear, my fellows," said Nanefer. "You and I are brothers, Prince Khamwas, and your friend Samlor is a friend to me."

His voice was awkward, as if it were being driven by a cracked bellows which had to be recharged after every few syllables, but his enunciation was so pure that his words were easily understood.

Samlor unlatched Khamwas' chinstrap and set that brazier on the floor before he delt with his own. Khamwas' hands cupped but did not grip the crystal book.

The brass censers were as cold as if they had never been lighted. They looked forlorn, sitting beside the blackened lamp which the men had abandoned on their first visit to the tomb.

Ahwere moved closer to her husband, walking instead of drifting as her shape had done in the past. Merib clutched her chest and shoulder but his chinless face was turned toward the living men with an expression of doubt rather than terror on it.

Khamwas swallowed. He stepped forward as Ahwere put her arm around the shoulders of the seated corpse.

"Prince Nanefer," Khamwas said, "the book is yours. Take it with our apologies." He laid the crystal, cushioned but not enveloped in its silk wrapper, on Nanefer's lap.

"We have bought the Book of Tatenen, my kinsman," said Ahwere's ghost, her voice a wistful echo in the minds of the living men.

"We will leave you now in peace," said Khamwas. He backed away stiffly, trying not to rub his left wrist. The corpse's leathery hand had brushed him there as it grasped the crystal.

Nanefer's dark face smiled, but he did not speak in the white, sourceless glow which filled the tomb chamber.

"Let your benefaction reach him who has need of it," said Tjainufi, looking straight into Samlor's eyes.

"What can we do to make amends for the trouble we have caused you?" Samlor blurted, surprised at his words but certain that he was right to speak them.

"You can bring my wife and son to me," wheezed Nanefer.

"You can bring me to my brother, my husband, my life," whispered the words Ahwere had no mouth to voice.

"You are my kinsman, my brother, Prince Khamwas," the corpse said. "Bring my wife and son to me that we all may find peace. After a thousand years we may find peace. . . ."

"Peace . . . ," echoed Ahwere.

"What you ask, we shall do," Khamwas promised formally. He bowed, rose, and then ducked low again to crawl out the tunnel.

Samlor could hear the music again as he followed, but he could also hear a voice murmuring "Peace. . . ."

CHAPTER 31

SEVERAL OF THE barge's deck planks near the bow had been replaced recently enough that the polished wood shone paler than the surrounding planks. It was the same vessel Samlor had traveled aboard in the dream that ended on Tabubu's bloody floor. When he realized that, he started sharply enough to splash a dollop of fruit juice from the cup a servant had offered to cool him.

"Yes, but it's all right," said Khamwas grimly. "The details were right, even when we didn't know them; but it was only a dream."

"I've had men searching as soon as the messenger brought us words of your requirements," said the sallow priest from the Office of Religious Works. His face was blank and his voice so reserved that his extreme concern was obvious. "I'm very much afraid that—long before my tenure in office, I assure you—property of the temple on this side of the river was converted to private use."

"But you know where the boundaries are?" Samlor said, glowering at the priest. Lost records had a way of turning up when officials weighed the bribe a landowner had given them against the chance of being tortured. Samlor's scowl promised torture and worse if the priest failed.

"'Ware in the bows!" shouted a crewman at the mast-head. "Next landing but one!"

"This is . . . ," said Khamwas, squinting at the shore the royal barge passed in a controlled drift. The walled enclosures, most of them with private docks for the convenience of Ankhtawi's wealthy residents when they visited the capital across the river, varied only slightly in style from one to the next.

"This is where Tabubu lived," Samlor said, thinking that he was completing his companion's thought.

"Tabubu lived only in our minds," Khamwas corrected. "Look."

The bank here was walled by huge stones so black with age and ages of flooding that the interstices between the blocks had vanished to the eye. The central relief of Tatenen which had grinned, then blazed as Nanefer sailed toward it, was worn to a surface as smooth as the silt covering the wall.

"We believe we know where the temple precincts lay," said the priest who stared at the horizon in front of him so that he needn't meet the eyes of the men who had been questioning him. "The problem is that at one time—very long ago—this whole region was owned by the local Temple of Tatenen. So it's very difficult—even where the records exist—to separate the precincts of the ancient temple from the croplands which supported it."

"The area has changed since we last saw it," Khamwas said. His words were normal enough, though no one alive save Samlor could understand their true meaning. "But I'm sure we can find what we need."

He smiled and stroked the ferule of his staff. Where his hand touched it, the wood shimmered green.

CHAPTER 32

THREE DAYS LATER, Samlor rested on an ornamental urn while Khamwas glared at the back of a grave stele whose face was cemented into the garden wall. A messenger, one of the men whom the Prefect of Ankhtawi had assigned to help the prince, stepped around a terrace of dwarf chrysanthemums. He saw the men and called, "Prince Khamwas? We've—"

Khamwas turned and pointed his staff at the messenger. The man screamed, flung down his baton of office, and ran off. Baby toads were hopping from his hair and bouncing down his face and tunic.

Someone else peered bug-eyed around the terrace, then jerked his head to cover.

"You think I overreacted, don't you?" Khamwas snarled at Samlor, holding the staff crosswise in a white-knuckled grip.

Samlor shrugged. "Not if you told 'em not to disturb you with search results," he said mildly. He met his companion's eyes without blinking.

"I didn't!" Khamwas said in the same challenging voice.

Samlor shrugged again. "Well, it didn't look like it was permanent. And anyway, life's a dangerous place."

Khamwas' anger melted. The princely scholar sagged without the emotion to sustain him. "It's not permanent," he said. "And of course I overreacted."

Samlor patted the rim of the urn beside the one on which he sat. The broad-mouthed jars made comfortable seats, although they would prove confining after ten minutes or so.

"Your . . . ," Samlor said as his friend did sit down. "Ah, you seem to be in good form. This must be a good place for . . . what you do."

Khamwas' smile was as tired as that of a man who's carried a hod of bricks all day. "In a way," he said in what was not agreement. "The *power* in this place is, is beyond. . . ."

When he could not find adequate words, he pointed the end of his staff at the stele he had been examining. The worn surface brightened, then spangled itself with the green, glowing symbols of ancient Napatan writing.

"They're reversed, of course," Khamwas said off-handedly as he peered at the stone. "Everything that was carven on the face shows through the back of the stone. It's easier than ripping it out of the wall."

He grimaced and the glyphs vanished. "Also quite useless. It came from the tomb of a temple scribe who died over a century later than Ahwere. Useless. Like all the others we've found.

"I can *do* almost anything here," Khamwas went on, letting out his frustration gently instead of in a blast of anger that sent innocent bystanders screaming away. "But I can't look *through* a, a sea of power like the one that surrounds us."

"There's also the problem," said Samlor carefully, "that most of the tombstones here seem to have been moved. From the tombs."

Khamwas dismissed the concern with a flutter of his hand. "If we find the stele, I can follow it to where it belongs," he said. "If I had some object of Ahwere's, I could find *her*. But not blindly. It's—"

He paused, then said in an understatement that proved he had recovered his temper, "—an irritating situation."

"I shouldn't have asked, ah, Nanefer what we could do for him," Samlor said lightly. His face crimped, and his mind wondered what price the mumified corpse would exact for failure.

"You did right," Khamwas replied in a tone of certainty. "There has to be retribution for what we did—I did—"

"*We* did. You weren't alone."

"At any rate. Retribution whether or not Nanefer wills it." Khamwas smiled wistfully. "The cosmos abhors imbalance. That's what Ahwere was trying to show us, but I was too—settled on my course to listen."

Samlor heard a sound and rose quickly to his feet. He stood between Khamwas and the new intruder. Not that Khamwas was likely to blast the fellow in a flash of anger just now, but—he'd feel really bad about it later if he did, and there was no point in that happening.

Instead of a messenger from the Prefect's entourage, an old man whose robe had been pounded to gauze with repeated cleanings edged cautiously around a hedge of dwarf acacias to the side. Had the Prefect decided to thrust a beggar into view to determine whether or not it was safe to approach Khamwas yet?

"Heh-heh-heh," said the old man, a laugh because his mouth was twisted into a grin. "Used t' play back here, but that were a long time since. It were all differ'nt then."

He began a gesture which jerked to a halt short of the hedge. Thorns already plucked his robe, and he began to remove them with patience and concentration.

"What are you doing here, my father?" Khamwas asked, relaxed by the interruption. If it turned out somebody had used the fellow to draw fire, though—that somebody would answer for it.

"Oh, all the commotion," the old man said. He tugged gingerly at his worn hem, then bent to remove the remaining thorn. "Muck-de-mucks from acrost the river, don't ye know? Used to play in this garden—as it is now, but it wasn't, don't ye know? Slipped by in the confusion, I did. Wouldn't 'e hev conniptions if 'e knew I was here, the Prefect?"

The old man turned and straightened. He had begun to laugh again, but now his face turned stern. "They shouldn't build here, ye know. It's sacred. There was a temple here, right here—" he stepped forward so that his sleeve wouldn't snag again when he gestured "—and the ground's sacred."

"You remember when the temple was here, ah, my father?" asked Samlor, copying his companion's use of the local honorific. He spoke with a flash of sudden hope, but Khamwas' wistful smile warned him even before the gesture was complete that it was vain. The time scale they were faced with was much longer than human memory could illuminate.

"Ah, that were *long* since," said the old man, capping his words with a laugh that disintegrated into a spell of coughing. "D'ye know," he went on when he could raise his head, "that everything you see were swamp long since? But they drained the land, they did, and now there's a city acrost the river—and nobody left as knows there was a temple here as my father's father kept the grounds of."

Neither Samlor nor Khamwas moved.

"Heh-heh-heh," laughed the old man.

"Did your grandfather ever talk to you about the grounds of the Temple of Tatenen?" Khamwas asked in a voice from which he had rigorously purged hope.

"My father did, bless his memory," the old man said proudly. "Many a time, he did that."

"Did anyone ever mention to you the tomb of Princess Ahwere and her son Merib?" Khamwas went on while Samlor tried to blank his mind of the prayer he would have spoken—except that the gods would surely dash this possibility if they were aware of it.

"Aye, aye, so 'e did, my father," said the old man with a nod of cracked solemnity. "It were a terrible thing, 'e said, that they'd build a house on the sacred ground of a temple and set the south corner on the very tomb of that sad young princess ez they did."

He pointed beyond the chrysanthemum terrace. "The very house the Prefect lives in now and thinks 'imself too good to let an old man walk about 'is garden harming no one."

"You're lying," said Samlor quietly. He walked toward the old man with his hands at his sides as if it required all his control not to batter the fellow to a pulp.

"You're *lying*!" he shouted, inches from the old man's face. "You think you'll get back at the Prefect by having his *house* down around his ears, don't you? *Don't* you?"

"If you doubt my word," said the old man, with unexpected dignity and an even more surprising absence of fear, "then hold me for execution if the tomb is not as I say it is."

"We'll do just that, you know!" Samlor shouted, though by this time the noise was self-reassurance. He was disconcerted by the old man's attitude . . . and by the information which if true—as he *would* not believe was possible—meant the search here was over.

With his hand gripping the other's fragile shoulder, Samlor frog-marched the old man up the path toward the house. He was too intent on his business to look back and see how Khamwas was reacting—or even whether he was following them.

This couldn't work, but by Heqt! if it did. . . .

There was a lily pond in the Prefect's garden, but neither it nor the two-story mansion beyond resembled Tabubu's except in basic function. The Prefect, looking stiff in his robes of office, paced beside the pond. He was throwing in bits of a flower his fingers worried. His wife was seated in the nearby gazebo between two of her maids, all dressed in their best.

At a little distance from the pond were two distinct clots of servants—household personnel and those wearing the indicia of the Prefect's office. One of the latter, the messenger, screamed and threw himself behind a rose arbor when he saw Khamwas again.

The Prefect was an obtuse man and much the happier for it. He brightened and came forward, saying, "I trust your highness has met at last with success?" though nothing in the tableau hinted at that possibility.

"You've been directed to afford my master every facility, have you not?" said Samlor brusquely.

The Prefect looked unwillingly from Khamwas to the underling—the *foreigner* who was addressing him. "Yes, yes, of course. Any help I can give." He paused, frowning as he looked at the old man in Samlor's grip. "But who is this?" he asked. "Was he with you? I don't—"

"We want you to hold him, " Samlor ordered. "Someplace he can't get away."

"At once," the Prefect agreed. He snapped his fingers. A pair of official servants stepped forward with the nervousness of men who had seen their fellow raining toads. "Take this fellow," continued the Prefect imperiously, "and lock him in my basement storeroom."

"Someplace other 'n that," the caravan master said, grinning in spite of himself. "Also, we'll need a hundred men equipped for a digging job. Demolition job, in fact."

"At once," the Prefect repeated. "Where do you want them to assemble, my good man?"

Khamwas said, "At the south corner of your house, my good man." He gestured with his staff. "We're going to demolish it."

For some long seconds, the Prefect blinked and waited to hear the rest of the joke. Only when his wife began to scream did the man realize his lord was quite serious.

CHAPTER 33

THE INNER WALL was too far back to be a threat to the diggers, but it blocked the route up which baskets of earth and rubble were handed to clear the excavation. The mud brick structure toppled backward with a crash and a cloud of white dust from the molded plaster covering.

The team of workmen cheered as they coiled their ropes. The Prefect's wife broke into a renewed set of wails. She had refused to allow her bedroom at the south corner to be emptied in the few minute Samlor allowed for salvage. She might regret the decision later, but Samlor had to admit that when your home was being devastated, there'd be small comfort in preserving your wardrobe.

"You've got that old man locked where he won't get loose?" Samlor asked the military officer standing beside him.

"Yes, sir," the soldier agreed. His ostrich plume headdress trebled the height of his nod. "We put him in an empty cistern—" his short spear pointed toward a back corner of the garden "—and there's a guard at the mouth of it."

"Stone!" called a man from the pit. "Smooth stone!"

"Then bloody clear it!" Samlor bellowed. "That's what we're about, ain't it?"

Khamwas stood silently with his hands clasped and the

staff held upright between them. He was facing the
excavation, but his eyes were closed. No one came near
him. Raised voices dropped if the speaker chanced to glance
across the scholar's forbidding figure.

"My lord," the Prefect said to Samlor, wringing his
hands. "You *have* to believe that I wouldn't have occupied a
temple site. There must be some mistake."

"That's between you and the Office of Religious Works,"
Samlor replied with a shrug. "Though . . . if it turns out
to be what we hope, I think you'll find the Prince—" he
nodded toward Khamwas "—is real well disposed toward
you."

"We've found a sarcophagus!" called the foreman from
the pit, his voice an octave higher than during the previous
announcement.

"Oh, I'm ruined!" moaned the Prefect, but Samlor was
running toward Khamwas at the edge of the excavation.

It had seemed quickest to collapse the house into its
basement and then to cart away the rubble while digging
further. As a result, there were plaster chips, fragments of
storage jars and even a forlorn piece of statuary at the
bottom of the pit.

The house was built on a brick foundation, but below the
corner which had been ripped down was an angle of
polished red sandstone, the remnant of previous construction. Samlor whispered a prayer, remembering the lamplit
interior of the tomb which Tekhao had offered for the burial
of his lord's child and wife. He could almost smell the
incense again. . . .

Khamwas pointed his staff.

The crew in the pit was six men whose shovels and
mattocks filled baskets for a hundred other men and women.
The earth was handed out in long, snaky lines until it could
be safely dumped. The diggers scrambled up the sides of
their excavation in near panic to avoid whatever the
magician was going to do.

Green light flared at the base of the pit.

There were two stone slabs, though only a corner of the
second had been uncovered as yet. They were of the same

fine-grained sandstone as the blocks of the walls, a striking contrast to the yellow clay in which they were now imbedded.

The cold light which followed the line of Khamwas' staff made the carvings on the stones stand out despite being worn shallow and covered with clay still baking dry in the sun.

"May the god Tatenen be merciful to the spirit of Merib," Khamwas read, chanting the revealed glyphs as loudly as a priest before his god. "May his innocence find peace in the god."

Samlor gripped his friend's shoulder in triumph, then strode back to the soldier to whom he'd spoken earlier. Behind him, Khamwas was reading out the inscription of the second sarcophagus while green symbols blazed through clay and uncleared rubble.

"We're going to let the old bastard go," Samlor said, gesturing sharply enough to catch the soldier's attention and start him moving without hesitation. "I don't guess he's owed much of an apology, but he'll get one . . . and he'll get whatever bloody else he wants, or I miss my bet."

The guard stood in a nook shaded by Rose of Sharon. The insects buzzing in the rich purple flowers had lulled him into a doze, but he snapped to full alertness when Samlor and the plumed officer stepped into view. "Sir," he said crisply.

"How's your prisoner?" Samlor asked. The cistern's pottery lid was ajar. He bent to remove it.

"Just fine, sir," the guard said to Samlor's back. "Hasn't said a word since we put him down there, except to ask that I put the lid back partway so the sun didn't cook him."

The cistern was a buried terra cotta jar, eight feet tall and five feet at its greatest diameter. Its interior was plastered to hold the water which could be fed in through pipes around the rim. Empty, it was the perfect prison for a frail old man who couldn't climb out unaided.

But the cistern was completely empty now.

Samlor backed away.

The military officer glanced in and gasped. He began shouting threats at the guard who defended himself with blurted astonishment.

But when Samlor thought about it, he realized that the proper place to search for the old man would be in a rock-cut tomb near the ancient capital of Napata.

Which is where he and Khamwas were about to return, bearing the bones of Merib and Ahwere. . . .

CHAPTER 34

AHWERE'S REMAINS WEIGHED almost nothing after a thousand years in what had been a swamp till silt pushed the Delta further out into the Great Sea. The casket in which Khamwas placed them was very small, but it was made of thick gold and ivory. Supporting half its weight while holding a lamp in the other hand—*and* crawling up the passage to Nanefer's tomb—made a damned difficult job.

But Pemu and Serpot were struggling along behind with Merib's similar casket. If they didn't complain, then Samlor surely had no right to.

As before, the sound of music outside the tomb dimmed to silence when Samlor and Khamwas stood within the chamber. The lampflame waved languidly, the only light in the room.

The children staggered out of the passage. They were sweating and the crawl had disarranged their garments of blue and gold, but they did their best to look royal and solemn as they caught their breath within the tomb.

Samlor had worried that the chamber would glow in an unearthly fashion, frightening the children . . . and reminding him of their terrified faces as he cut their throats from ear to ear in his dream, only a dream. Perhaps Prince Nanefer had shared the same concern, because the tomb was as cold and dark as a cavity in rock should be.

Nanefer wouldn't have been a bad guy to know.

Nanefer hadn't been a bad guy to *be*, though he sure wasn't Samlor hil Samt . . . and anyway, that had been a dream, too.

"Prince Nanefer," Khamwas intoned, "my kinsman, we have come to reunite you with the Princess Ahwere."

There was no echo, none at all.

Speaking together—Serpot starting a half syllable ahead of Pemu, but the two of them coming into synchrony almost at once—the children said, "Prince Nanefer, our kinsman, we have come to reunite you with the Prince Merib."

"Your little boy," Serpot said in a piping solo.

The children, sagging toward the heavy casket between them, looked at their father. Khamwas nodded, and the party advanced as evenly as possible.

The adults set Ahwere's coffin to the right of the throne and the seated mummy. Pemu and Serpot managed to put their burden down on the other side without dropping it, but the boy heaved a great sigh of relief and began kneading circulation back into his right palm.

Nanefer's corpse was as still as carven wood. With luck, Pemu and Serpot thought the ill-lit form was indeed a statue.

Khamwas bent over his children and hugged them. "You can go out now, darlings," he said. "Samlor and I will be with you very shortly."

Serpot turned, but Pemu tugged her around again. They made deep bows toward—Nanefer? The caskets? Samlor couldn't be sure. Only then did they back to the passage and duck away.

Samlor wasn't surprised that his lamp snuffed itself as soon as the children disappeared, nor that the frescoed walls took on a pale, shadowless light.

"Prince Nanefer," said Khamwas, bowing to the seated corpse. "We will leave you to your peace."

"You have done well, my kinsman," the corpse rasped softly.

A point of white light sparkled on the surface of either casket, then expanded solidly into the living form from which the bones within had come. Ahwere stepped in front of her husband, lifted Merib onto her hip, and placed her free hand on the mummy's shoulder.

"Go in peace, kinsman," Nanefer said.

"Go in peace," echoed Ahwere, smiling warmly. She and the infant faded away, but for a moment the translucent memory of her lips hung in the air.

Samlor turned to follow his companion out of the tomb chamber. He had expected his tension to release when the corpse had accepted their offering, but his gut was no less tense than it had been when he steeled himself to enter the tomb for the third time.

"Wait with me, Samlor hil Samt," said the leathery voice.

Great. He could trust his gut. As if *that* was news.

"Prince Nanefer—" said Khamwas as he whirled.

"You told your kids you'd come out quick," said Samlor; fear made his voice snarl. "Get *out* with 'em, then!" His big hand closed on his companion's shoulder, forcing Khamwas to meet his eyes.

"But—" Khamwas said, begging his friend to be allowed to plead with the corpse at whom neither of them dared look for the moment.

"Don't speak when it's not the time for speaking," said Tjainufi sharply from the opposite shoulder.

"Your kids need you," Samlor said harshly. "I don't need *nobody* t' take my heat."

Khamwas clasped Samlor's hand, then bowed with cold formality toward the seated corpse. He ducked down the passageway, leaving Samlor in a chamber which contained no other living thing.

"How can I serve you, your highness?" Samlor asked. His voice sounded reedy in his own ears, but at least it didn't break.

"You have served me, Samlor hil Samt," Nanefer whispered. "Do you recognize me?"

"I know who you are," Samlor replied as coldly as if he were disposing a caravan against foes sure to overwhelm it.

The horny flesh of the corpse began to soften and swell like a raisin dropped in water. The skin lost its wooden swarthiness and paled to a warm, coppery tone much like that of Khamwas and his brothers.

There could be no doubt that this was the man Samlor had met in the Vulgar Unicorn; but there had been no doubt of that anyway.

Samlor drew the coffin-hilted dagger. "Look," he said, beyond fear and beyond even resignation. "The night I took this, I did what seemed like a good idea to do at the time. I don't expect you to like it—but I'd do the same thing again if I thought it'd do a damn bit a good."

Nanefer gave the laugh of a happy, healthy man. "You did what I wanted you to do," he said easily. "What I chose you to do."

Samlor said nothing, because his lips clamped shut on, "I don't understand—" which was too evident to need stating.

"My kinsman is a good man," said the figure which had been a corpse, "and a great scholar. But without a friend like you, Samlor, he would have left his bones to be gnawed by the rats of Sanctuary. He couldn't have taken the Book of Tatenen from me."

The crystal in his lap blazed, visible through the silk and the hands grasping it, though the sunwhite radiance didn't change the illumination of the rock chamber.

"But you fought him?" said Samlor, uncertain in his own mind as to whether he was really asking a question.

"With all my strength," Nanefer agreed. "No one else could have defeated me—nor Khamwas had he been alone.

"And until I was truly overborne, neither I nor my wife and son could ever find peace."

"I . . . see," said Samlor when he was sure that he did.

"A thousand years isn't a very long time," Nanefer murmured. His well-shaped hands caressed the crystal whose effulgence glowed through him. "When it's over."

"Then I'll give you back your knife," Samlor said, "and leave you to your rest. You—"

He paused, then blurted out the observation he knew he had no right to make: "You're a pretty good man, your highness. I'm glad to have known you."

"Keep the knife, Samlor," said the seated form. "May it serve you as well as you served my kinsman."

The light began to fade from the walls. Nanefer's features shrivelled and darkened away from the semblance of life. The entrance to the passage was a square of light trickling from the rockface beyond.

When Samlor bent to crawl out of the tomb chamber for the last time, his eyes fell on the blade of the dagger bare in his right hand.

Letters wavering in the steel read, *Go, blessed of the Gods.*